---------- ★ ----------

McAlpin's smile evaporated. His face turned hard, ugly. He reached out and grabbed her hand.

"Gi' me the brooch, lass," he said quietly.

Lucy tried to pull away. She started to scream, but McAlpin clasped one hand over her mouth and spun her around, pinning both her hands behind her back with the other.

Lucy looked over her shoulder in helpless panic. McAlpin's teeth were clenched, his face grim, determined. He was going to pitch her into the atrium!

---------- ★ ----------

"Crammed with incident, narrated in lively conversational style: a first novel that blends elements of gothic romance with vivid characters and the contemporary scene into a dazzling story..."

—Kirkus Reviews

CHARLES MATHES

THE

girl

WITH THE

phony

name

WORLDWIDE®

TORONTO • NEW YORK • LONDON
AMSTERDAM • PARIS • SYDNEY • HAMBURG
STOCKHOLM • ATHENS • TOKYO • MILAN
MADRID • WARSAW • BUDAPEST • AUCKLAND

THE GIRL WITH THE PHONY NAME

A Worldwide Mystery/August 1997

First published by St. Martin's Press, Incorporated.

ISBN 0-373-26246-9

For Arlene and our Grandfather

PROLOGUE

It was one of those autumns thirty years ago when cars still had tail fins and kids wanted to be policemen when they grew up and America had never lost a war. The exact date was October 23. It was a Thursday.

Al Stogner and his wife, Janet, were driving through Massachusetts on their way back to Dayton, Ohio. They had been away for two weeks now, staying at hundred-year-old inns, picking up antiques, but mostly just watching the season unfold across New England. Al and Janet were what the locals called "leaf peepers."

Thousands of peepers descended upon Massachusetts, Vermont, New Hampshire, and Maine each fall, often doubling the populations of the tiny villages and towns. They came in tour buses, private cars, even limousines.

Rich and poor stood equal in awe as a hundred billion leaves exploded into achingly beautiful reds, quiet russets, eccentric oranges, wildly blazing yellows. Maple and birch, oak and gum and beech, white ash and poplar raised a canopy of color above the crazy-quilt forest floor.

It was nearly seven. The Stogners were heading south on Route 7 and had just passed the historic town of Lenox. They were minutes from Stockbridge, where they had reservations for the night at the Red Lion Inn. It was raining, which had put them behind schedule; they had hoped to make the inn before dark.

An hour ago the show of sunset and changing leaves had been upstaged by a sudden, ferocious thunderstorm. Lightning still illuminated the autumn landscape every few minutes. Rain fell in sheets. Al, who had been driving for six hours, hummed "How Much Is That Doggie in the

Window?'' Al considered ''How Much Is That Doggie in the Window?'' to be one of the great tunes of all time.

Janet was resting her eyes, but was not asleep. It had been a long week, a wonderful week, despite her husband's humming. She was almost sorry that in a few days they would be home.

The narrow, wet road, shining in their headlights, snaked through the storm. Al ran a hand through his sandy hair and pushed his wire-rimmed glasses back up to the bridge of his nose. He was tired, ready for a big dinner and a comfortable bed at the Red Lion. It was getting cold; the car was unheated. Perhaps he was going too fast, but there was little traffic.

Suddenly the road veered right and Al saw another car's lights directly in front of him. His foot touched the brake pedal. The car slid over the road as if the water had turned the pavement to glass.

One moment Al and Janet were in the serene safety of a three-year-old Buick and the Massachusetts autumn, the next they were in a nightmare, upside-down in a ditch. Al never remembered the actual crash. He did remember dragging Janet to a tree, where he frantically patted her hand and yelled her name through the gruff roar of the storm until she declared she was all right. Only then did Al smell the smoke. It was coming from the other side of the road.

He stumbled up the banks of the ditch and ran through the puddles to the car they had hit. It had smashed into a thick elm on the other side of the road. Black smoke billowed from beneath the long hood.

In the front seat were a man and a woman. The windshield was shattered; their faces were gone, indecipherable in the blood. Someone else might have been unable to function further, but Al had gone through Europe with the Eighth Army. He had seen carnage before. His senses were clear, his reflexes were conditioned against panic. Each detail in the bloody car was crisp, brilliant. He heard a faint whimpering from the backseat.

The back door would not open. The smoke was getting thicker. Al knew there was a great risk of explosion if flames reached the gas tank. Afraid that he might have only moments to act, Al jammed the rear side-window with his elbow as hard as he could. It shattered.

Time slowed down. It was almost as if another man pounded on the inside handle, brushed aside the shards of broken glass, wrenched the door open.

Behind the driver's seat was an infant. It was strapped into a kind of basket, a sturdy cradlelike carrier secured to the floor. Al took a handkerchief from his pocket and put it over his mouth. He was coughing violently now from the thick smoke. His eyes watered. Calm in his dreamlike state, he fought to unbuckle the straps holding the cradle. At last he got them far enough apart to remove the infant, swaddled in a white blanket, wailing loudly now.

Al could barely see his way through the black smoke, but he ran, the baby under his arm like a football. He had crossed the road and was heading down the muddy side of the drainage ditch toward Janet when the smoking car exploded. For an instant Al was back in the middle of World War II. He curled into a ball around the baby as the force of the explosion knocked them to the ground.

After a moment, Al stood, shaken and bruised. He had survived. Again. He hobbled up the side of the ditch, still holding the child. It had stopped crying now and was very still. Al feared it was dead.

He ran across the road toward the flaming car, but could not get within twenty feet. The heat was too intense. He watched the fireball, shaken by the acrid smells, the smells of a war he had almost forgotten.

After a moment, he turned and walked back across the road. Janet was still under the tree where he had left her. She was holding her arm and he could hear her sobs, though whatever tears she cried were lost in the rain. Her blonde hair was plastered down flat. She had rolled up her sleeve, and Al could see a bone protruding from her skin.

Al sat down next to her, the baby in his lap. He was suddenly aware of pain in his own arm. He had cut it breaking the window, even through his thick corduroy sport jacket. His sleeve was torn and bloody. He hurt all over.

The rain began to let up.

Janet reached over him with her good arm and moved the blanket. It was fastened with a heavy silver brooch covered with fantastic designs like nothing she had ever seen before. The baby opened enormous blue eyes, smiled broadly, and gurgled.

The flames from the death car rose into the Massachusetts sky. Al began to weep. Janet stared at the child, her face a blend of awe and terror, pity and fear. What had they done?

ONE

"WELCOME IN to Welcome Inn, Miss Trelaine!"

"Thank you," replied Lucy MacAlpin Trelaine politely, making a mental note to give the pretty blonde desk clerk a ten for Employee Attitude. The girl was so perky you could probably fry an egg on her face.

"Joey will take you to your room! My name is Jill! Thank you for choosing the Kankakee Welcome Inn! Have a great stay!"

"Thank you so much," said Lucy. A tall, pimply teenager had already grabbed her bags.

"Hi! I'm Joey! Follow me! Welcome in to Welcome Inn!"

Lucy followed the boy through the standard Early American lobby into the standard oak-paneled elevator. There was even the standard Welcome Inn smell, a mixture of fried chicken and rug shampoo. Did someone buy industrial-sized drums of it in concentrated form? "Eau de Motel?"

"Have you ever stayed at Welcome Inn before?" asked Joey, eyes wide, Adam's apple bobbling up and down like a lottery ping-pong ball.

"No," she lied. She had stayed in hundreds. It was her job.

"Well, you're in for a treat!" the boy exclaimed with frightening enthusiasm.

The elevator opened onto the third floor. Lucy's room was only a few steps down the standard beige hallway. Joey unlocked the door, hung her Valpak in the closet, and placed her suitcase on the luggage rack at the foot of the bed.

"This is your TV! This is your phone! This is the key to your honor bar! Plenty of beverages and snacks in there! It's refilled every morning and your room is automatically billed for what you've used...."

Lucy glanced around, listening to Joey's spiel out of one ear. The room was identical to the one last night in Terre Haute and the room in Roanoke the night before that. Everything looked satisfactory on the surface, but she'd make a more thorough inspection later.

"...Check-out time is one o'clock! Thank you for choosing the Kankakee Welcome Inn! Have a great stay!"

Joey stood grinning ear to ear at the door, towering over her five-foot-one-inch frame.

"Thank you very much," said Lucy. "I know the sign said 'no tipping,' but I'm sure you wouldn't mind if I gave you a little something for being so helpful?"

Lucy pressed two dollars into his hand.

"Thanks," said Joey, his eyes narrowing almost imperceptibly. He handed her the key and left smiling.

"Joey sleeps with da fishes tonight," said Lucy sadly to a lamp. The lamp didn't answer.

Part of what made Welcome Inns such hospitable places was the absence of outstretched palms every time you turned around. Welcome Inn, Inc., considered "No tipping" on a par with "Thou shalt not make any graven images" in the great scheme of things. Joey would probably lose his job when she filed her report.

He had only himself to blame, Lucy told herself, nibbling her lower lip. She had to zap a few employees every month or they wouldn't take her seriously at corporate headquarters. She had let two screw-ups off the hook this week already, for crissakes.

Lucy dug out a petty cash slip from her jacket pocket.

"Should I put in for four dollars instead of two?" Lucy asked the lamp. "One hundred percent on my money. Who would know?"

The lamp still didn't answer. Lucy had been talking to furniture a lot recently.

"I'm not cut out for this," said Lucy, recording the tip as two dollars on the slip. "I'm too honest."

Welcome Inn paid Lucy $35,500 a year plus expenses. Big money to Joey, she thought cynically, but what were her ex-classmates from Harvard pulling down now? $50,000? $100,000? To say nothing of exploding bonuses and stock options.

Even now that she had finally paid off her student loans and built up some savings, Lucy still felt poor. She had been working since she was fifteen, trying to give herself a little security, but it was never enough. She never felt safe.

Lucy glanced at the mirror over the dresser. A caricature looked back: a mop of tangled black hair over a pair of enormous blue eyes. She looked tired down to the tip of her long, straight nose.

"Lucy," she said earnestly to her reflection. "What is your problem?"

Mirror Lucy looked frightened and angry but said nothing, just stretched her hands over her head, then popped her trick shoulders. Her arms fell unnaturally behind her back.

Lucy had nearly blown her interview for Harvard with a demonstration of her double-jointedness. She hadn't thought she had a chance and hadn't taken the procedure very seriously. Why would Harvard accept a kid who hadn't completed more than six months in any one high school?

"We are only interested in people who are in some way special," the interviewer, a small Pakistani with an expensive toupee and a complexion like dried fruit had said. "What makes you special?"

Instead of concocting some suitably pretentious answer, Lucy had clasped her hands behind her back at waist level, then moved them over her head into her lap without letting go. When the little man didn't laugh, she'd bent her wrists backwards, made her fingers into little sevens, and rotated her elbows 240 degrees.

"Shall I call paramedics?" the interviewer had asked, blinking three times in rapid succession and nervously adjusting his hair.

"No," Lucy had muttered. "I'm all right now. Being able to cope with my condition and still lead a relatively normal life makes me feel very special indeed."

Inspecting motel units for Welcome Inn was Lucy's sixth job since Harvard. She had been fired from two sales jobs, quit on a financial planner, and been laid off by a computer service bureau. She had lasted a few years as an assistant to an accountant, but then he had retired, leaving her to comb the want ads in the *Boston Globe* until she found her present position.

At least this job was out of the line of fire. Lucy was useless at office politics and didn't mind traveling, although lately it had been getting a little lonely.

"The next thing you know I'll be talking to myself," she confided to the clock radio, which hummed sympathetically.

It took Lucy six and a half minutes to unpack and check the television reception, the extra pillows and blankets in the closet, and all the light bulbs. After three years of being on the road five days a week, Lucy had her routine down to a science.

She orbited the room counterclockwise, inspecting the wastebaskets, ashtrays, and drawers for litter. Using the toilet gave her a perfect opportunity to see that there was a proper supply of towels, soap, Kleenex tissues, and toilet paper.

"What?" Lucy gasped, seated on the throne. "TP end not folded into a reassuring triangle? Someone will pay for this flagrant challenge to propriety and Western civilization!"

She recorded the offense on one of the preprinted evaluation forms and moved back to the bedroom.

Unlocking the honor bar revealed another problem. The ice trays were frozen together. How many times had she seen that! It would cost them one quality point.

Leaving the honor bar unlocked—every once in a while she could nab a maid for stealing something—Lucy took the ice bucket down the hall and filled it from the ice machine.

She returned and poured herself a Coke, then picked up the phone and dialed 8 for valet service. It was Thursday, which meant the blue dress. She might be poor but at least she would remain unwrinkled. How many Harvard grads got free dry cleaning as a job perk?

"This is Miss Trelaine in Room three-o-nine," Lucy said, filling out the laundry ticket as she spoke. "I have some cleaning that I need tomorrow morning. Could you please send someone? Yes, three-o-nine. Thanks."

It would be a few minutes until the boy arrived and Lucy didn't believe in wasting time. She tossed yesterday's bra and panties into the sink with a capful of Woolite, then dug into the night-table drawer for the local phone book.

Checking phone books was Lucy's only hobby. It cost nothing and gave her a little hope. Everybody needs a little hope, Lucy had often confided to furniture. Everywhere she went Lucy ritually checked the phone books.

The nuns at St. Anthony's claimed she had no family, but Lucy never believed a word the nuns said about anything. Everyone had somebody. People didn't just pop out of nowhere, regardless of what her records said.

Records! That was a laugh. Lucy kept a photocopy of her admission file from the orphanage in her wallet. It consisted of four sentences:

Lucy MacAlpin Trelaine, October 23. Parents killed auto crash, Western Mass. Admitted St. Anthony's. No known relatives.

It was the only real information Lucy had ever found about herself, and it had taken the threat of legal action to get it from the nuns.

Where Lucy had spent her first year and a half was still a mystery. Boston child welfare couldn't even come up with the paperwork of her transferal to St. Anthony's. Somebody had obviously bungled. Going through phone books was the only hope Lucy had of finding her family.

Thanks to her job with Welcome Inn, Lucy had been able to check phone books in over five hundred cities. She had never found any Trelaines.

Trelaine sounded like a normal name, but there the resemblance ended. There were Trelauns, Trelevens, Trelegens, Treloars, Trelins, Tralins, and Tralongos. There were plenty of Tremaines. There were no Trelaines. Anywhere.

Lucy had researched the name thoroughly in the best genealogical libraries in the country.

She had pored over Black's *Surnames of Scotland,* the *Dictionary of English and Welsh Surnames,* Elsdon Smith's *New Dictionary of American Family Names, The Dictionary of British Surnames, Surnames of the United Kingdom, Irish Names and Surnames,* and both of Edward MacLysaght's books, *The Surnames of Ireland* and *More Irish Families.* She had even tried the *Dictionnaire Étymologique des Noms de Famille et Prénoms de France,* as well as books on Dutch, Spanish, Italian, Russian, and Scandinavian names.

Trelaine simply did not exist as a surname.

MacAlpins were another story. Although the exact spelling was rare, the phone books were full of plausible variants like McAlpin and MacAlpine. Over the years Lucy had talked to hundreds of them.

MacAlpins had become her pen pals, McAlpins had had her over for dinner. McAlpines had brought her to their country clubs. Some had talked a blue streak and some had hung up in her ear, but no one had ever thrown any light on her origin.

There were no Trelaines in the Kankakee phone book.

Lucy wondered what she would do if she ever found a Trelaine. Have a heart attack, probably. No doubt it would turn out to be the wrong Trelaine, anyway.

There was one listing for a McAlpin, Roy, and another for McAlpin's Barber Shop. Since Lucy had been in Kankakee before, she powered up her little Toshiba laptop to check if she'd already spoken to the man. Several megabytes of the hard disk were devoted to her family-research database.

In seconds Lucy was in the right subdirectory and had found Roy McAlpin's name, address, telephone number, date of contact, and a memo that she had turned down his offer of a haircut. She had rated him a "three" on her MacAlpin scale—"one" being a possible, "three" being an unlikely.

Over the years Lucy had accumulated information about more than a thousand MacAlpins, first in notebooks, now on the computer. There were maybe two dozen "one's" altogether.

Andrew Macalpin, for instance, was a "one." He lived in western Massachusetts, Springfield, and had a sister with whom he had lost touch.

"She got herself pregnant," Andrew Macalpin had told Lucy in the coffee shop of the Springfield Welcome Inn. "Had a child somewhere in the sixties, I heard." Lucy never found the woman.

Barbara McAlpin in Atlanta was a "one," too. She remembered a distant cousin who'd been killed in a car crash up north. Unfortunately she couldn't remember the cousin's married name. How do you track something like that?

A knocking sound interrupted Lucy's thoughts.

"You called for some cleaning?" said another pimply teenager when Lucy opened the door. His name tag read, Bob Welcomes You in to Welcome Inn!

"Yes," said Lucy, handing him her blue dress. "I need it tomorrow morning. Can you do that?" Lucy knew very well that Welcome Inns did dry cleaning twenty-four hours a day, but took nothing for granted when she was on duty.

"There's an extra charge since it's after noon, ma'am."

"That's fine as long as I get it back before ten a.m. tomorrow. Let me give you something extra just…"

"No, thank you, ma'am!"

"Are you sure?" Lucy batted her huge blue eyes innocently. The boy didn't even blink.

"Yes, ma'am! It's our pleasure to serve you without gratuities! Have a great stay!"

Lucy shut the door behind him. That made up for Joey. Maybe Bob would make employee of the week when she filed her report. Did she really look like a "ma'am"?

Lucy was at the mirror, trying to decide whether she was over the hill, when the phone rang.

"Hello?" she said tentatively.

"Hello, Lucy. It's Tug."

Lucy didn't like this already. Tug Berwin was her boss, an ex-army officer with a cleft in his chin as deep as a Welcome Inn closet. They rarely spoke. Lucy mailed her evaluations and expense documentation to Tug at company headquarters in Dallas every week. He wired paychecks and expense reimbursements to her New Hampshire bank and forwarded her itinerary. For him to be calling meant something was wrong.

"Hello, Tug," she said, trying not to sound concerned. "What a nice surprise."

"So, Lucy, how ya doin'?"

"Fine, thanks. And you?"

It must be really bad, Lucy decided. Tug Berwin didn't give a shit how anyone was doing. Tug Berwin had actually missed his daughter's performance as the Sugar Plum Fairy to attend a Monster Trucks rally for goodness sakes!

"Look, Luce, we've been together a long time," said Tug. She could practically hear his perfect posture over the phone. "I respect you too much to pull any punches."

"You mean you'll let me have it right in the kisser? I appreciate that, Tug."

"Fact is, Lucy, the company's reorganizing. Your job's been phased out."

"I see," she said, stunned. "When is this going to happen?" Maybe he would cut himself on the creases in his trousers and die before the paperwork was completed.

"It's already a done deal. You can drop off the car in Chicago—the long-term lot at O'Hare. Send me the keys and the parking claim-check with your final expense report. Cut your company credit cards up and send them, too. You're due for four days' severance. I'll wire it with your final expenses."

"Just like that?" Lucy asked, stiffening her upper lip.

"Just like what?" responded Tug, genuinely confused.

Lucy managed to muster a smile. The warmhearted American corporation! In a way she was almost relieved. Something like this was bound to happen. It always did. She had always survived. She would again.

"I've already checked in here," said Lucy after a moment. "Would you mind if I..."

"Relax, kid," said Tug magnanimously. "Take your time. You don't have to be in Chicago until tomorrow. Have a great stay."

TWO

THE DRIVE from Kankakee—long, straight roads bisecting cornfields—was endless, cloudless, featureless. It was April, so there weren't even crops yet to challenge the vast, flat horizon.

Lucy felt strange about suddenly not having a job, like someone had come and taken away the rest of her dinner. What, all this spinach and no dessert? Not that people who served spinach for dinner would come up with anything very appealing for dessert anyway. Lucy suddenly realized that being fired by Welcome Inn might be a blessing in disguise.

"I could have been inspecting hotels for the rest of my life," Lucy said into the din of radio preachers that passed for entertainment in this part of the world. "This is just God's way of getting me out of my rut."

Lucy pushed the buttons on the radio, feeling a little excited, a little frightened, a little sad. With all the nuns, the foster homes, and the succession of reptilian employers that passed for her career, it was hard to believe that God really cared all that much about her. She gave Him the benefit of the doubt, however.

The miles rolled past her windows. Lucy couldn't remember a thing about this stretch of highway, though she had taken it dozens of times. All America looked alike. The last few years of her life looked alike. What would they look like now?

It was early afternoon when Lucy finally checked into the Chicago Towers Hotel and dropped off her luggage. There were four bags altogether. She usually left two in the trunk of the car, but now that would be impossible.

After going to the bathroom and splashing some water on her face, Lucy drove out to O'Hare per Tug Berwin's orders and parked George Bernard Shaw, her red Reliant K, for the last time.

She was surprised by the slight pang she felt in her chest, like her heart was being pinched. She knew it was stupid to be sentimental about a Plymouth, but she couldn't help it. She just sat for a few minutes, her hands on the wheel.

"I never got so much mileage out of a man before, George," she whispered. George maintained a respectful silence.

Lucy went through the glove compartment and looked under the seats, not wanting to leave the car in too disgraceful a condition. Evidence of her tenure was everywhere: neglected receipts, fugitive M & M's, a pair of mittens, some tampons, her Sony Walkman. Lucy had bought the little tape player a few years ago, intending to take up jogging and listen to great literature. The impulse had lasted about a hundred yards.

After filling two plastic bags with personal debris, Lucy finally took a deep breath, got out of the car, and locked the door for the last time. It was a long walk to the arrivals area, where she caught the courtesy shuttle back to the hotel. Lucy put on the earphones and listened to the first ten minutes of *Pride and Prejudice* on the bus before the Walkman's batteries gave out.

The Chicago Towers was a nice change from a Welcome Inn. The pillows were deliciously fluffy, there was actually marble in her bathroom, and of course they offered a special weekend rate.

Welcome Inns had given Lucy an extra $100 a week as travel allowance, and it made more sense to just live in hotels over weekends than to commute back to some expensive apartment. She hadn't needed a permanent residence anyway. She'd gotten along fine all her life without one, going from foster homes to dorms to furnished apartments.

Lucy knew she wouldn't be staying long in Chicago, so she only unpacked two bags. It took six and a half minutes. Then she phoned her accountant, Billy Rosenberg.

Billy's office in Manchester was Lucy's legal address. It was where Tug Berwin wired her salary. She had chosen Manchester because New Hampshire had no state tax. Billy took care of her tax returns and whatever personal credit-card bills she ran up.

"Wh-wh-what are your plans?" Billy said when Lucy told him the news. He was a little self-conscious about his stutter, but Lucy thought it was dear.

"I'll get a job, I guess," she said. "I just didn't want you to worry when the money stopped coming from Dallas."

"Hey. Wh-why don't you come up here and st-st-stay for a while?" Billy asked carefully. "There are plenty of jobs available h-here."

"You're sweet," said Lucy uncomfortably.

"I'd love to see you. I r-r-really mean it."

"Well, I'll think about it."

There was an awkward pause.

"There are some tax forms I need you to sign," Billy said after a moment. "Wh-where should I send them?"

"I'll be in touch."

"Don't wait too long."

"I'll try not to," she said and hung up.

Men, she winced. What did Billy see in her, anyway? Lucy couldn't understand his interest and didn't want to think about it. She had enough troubles without getting involved with an accountant. Besides, she was hungry.

Lucy changed out of her traveling clothes and went downstairs. It was after three o'clock. She went over to the newsstand and picked up a *Tribune* to read over lunch.

There were three restaurants in the lobby. Lucy automatically chose the expensive one. She kept meaning to economize on weekend meals, but she couldn't make it to Monday without a shrimp cocktail or two.

Lucy ordered half a carafe of white wine to celebrate her release from wage earning and browsed through the paper.

The end section contained the classifieds. Lucy casually leafed through the wants ads. She knew she should start looking for a new job right away, but the thought of working in the Midwest was depressing. It was too flat, too wholesome. She'd never fit in. She'd do better to try the West Coast. Or the Rockies. Or Mars.

The ad was in a section titled "Public and Commercial Notices" and it was practically a miracle Lucy saw it at all. The funereal black box around it must have matched her mood and thus caught her eye. She sat bolt upright and read it again, her mouth agape.

Will anyone knowing the whereabouts of Lucy MacAlpin Trelaine kindly contact Dwyer Parrin & Calabrese, attys.

There was an address and phone number in Pittsfield, Massachusetts. Lucy couldn't believe it. After all these years of looking, someone was looking for her. Someone in western Massachusetts!

The waiter was returning with her wine. Lucy almost knocked him over on her way out, hollering over her shoulder that she'd be back.

She ran through the mirrored lobby like a schoolgirl and waited for what seemed like days for an elevator. It all seemed so incredible. If she hadn't lost her job she wouldn't have been in Chicago, would never have seen the ad. Who wanted to find her? she wondered impatiently. And why? Finally she was in her room and dialing.

Chicago was on Central Standard Time, so Pittsfield would be an hour later. It would be after four. And on a Friday. Would they still be there?

The phone was answered on the fifth ring. "Dwyer Parrin & Calabrese, please hold."

Lucy stared at the receiver. Muzak blared at her. She choked down her excitement. What had gotten into her, anyway? This was probably just another false alarm. It was another two agonizing minutes before the voice returned.

"Dwyer Parrin & Calabrese. Can I help you?"

"I'm calling about the ad in the *Chicago Tribune* for Lucy MacAlpin Trelaine?" Lucy said breathlessly.

"Yes," droned the voice. "You want Mr. Parrin. One moment, please."

There was another pause. Then a faint male voice answered.

"Yes, hello?"

"Mr. Parrin?"

"Yes, hello?"

"Yes. I'm Lucy MacAlpin Trelaine and I'm calling about the ad in the *Chicago Tribune*."

"Oh, yes," squeaked the voice. "Now let me see. Do you claim to be Lucy MacAlpin Trelaine?"

"I *am* Lucy MacAlpin Trelaine," she said, struggling to keep calm. "I promise you there aren't any other Trelaines. Believe me, I know."

"How old are you, Miss Trelaine?"

"Pardon?"

"It is essential that I have that information. I hope you don't mind my asking."

"I'll be thirty in October," Lucy said, not minding any more than she minded the root canal her dentist promised to inflict the next time she got back to Boston. "Look, what's this all about, Mr. Parrin?"

"And can you tell me who your parents were?"

"No. My parents were killed in a car crash when I was a baby."

"Do you know where that crash took place?"

"Western Massachusetts. Look, will you please tell me…"

"Can you produce proof of identity? Birth certificate, passport, or the like?"

Lucy tried to distance herself, to appear uninterested, but she couldn't.

"Would a driver's license and credit cards do?"

There was a pause.

"I suppose so."

Lucy tried not to exhale her relief audibly. Ultimately the Massachusetts department of motor vehicles had accepted the St. Anthony admission file as proof of birth, but not before making her go through a nightmare of paperwork.

"Very well, then," continued Parrin with a sniff. "We represent the estate of Dorothy A. Wieters. Lucy MacAlpin Trelaine has been named in the will of Miss Wieters. If you can prove your identity you may come to our office and claim your inheritance."

"An inheritance? What is it?"

"I'm afraid you'll have to present your credentials before I can discuss the matter further."

Lucy practically peed in her pants. This had to be someone who was related to her. And there could be money involved!

"What was this lady's name again?" she stammered.

"Dorothy A. Wieters."

"I'll be there on Monday morning," said Lucy.

"Fine. I'll transfer you back to my secretary to make an appointment."

"What time do you open?" said Lucy.

"We're here at ten, but..."

"See you then!"

Lucy startled herself with a whoop of pure joy, then collapsed, giggling, onto the bed, at once embarrassed and delighted at the emotions roiling inside her. How could she ever wait until Monday? Was there a direct flight to Pittsfield? Who the hell was Dorothy A. Wieters?

THREE

"IT WOULD SEEM that our client, Dorothy Abigail Wieters, was a thief, Miss Trelaine," said Walter Parrin, squinting like a rabbit, his spectacles riding half an inch up his fleshy pink nose.

It figured, thought Lucy. The whole deal now looked like it was probably just a cheap con. How could she have been such a sucker?

Yesterday Lucy had shelled out $375 for a one-way ticket to Albany—Pittsfield had no airport. Her rented car was another $60 a day. Plus mileage! At least Tanglewood and the Berkshire Festival weren't in session yet, and she could get a fairly inexpensive room at one of the big, old-fashioned hotels in Lenox.

Dwyer Parrin & Calabrese turned out to be a little clapboard house on a commercial thoroughfare. Walter Parrin was a gray puffball with dandruff on his shoulders. He had arrived at 10:20 and kept Lucy waiting another half hour, then spent a full ten minutes scrutinizing her driver's license, credit cards, and the admission file from St. Anthony's. And now the punch line: Her benefactress was a thief!

"What did she steal?" asked Lucy warily.

"This," squeaked Parrin, taking a large manila envelope out of a drawer and dumping its contents on the desk between them.

"What is it?" said Lucy, not moving.

"A piece of jewelry," said the little man. "A silver brooch."

Lucy stared at the hideous thing. It looked like a massive silver belt buckle. It was the shape of the letter *C* and nearly three inches across. The thick pin turned the brooch into an *E* or a cent symbol, depending on where you slid it. The elaborate terminals held bits of what looked to Lucy like colored glass. The entire mass was covered with strange, interlacing animals and spiraling filigree.

"What does this…this article…have to do with me?" asked Lucy, struggling to stay cool. She had some taste, after all.

"This brooch constitutes your inheritance from Dorothy A. Wieters, deceased."

"You mean there's no money?"

"The estate wasn't large. Whatever remains after legal expenses and the cost of locating beneficiaries such as yourself will go to a niece in Baltimore. Actually, we had been running the ad to which you responded in five major city newspapers for a month and were about to give up on you. You're very lucky."

"Yeah, if I hadn't been so lucky to be in Chicago because I lost my job, I could have saved the five hundred dollars it cost to get here."

"Beg pardon?" said Parrin, obviously not interested.

"If this thing, this brooch, is stolen, then how can this Dorothy Wieters woman leave it to me?"

"Because it was stolen from you. Miss Wieters made a deathbed declaration that she had stolen it from you."

Lucy was baffled. "I've never seen it before in my life," she snorted.

"There is a tape recording Miss Wieters made at the hospital," Parrin droned, digging into another desk drawer and bringing out a cassette recorder. "It should explain matters sufficiently. May I play it?"

"It's not going to cost me anything, is it?" muttered Lucy.

Parrin didn't seem to hear. He pressed a button. A frail voice came from the little machine. It was the kind of voice that set Lucy's teeth on edge. Ignorant. Whiny. It reminded Lucy of half a dozen of her foster parents.

"My name is Dorothy Abigail Wieters. I used to be the

night cleaning-lady at Pittsfield General Hospital. This all happened one fall 'bout thirty years ago, I remember. I was walking through the charity ward, gonna get my bucket, when they brought this little baby in, her parents was killed in a crash. I sees that her little blanket was fastened with a beautiful piece of jewelry. I figured that she didn't need that silver and later, when nobody was around, I took it. The baby didn't mind. She just laughed and laughed. I took it and I hid it and I never told nobody. And I got to feeling worse and worse. So after a few weeks I come back to the charity ward to give it back to that baby, but she was gone. Supervisor said she was took by the state welfare people. So I never told nobody about the brooch. I kept it all the years. And I always felt bad, but I was afraid I'd get in trouble if I tried to do anything about it, so I didn't. I don't want to go to my grave with this thing on my mind, so I wants it should go to that child when I'm dead if she can be found. I know they never found her people, but I heard them calling her like it says on the brooch."

Lucy felt gooseflesh running down her back. She picked up the brooch on the table. It was very heavy. She turned it over. The reverse was a spiderweb of worn engraving and ornate, old-fashioned lettering that read *Dumlagchtat mac Alpin Bethoc.*

The name incised on the massive silver pin, however, was sharp and clear: LUCY MACALPIN TRELAINE.

"I'LL BE GODDAMNED," said the fat cop, slamming his desk with a sweaty palm. Paperwork scattered unnoticed onto the floor. "Lemme look at you."

Lucy winced. Parrin, the lawyer, had told her to check with the police for details about the crash, but no one at the station had been much help or even showed any interest—until she found Sergeant Simchick. She didn't have anything against cops per se, but Simchick was pawing her like he was some sort of long lost canine brother. He was pressing his palms into her collarbones now. Lucy feared for her shoulder pads.

"Little Lucy Trelaine. I don't believe it." The man shook his head. His jowls swayed in the breeze. Lucy could smell stale beer on his breath. "Hey, Lou. C'mere. I ain't seen this kid since she was a baby."

"Yeah?" said Lou, not looking up from the Smith & Wesson he was cleaning.

"She was just a little baby," Simchick's eyes teared up. "Hey, fellas. Say hello to Little Lucy Trelaine!"

There were a few grunts. Sergeant Simchick had clearly reached the useless-old-fart stage of his career.

"Like I said, Sergeant Simchick..." Lucy said, trying to smile.

"Call me Walt!"

"Like I said...Walt...I'd be grateful for any information you might remember about my...parents. You are the man to see, aren't you?"

"Sure, honey. They sent you to the source. Come on. You come with me. We'll go get the file. Hey, guys. Me and Lucy's goin' to the file room, case anybody wants us."

He lumbered off down the hall. Lucy followed reluctantly. None of the other officers even looked up.

At least the station was clean. Lucy had memories of sitting in filthy police stations in Boston after being picked up for running away from foster homes.

"I remember there was a whole big legal squabble about you," Simchick was saying. He ran a fat hand over his head, plastering down the few remaining hairs.

"What do you mean?" said Lucy.

"The driver of the other car...you know about the crash, don'cha?"

"I know there was a crash."

"Well, the guy wanted to adopt you. Felt guilty or something. The social workers didn't think that was such a hot idea. Some local priest got involved... I can't remember. Anyhow, there was a lawsuit. The venue got changed. The state got involved. I never found out what happened. Where did you finally end up?''

''Boston,'' said Lucy.

Simchick rolled his eyes. ''Figures.''

Lucy had spent the first eight years of her life at St. Anthony's. After that she had lived in a succession of foster homes until she had finally escaped to college. Lucy couldn't even remember the faces of any of the people who had taken her in for the few bucks a week the Massachusetts Department of Social Services paid.

They were standing in front of a door marked FILE ROOM. Simchick unlocked it with a key from his ring and flipped on a light. The place had a musty smell. It was packed to the ceiling with boxes and metal file-cabinets.

Simchick had to suck in his stomach to get down the narrow aisle. At the back of the room he knelt with a grunt, opened a drawer, and began fingering through the manila folders. Finally he found what he was looking for.

''Here we are,'' he said, rising laboriously. '''Car crash ten twenty-three. Route Seven. Two fatalities. Baby taken to Pittsfield General.' This is my own report. Jesus Christ. I was thirty-four years old, can you beat that? It was like yesterday.''

Lucy felt sick. All her life she had celebrated October 23 as her birthday. Now this fat cop was saying it wasn't her birthday; it was the day her parents died.

''The driver of the other car got you out before the fire started. I seem to remember there was some guy from New York involved,'' Simchick went on. ''Yeah, here it is. Cicarillo, the driver.''

''What are you talking about?'' asked Lucy softly, wanting to scream. She was suddenly full of unfamiliar emotions, feelings so strong and so immediate that they left her with no room to think.

''Yeah, it's all coming back to me now,'' said Simchick, reading further.

Lucy was afraid to speak. Her heart pounded. She didn't

want to know any more. She wanted to turn and run, but it was too late. Simchick was talking again.

"...burned beyond recognition, both of them. Two suitcases in the trunk, also burned. We identified the driver from the car's license plate. Here we go. Alex Cicarillo. Caucasian male, age forty-two. Lived in Brooklyn, New York."

"Cicarillo." Lucy rolled the unfamiliar word around in her mouth. "This...Cicarillo...was my father?" Lucy braced herself with a hand against a file cabinet so she wouldn't fall.

Simchick shrugged. "He sure wasn't about to tell us. We didn't even know for certain that the woman was your mother. All we had was two dead bodies. Let's see, we talked to Cicarillo's sister—" Simchick glanced down at the report again. "—Theresa Iatoni, Mrs. Stephen. Also of Brooklyn. Yeah, this was the problem. The sister claimed the baby couldn't be her brother's, him being unmarried and all."

"Then why was he driving the car?"

Simchick scratched his head. "Yeah, that was the problem. The sister claimed Cicarillo hired his car out for day rates. But he wasn't a licensed hack, so there weren't no records or nothing. The passenger—if she was a passenger and not some girlfriend the sister didn't know about—the passenger coulda been anybody. A tourist, a neighbor, just somebody looking to get to Vermont. One of our guys was even convinced the two had kidnapped you, but that never checked out. You never knew any of this?"

"No," Lucy said almost inaudibly.

"Jeez. Somebody shoulda oughta told you. Anyways, the sister wouldn't have any part of the dead woman or of you. Wouldn't even pay the burial fees. That's when the priest got involved."

"Where is this priest? Can I talk to him?"

"Father Hale, that was his name, I think. Hale, Hall,

something like that. Naw. He died in the middle of the lawsuit. He was just tryin' to help, that's all."

Lucy thought of St. Anthony's. The nuns used to lock her in a closet because she wouldn't thank God for her oatmeal. Lucy wondered where she would have landed without that priest's "help."

Simchick was still talking. Lucy struggled to pull her attention back.

"...but I ask you, if this Cicarillo was the father, how come nobody ever came looking for the woman? We're talkin' about a mother here, a newborn baby. You'd think that somebody would be expecting them somewheres and would scream bloody murder when they didn't show, right?"

"Nobody did?"

Simchick shook his head. "No missing person reports ever matched up. No lost baby stories came out of the whole Northeast that month."

"But how did you know my name was Lucy Trelaine?"

"There was something with a name... I can't remember...."

"This?" Lucy held out the silver brooch in her hand. Simchick's eyes lit up.

"Yeah. Son of a bitch!" He took the brooch and turned it over. "That's it." He held it at arm's length and squinted to read the inscription. "'Lucy MacAlpin Trelaine.' Yeah. We figured that beat Baby Jane Doe."

"But it's my name," said Lucy weakly.

Simchick waddled back toward the door.

"Maybe. Lucy MacAlpin Trelaine might be you. Or she might be someone who had a brooch that got stole. Or the name of a jewelry store. Or a silversmith. Hey, what's the matter, kid? Did I say something wrong?"

Lucy didn't hear him. She was crying. She was crying for the first time since she had flunked out of Harvard.

FOUR

AFTER LEAVING SIMCHICK, Lucy returned to her hotel in a daze and checked out. Then she drove to the little cemetery the cop told her about, next to the Church of the Holy Trinity. The plot she was looking for was not hard to find. It was marked by a small, flat stone marked JANE DOE, DIED 10-23, followed by the year.

Lucy stood on the grass in front of the grave for a long time, struggling to control the unfamiliar feelings inside her. Who was this woman in the ground at her feet? Where had she come from? Where had she been going? Had Cicarillo been her lover? Had she died seated beside a stranger?

Lucy bent down and traced the dates on the stone with her finger.

"Hello, mother," she said awkwardly.

Despite what her records said, Lucy had always believed she would be reunited with her parents one day, that they hadn't really been killed. All those years, shunted from foster home to foster home, ridiculed each year by a new group of schoolmates for being skinny, smart, different, Lucy had never given up hope. When she had failed out of Harvard, unable to keep up with the work load and hold down two jobs at the same time, Lucy had told herself that her parents wouldn't care, that her parents would still love her. Wherever they were.

"What am I supposed to use for hope now?" Lucy whispered to the gray stone. The wind rustled the locust leaves. A miscellaneous bird called in the distance. Maybe this was all happening for a reason. Maybe God was mad at her, after all.

"Listen to me," Lucy said abruptly. "You'd think I'd

never been an orphan before. Why should this get to me? Nothing's changed. I'm Lucy MacAlpin Trelaine. I don't need anybody. I can take anything life can dish out, god-damn it!''

The stone didn't reply. Lucy turned on her heel and stormed back to her car, unsure of what she was so angry about. A thousand questions raced through her mind. Why had that Cicarillo man's sister been such a bitch? Was there a jewelry store in New York called Lucy MacAlpin Trelaine? How old had her mother been when she died? People got married and had babies young in those days. Was she even married at all?

"Am I a bastard on top of everything else?" Lucy demanded of the rearview mirror. "Or are bastards just boys? What's female for bastard? Bastardette?"

The sky was blue with patches of pink. On the roadside, wildflowers danced in the light wind, the trees were just beginning to bud, blackbirds shunted among empty branches. But Lucy didn't see the spring at all.

Choking down her emotions, she drove south on Route 7, followed the road through Stockbridge, past the Red Lion Inn, and out of Massachusetts. After a while Lucy found herself on the Taconic Parkway. Only when she saw the sign did she finally understand where she was going: NEW YORK CITY, 60 MILES. What she intended to do once she got there, however, she had no idea.

LOOKING DOWN on the bombed-out buildings from the elevated highway, Lucy Trelaine was terrified. Had she taken a wrong turn somewhere amid the concrete confusion of the last ten miles? The road signs were ambiguous when there were signs at all, and it was already dark. Was she about to be dumped into the desolation below?

The traffic crawled ahead, painted an eerie yellow by the halogen streetlamps. Lucy hadn't driven into a big city for years. Welcome Inns were always located at superhighway exits. She hadn't even owned a car when she lived in Boston.

A useless map lay sprawled across the seat beside her. The New York City highway system resembled the insides of her computer, a million different-colored circuits, apparently all leading nowhere. At least the streets seemed to have numbers now. But what magic combination had to appear before she was safe?

Gradually the traffic thinned, the buildings grew taller, more electrified, until New York City loomed ahead like Oz. Lucy stayed on the highway until she found an exit marked UNITED NATIONS, figuring diplomats would always manage to park themselves in the right part of town.

For the next hour she drove through Manhattan, feeling out the orderly grid of streets, inspecting neighborhoods, trying to get her bearings.

Lucy had never been to New York before, but had heard enough stories to know how expensive hotels were. She didn't know exactly what her plans were, but it was a cinch she couldn't afford to stay at the Waldorf. She no longer had an income and the money clock was ticking.

She finally came across a TownLodge on West 57th Street. Lucy had occasionally stayed in TownLodges on weekends to save money. They weren't the most elegant accommodations in the world, but at least they were clean. There might be a better place somewhere in town, but Lucy was too tired to go looking for it. And she hadn't eaten anything since breakfast.

She pulled up in front of the hotel. A porter ambled out to the curb, took the four bags from her trunk, and wheeled them away in an open dolly. Lucy hoped she would see them again.

She drove to a rent-a-car location she had passed ten blocks away from the hotel and dropped off the car. Lucy was resigned to paying the $100 penalty for not returning it to Albany, but being charged the exorbitant 8.25 percent city sales tax on the entire rental made her mad enough to spit. Life wasn't nearly as much fun without an expense account.

She walked back to the TownLodge, dodging the outstretched palms of the homeless on every corner, trying to ignore the littered streets, the hostile stares, the noise.

"Yeah?" said the hotel desk-clerk. He looked like he hadn't had a perky day in years.

"I'd like a single."

"Front," said the clerk, but no porter appeared.

"How much is the room?" asked Lucy cautiously.

"One hundred thirty-five dollars a day, not including taxes. Check-out time is eleven a.m."

"Do you offer a weekly discount rate?" sputtered Lucy, looking around at the lobby. She had seen better furniture in airport waiting-rooms.

"You some kinda nut?" said the man and tossed her a key.

Ten minutes later, Lucy was sitting in disbelief on a rickety bed. The room was nothing like the TownLodge rooms she was used to. It was a dark little box with hideous Danish Modern furniture, like something that would spurt out if you squeezed 1958. At least the bellman had delivered all four of her bags. When she had given him a four-dollar tip, he'd scowled. She found a cockroach in the bathtub.

"Okay," she announced bravely. "This isn't so bad. I've stayed in worse places. And I'm in New York. That's what matters. This is where my mother left from thirty years ago, and this is where I'm going to find out who she was."

Feeling a little better, Lucy unpacked two of her suitcases—it took six and a half minutes—then paged through the tattered Manhattan phone book she found in the night table. There were no Trelaines. Lucy was relieved in spite of herself.

"But it doesn't prove there wasn't a jewelry store or a silversmith named Trelaine thirty years ago," she said to the cracked ice bucket, which would have cost a Welcome

Inn two quality points. She had to be Lucy Trelaine, she just had to be!

There were no MacAlpins in the phone book, either. Lucy started to flip to "McAlpin," but stopped after a few pages. The inscription on the brooch left no question about the spelling of her middle name. If it was hers at all.

Lucy looked at her watch. It was a little past eight. She was so famished that even the menu at the hotel coffee shop—seventeen-dollar flounder and twelve-dollar meatloaf—looked good. There was something she had to do before she could eat, however.

Lucy picked up the phone. The hotel would probably charge her fifty cents per call, but she didn't care. The chances that Cicarillo's sister would still be in Brooklyn were slim, Lucy knew, but she had to try. She dialed Brooklyn information.

"Do you have anything for a Theresa or Stephen Iatoni, I-A-T-O-N-I?" she asked, opening the drapes and revealing a grimy view of a brick wall.

"There are five listings under I-A-T-O-N-I," replied the operator, "but nothing listed under the name Theresa or Stephen."

Lucy took all the numbers and started calling. To her surprise she hit pay dirt on the third call, the listing for Iatoni, Alphonse. A deep female voice answered.

"Hello?"

"I'm trying to get in touch with Theresa Iatoni," said Lucy. "I'm wondering if you might be related to her."

"Yeah, sure. She's my sister-in-law. Lives on the island."

"The island?"

"Long Island. Amityville."

Lucy couldn't believe it had been so easy. "Might I trouble you for the number?"

"Who you say you were?"

"My name's Lucy Trelaine. I...I think I might be related to her."

"Yeah?"

"To her brother, actually. I suppose I can get the number out of the phone book...."

"I didn't know she had a brother."

"He's dead."

"Well, I guess you're okay. Wait a sec. I can never remember the number," The woman returned to the phone after a minute and read Lucy the number.

"Thanks very much," said Lucy, wondering what she was going to say to Theresa Iatoni. Would the woman even talk to her? After all, this was somebody who had wanted nothing to do with her thirty years ago when she was a helpless, newly orphaned baby. Her brother had been driving the car, but Theresa Iatoni had let Lucy's mother be buried in a pauper's grave.

"You know she's in California visiting the grandkids, right?" said the raspy voice in the receiver. "They don't got winter there. Ain't natural."

"California?" said Lucy, biting her lip.

"Yeah. 'Til the first. You want the number out there?"

Lucy's heart sank. The first of May was nearly a month away! She supposed she could call Theresa Iatoni in California, but how likely would it be for the woman to open up over the phone in a house full of surfer grandchildren? No, Lucy had to see the woman in person.

"I think I'll try her when she gets back. And if you happen to talk to her, don't mention I called, okay? I want it to be a surprise."

"Sure, no problem."

Lucy replaced the receiver in its cradle and stood up, wondering if coming to New York had been such a good idea. Fantasies of finding her family had helped Lucy through some tough, lonely times. Did she really want to find out the truth? She might be just an illegitimate Cicarillo whose own aunt had abandoned her.

Outside, a symphony of sirens, garbage trucks, and what sounded like gunfire rose from the streets. Lucy's stomach

rumbled like thunder, but something inside her relaxed. She
had made her decision.

Whatever the truth was, Lucy was going to find it. She
had to know who she really was.

FIVE

LUCY SPENT the next few days exploring New York, gawking at the buildings and shops, but mostly just watching
the people—break dancers and street musicians; stick-thin
models dressed to the nines; Arabs with thousand-dollar
briefcases; beggars pushing shopping carts full of litter. It
was like window-shopping at the circus. After watching a
teenager snatch a purse from a woman in front of Tiffany's,
Lucy even bought herself a bag of peanuts from a vendor.

She finally found herself standing in front of the main
library at Fifth Avenue and Forty-second Street, staring up
at a matching pair of stone lions. Lucy trotted up the long
stairs into the cavernous entrance hall of gleaming white
marble, twelve-foot-high marble candelabra, vaulted ceilings so vast that she could barely hear the echo of her
footsteps.

"Where can I find old telephone books?" Lucy asked a
guard.

"Main reading room, two flights up," mumbled the man.

The stairs took her into a rotunda of dark wood and fres-
coed ceilings, the white marble giving way to red. She
passed book catalogues and computers and walked into a
room the size of a football field divided by a center partition. There were wooden tables and chairs with reading
lamps every few feet. Halfway into the huge space was the
microfilm department.

"I'm looking for old phone books."

The bored teenager at the desk gave her a slip to fill out.
Lucy requested the phone books of Manhattan and Brooklyn of thirty years ago. The boy returned in a minute with
a stack of battered, square boxes.

"You can view these over there," he said, pointing at rows of ancient projectors. Lucy took the boxes over to an empty projector and opened one box. Inside was a thick roll of film, about the size of a can of tuna fish.

Lucy struggled with the projector for ten minutes. Finally she turned to the boy beside her, a redhead about thirteen years old.

"Can you show me how to thread this thing, please?" she mumbled. The boy rolled his eyes.

"You never went to school or nothin'?" he said and installed the microfilm in a matter of seconds.

"Rotten kid," Lucy muttered to the projection of phone listings after the boy returned to the computer magazine he was scanning. No wonder she had flunked out of college.

There were no Trelaines in any of the reels. Lucy went back to the desk again and again, until she had viewed all the phone books back to 1945. No Trelaines. It didn't prove that Lucy MacAlpin Trelaine wasn't a jewelry store, but still she felt a little better.

THE FOLLOWING MORNING Lucy got out the Yellow Pages and started calling hospitals. Her mother had left from New York. Cicarillo was from New York. It was reasonable to assume that she had been born here, and if she had there would be a record of the birth somewhere.

To her disappointment, however, none of hospitals she reached kept old records. "Check the health department," said one polite gentleman with a Spanish accent. Lucy found a listing for birth and death records in the back of the phone book and dialed the number.

"...the information required for obtaining a birth certificate," said the recorded voice, "is the full name as listed on the certificate, date of birth, mother's maiden name, father's name, borough of birth, name of hospital or building address where the birth occurred, and the reason the certificate is needed."

The recording gave another number for further assistance. Lucy dialed. A human being finally answered on the fourteenth ring.

"You must give specific information in order for us to find a birth record," said the woman patiently.

"But I was orphaned as a child and I don't know the specific information. That's why I need you to check."

"You should ask your adoptive parents for more specific information."

"I wasn't adopted," said Lucy, collapsing onto the bed in frustration. "And there weren't any records in the first place."

"All adoptions go through Albany," said the woman, oblivious. "I can give you the number there."

"Thanks anyway," said Lucy, putting down the phone unhappily. This was obviously going to be harder than she had thought. And more expensive. The Cokes in her room's honor bar were $2.50 and they were charging her a dollar a phone call. By the time Theresa Iatoni got back from California, Lucy's hotel bill would be over $2,000. And what if Theresa Iatoni wouldn't meet with her or didn't know anything?

She sighed and rolled to the other side of the bed, where there were still some springs. New York seemed impossibly large. Lucy blanched at the thought of renting and furnishing an obscenely expensive Manhattan apartment, but she would have to find a cheaper arrangement—and a job—if she expected to survive here. And Lucy was a survivor.

LUCY DUMPED the monster Sunday *New York Times* on the bed. The room was too hot. The odor of garbage wafted up from the alley below. So did the characteristic sounds of Love Choo-Choo, at it again. Lucy had been here nearly a week now but still couldn't figure out whether Love Choo-Choo was a prostitute or just an enthusiastic house-wife.

"I can do it! I can do it!" callioped Love Choo-Choo at

unlikely hours of the day or night, until a final "Woooo Wooooooo!" indicated that she had left the station.

Lucy took out the Help Wanted section and started going through the classified ads. She didn't know exactly what type of job she was looking for, but figured she would recognize it when she saw it.

The listings weren't too promising. Lucy figured she'd need at least what she had been making with Welcome Inn to get an apartment and pay the exorbitant city taxes. The problem was she wasn't qualified for anything.

Lucy glanced at the résumé she had worked up on her computer. Six jobs in eights years wasn't going to impress anyone. The printout from her little dot-matrix Diconix wasn't going to impress anyone either. At least "Harvard" looked good under "Educational Background"—as long as no one asked what degree she had earned. She was too honest about some things.

After half an hour with the paper, Lucy's fingers were black with newsprint and her spirits decidedly dampened. There were no ads for hotel inspectors. Or college dropouts. Or orphans.

"What kind of secretary do you think I'd make?" Lucy asked the dresser. The dresser maintained a discreet silence, obviously aware of how rotten her typing was.

Lucy ignored the hollow feeling in her stomach and started through the listings again. There had to be something she could do, even if it wasn't the best thing in the world. She had to find something.

Suddenly she saw it. Lucy read over the ad, again, amazed that she had missed it the first time:

Entrepreneur needs clever assistant. Free room and board. Weehawken, New Jersey. Contact Mr. Wing

There was a phone number with a 201 area code. Wing was a Chinese name. What kind of entrepreneurs did they have in New Jersey? Where was Weehawken, anyway? Could she commute to the city from there?

Lucy read the magic words again. "Free room and board." Free room and board! That would solve all her problems. Whatever the job paid, she would come out ahead if she didn't have to pay rent and buy furniture. The taxes might even be less in New Jersey.

Lucy picked up the phone, then put it back down.

What was she getting herself into? This was New York City, after all, not Kankakee. For all she knew this Wing person could be a white slaver. Or an opium merchant. She'd have to be crazy to go off blindly to some strange city on the strength of an ad in the paper!

Lucy looked at the magic words one more time—"Free room and board"—then dialed the number.

So she would be careful. She didn't have to take the job if she didn't like the looks of things. They might not offer it to her anyway. It couldn't hurt to check it out, could it?

No one would be there on Sunday, Lucy knew, but maybe she could leave her name on a machine or with an answering service. Some ads got hundreds of responses. It was important to stand out, make them remember your name. Maybe she'd leave several messages.

"Yes, yes, yes?" answered a voice abruptly and none too happily. Lucy was too surprised to hang up. Who worked on Sunday night?

"Hello. My name is Lucy Trelaine. I'm calling about your ad in the paper."

"You clever person?" It was a comic-book Oriental accent, guttural, the *l*s crimped, the stresses in the wrong places.

"Clever enough to call on Sunday," she said warily.

"You have experience?"

"Experience at what?"

"You ever raise money for new venture, maybe?"

"No," said Lucy carefully, "but I have worked extensively in finance and have a good deal of accounting knowledge.''

''Woa!'' came the throaty exclamation.

Lucy felt a little guilty. The financial planner she'd worked for had made his money selling unnecessary insurance policies to little old ladies and the accountant had used her as a human adding machine. But you had to put the best face on your experience, didn't you?

''I run quality business,'' the voice was chattering in her ear. ''You quality person?''

''As a matter of fact, my most recent position was monitoring quality for a national hotel chain.''

''No kidding?''

''No kidding,'' she said honestly.

''You brave person?''

''What?''

''You scared of lot of stuff, maybe?''

Lucy removed the receiver from her ear and stared at it for a moment, then spoke again.

''May I ask what kind of business we're talking about here?'' she said.

''Very nice business, please. Service everybody needs, sooner or later.''

''Oh? Exactly what service—''

''Rucy Trelaine,'' he said, mangling her name. ''Nice name. Why should I hire you over plenty of others, Rucy Trelaine?''

''Well, I don't really know. I don't know what your needs are.''

''Need clever assistant.''

''Well, I did go to Harvard,'' Lucy muttered.

''Famous American university?''

''Yes.''

''Okay. You come Weehawken tomorrow at ten a.m. Thirty-two Boulevard East. Take cab, I reimburse. My name Wing. Bye-bye.''

The line went dead.

Lucy put down the phone and stared out at the air shaft for a long time, hoping to hear a reassuring "I can do it." Where was Love Choo-Choo when you really needed her?

"So I puffed up my credentials a little," she finally said to the ceiling. "So what? Everybody does it. I need the job."

The ceiling peeled disapprovingly. Lucy swallowed hard. Why did she feel so guilty? And what was she getting herself into?

SIX

THE NEXT MORNING, against her better judgment, Lucy Trelaine was in a cab going through the Lincoln Tunnel on her way to New Jersey.

She had no idea where Weehawken was. Her New Hampshire bank belonged to a national network of cash machines and Lucy had withdrawn $100 at a local Irving Trust. She hoped it would be enough. As for this Mr. Wing, Lucy was prepared to give him the benefit of the doubt but had a fork in her purse just in case. She hoped it would be enough, too.

Lucy had figured on a long trip, but it took practically forty minutes just to get out of Manhattan. She had only an hour left to make it to Weehawken. Would she still be reimbursed if she showed up late?

The cab crawled through the narrow, poorly lit tunnel. Lucy tried not to breathe or think of the billions of tons of Hudson River above their heads. The air seemed like it was almost pure carbon monoxide. She marveled at the strange state life had brought her to. As if to confirm the fact, the cabbie tilted his head back and hollered through the bulletproof partition.

"This is Joisey. I get double fare from here."

Suddenly they were out of the tunnel and the sun was shining in her eyes again. She took a deep breath; the air still smelled awful. The cabbie took the first exit. They drove up a hill onto a small residential road and stopped. Lucy's watch said 9:05.

"That comes to twenty-nine bucks."

"This is it?"

"Thirty-two Boulevard East."

"This is Weehawken?"

"Yeah? So?"

"Weehawken, New Jersey?"

"You mean as opposed to Weehawken, France?"

Lucy gave the driver a six-dollar tip. She would be reimbursed. She hoped.

Boulevard East was a quiet street at the top of the Jersey cliffs. There were large, old houses on only one side of the street and they all looked out across the Hudson River to Manhattan. Number thirty-two was a gigantic, multigabled Victorian mansion covered with decorative fretwork and topped with elaborate turrets and chimneys. The trim was white, the clapboards were blue. Stately trees grew all around. A discreet sign next to the driveway read NEAT 'N' TIDY.

Lucy studied the quaint architecture for a minute, trying to guess what sort of business went on behind the gingerbread walls. She was baffled, though reassured, by its appearance, which was in fact neat and tidy. One chimney was taller than the others. It was white metal, clearly not an original feature of the house. Braced with metal struts, it extended ten feet above the roof.

Realizing that she couldn't possibly show up an hour early, Lucy turned and started up the street. Across from the house on the cliff behind a tall iron fence was a weathered bust seated on a rock. She strained to read the inscription.

Upon this stone rested the head of the patriot, soldier, statesman and jurist Alexander Hamilton after the duel with Aaron Burr.

"Great place to die," said Lucy unhappily to the spectacular view of Manhattan across the river. The panorama stretched from New York harbor past the towers of the

World Trade Center, all the way up the West Side to the George Washington Bridge and beyond.

She followed the sidewalk along the top of the cliffs and through a little park. The street became shabbier, the big old houses giving way to boxlike apartment buildings and prosaic brick two-family homes with porches.

After a few more blocks Lucy came to a restaurant. She could use a cup of coffee. And a chocolate doughnut. The lone waitress was Spanish and didn't "habla inglés." Coffee was no problem, but the woman didn't seem to understand what a doughnut was. Lucy tried to think up a convincing pantomime, but couldn't.

Luckily she didn't have to illustrate that she wanted to go to the bathroom—there was a door marked DAMAS in fancy script. Lucy read it "Dames" at first—it took her a minute to figure out the sign was in Spanish, not in Frank Sinatra.

Lucy studied her appearance in the small mirror over the sink. Not too bad for a dame. She was wearing her navy interview suit and had figured out how to secure the blouse's neck scarf with the big silver brooch, hoping it would bring her luck. It had to be good for something. She took out a comb and tried to convince a few recalcitrant black hairs to cooperate with the rest of her head, then gave up.

"Do you have a local phone book?" Lucy asked, returning to the counter. Somehow it seemed more important than ever to look for Trelaines. The waitress smiled in polite incomprehension. Lucy threw her hands up in the air, miming forgetfulness, then opened a book and walked her fingers through the listings. Finally she picked up an imaginary phone and dialed. The woman laughed and clapped her hands, then handed Lucy a greasy Hudson County phone book from a shelf under the cash register.

Lucy sipped her coffee and browsed through the phone book. There were no Trelaines in Hudson County, but there was one listing under MacAlpin. She went over into the

old-fashioned phone booth next to the door marked HOM-
BRES and closed the door. A little light went on above her
head. Lucy deposited her quarter and dialed.

"Hello?" answered a female voice on the second ring.

"Hello. Robert MacAlpin, please."

"He's at work."

"Are you Mrs. MacAlpin?"

"Yes?"

"Perhaps you can help me," said Lucy, launching into
her standard routine. "My name is Lucy MacAlpin Trelaine. My parents were killed in a car crash when I was a
baby. I'm trying to find my family. Has your husband ever
talked about a woman relative with a newborn who disappeared thirty years ago?"

"No, I don't think so. You'd have to ask him. He doesn't
talk much about his family."

"When will he be home?"

"Not till after six. He's at the office now. In the city.
You can get him there if you like."

Lucy looked at her watch. There was still plenty of time
until ten.

"Sure, why not?"

The woman gave her a Manhattan phone number. Lucy
thanked the woman, hung up, and dialed, giving the operator her phone credit-card number.

"Home Trust," answered a female voice.

"Robert MacAlpin, please."

The line went dead for a moment, then a curt voice answered.

"MacAlpin."

"I'm sorry to disturb you at work, Mr. MacAlpin," began Lucy, and went into her spiel about the crash thirty
years ago. For the first time she had something new to add.

"Apparently I was also wearing a large silver brooch,
which has just come back into my possession. It's sort of
semicircular with a thick pin. It has my name...it has Lucy
MacAlpin Trelaine written on it and something else—

'Dum...lag...chtat mac Alpin Bethoc.' I have no idea if I pronounced that right. Does any of this ring a bell?''

There was no response. For a moment Lucy thought they might have been disconnected.

"Mr. MacAlpin?"

"I'm here," said MacAlpin, a slight burr noticeable in his brusque voice. "My secretary just put something in front of me. Hoo did you coom to call me, Miss Trelaine?''

People were naturally suspicious of strangers asking questions. Over the years Lucy had found that the best way to deal with them was openly and honestly.

"I just happened to be in Weehawken and your name was in the phone book," she said. "I call MacAlpins everywhere I go. I've talked with hundreds."

"Then you're not from around here?"

"No. Actually I'm staying at a hotel in Manhattan."

"Oh? Which one?"

"The TownLodge."

"On West Fifty-seventh Street? Know it well. So you been lookin' for your people for a long time, then?"

"Years. Actually I was just thinking how ironic it is that I hardly ever talk with real Scots."

For the first time there was a chuckle and the voice softened. "Nae, I'm as American as apple pie, coom over here when I was a young lad. I'm a citizen, ye know."

"Can you help me, Mr. MacAlpin?"

"Nae, I'm sorry, lass," said the man. "It's a real mystery, this one." His initial abruptness was entirely gone now, and the voice was friendly, soft, almost lazy.

"Well, thanks for your time," Lucy sighed.

"Searchin' for years, eh? You're a verra unusual person, Miss Trelaine, I can tell."

"Thank you."

"Most people aren't so thorough. They dinna even keep track of the basics. Like where their children aire, and whether they're losing heating dollars oot an uninsulated attic, even necessary life coverage, can you believe it?''

"Yes, I'm sure that's true, Mr. MacAlpin, but..."

"A course I'm sure someone as careful and methodical as yourself has considered her basic insurance needs verra completely. I mean there you aire, a young girl in a dangerous city with a valuable piece of jewelry—wouldna this be the right time to consider..."

For the next five minutes Lucy tried politely to extricate herself from MacAlpin's insurance pitch.

"Well, I dinna want to press you, you understand," said MacAlpin, finally giving up. "I'm sure ye know what manner of coverage you need."

"Thank you," said Lucy.

"Where can I reach you, in case I ever hear of anything that might help with your search?"

She gave him Billy's address. All her mail from MacAlpins went to Billy, who forwarded it. There was usually a letter a week. Only a few were ever obscene.

"Say," said the mellow voice. "Since you're in Jersey, maybe you'd like to coom for supper...."

The man was like flypaper. "Thanks, but I'm only here for the morning."

"Maybe next time, then. Good luck to you."

"Thanks," said Lucy, hanging up the receiver.

Lucy returned to her coffee. It was cold. Maybe she would be lucky and Robert MacAlpin wouldn't start sending her insurance brochures. It was almost too much to hope for.

Lucy paid the tab and headed back up the street. It was nearly ten. There was that sign again—Neat 'n' Tidy. A featureless white station wagon was now parked in the driveway. The smokestack was belching white smoke.

Still worrying that she was making a terrible mistake, Lucy walked up the steps to the polished wooden door and rang the bell.

A pale young girl in a black dress came to the door. She was only about Lucy's height, her black hair was cut very short like a boy's, and she wore five gold earrings in her left ear. Lucy could barely see the girl's dark eyes behind the thick, round lenses of her glasses.

"My name is Lucy Trelaine...."

"Yes, we're expecting you," said the girl in a tiny voice and showed Lucy through a bright, cheerful lobby into a huge, pleasantly appointed waiting room. Lucy sat uneasily on the couch and looked out at an astonishing view of Manhattan through the picture windows.

Suddenly a pudgy Oriental man bounded out of an inner office. Lucy jumped in spite of herself. The little man set upon her, shaking her hand with both of his.

He was about five foot, four inches tall and was shaped like a dumpling. His outfit was incredible: a Prince Albert coat, striped trousers, an old-fashioned black-silk top hat. He looked like a miniature Englishman on his way to the races at Ascot. A goatee, graying at the tips, brought his round face to a point. His bright eyes danced merrily in a tangle of smile lines. Lucy couldn't honestly tell whether he was an old twenty or a young sixty.

"Hello, hello, hello!" said the man, bouncing up and down.

"I'm Lucy Trelaine," Lucy replied, finally freeing her hand from his powdery grip.

The little man suddenly bent one knee, stretched his arms out in front of him like a cheap painting of Jesus, and exclaimed, "Take Wing!"

Lucy was about to head for the hills before she realized it was his name.

SEVEN

Tak Wing (whose name was pronounced "take" but spelled without the final *e*) always wished he could remember more about his father.

There was only the one clear memory. It was an afternoon in 1937. Tak Wing was six years old. He and his father were sitting under a plum tree in the courtyard garden of their house in Nanking. Yellow carp swam in the small pool from which a great gnarled stone seemed to grow.

Tak Wing always thought it was funny that he could remember the ladybug crawling up his finger but not his father's face. There was the uniform, the polished boots, the quiet voice, but no face.

"The only thing that doesn't change," his father was saying, "is the fact that everything changes. That is the Tao. You can accept the Tao or fight it, but still everything will change."

Things did change. A formation of Japanese Zeros appeared out of the clouds. The planes strafed the garden. Tak Wing's father fell facedown in the chrysanthemums. Moments later the Wing house exploded. When the invaders took the city, Tak Wing was still sitting by his father's body, hoping things had finished changing.

Soldiers dragged the little boy from his garden and brought him before General Todesciu Morehi.

"Do you want to live as a Japanese or die as a Chinese?" demanded the general through an interpreter.

"When I die, won't I still be me no matter who I am?" he replied.

General Morehi thought this was immensely funny. It

was funnier still to make a high-ranking Chinese officer's son into a servant. When the general returned to Tokyo six months later, Taki, as he had come to be called, went with him as a houseboy.

Since fighting the Tao was pointless, Taki abandoned his own language for Japanese and became a cheerful and efficient servant. He did what he was told without complaint, which General Morehi took as further evidence of Chinese cowardice.

The war took its course. Two days after the Emperor commanded the Japanese to surrender, Morehi-san committed *seppuku.* Worried that the Americans might send him back to China, Taki ran away to Tokyo to seek his fortune. But he was not Japanese. In the slums of Tokyo he was shunned as only the Japanese can shun foreigners.

Taki was finally taken in by a refugee Chinese family, but he barely remembered the language and was treated like a dog. He soon left, preferring life in the streets to further humiliation.

He lived in bombed-out buildings, begging for food, stealing when there was something to steal. His only asset was the sense of humor he had developed to survive in Morehi's house. If you could make someone laugh, they were less inclined to beat you.

Ironically it was the Americans who laughed the easiest and were the most generous. Taki spent each day loitering near the U.S. Army base. The MPs threw him out periodically, but Taki picked up enough handouts—and English—to make persisting worthwhile.

When he was seventeen he hooked up with a Negro sergeant named Caesar St. Vincent Marvelle. Marvelle was a "dog robber," an army scavenger responsible for keeping spare parts in the motor pool and steak in the officers' mess.

Taki, who was small and looked younger than his age, cornered Marvelle outside the Quonset hut where the NCOs held their regular Friday-night poker game.

"GI, GI," said Taki, tugging at Marvelle's coat. "You

will be lucky tonight.'' He actually said, ''You wirr be rucky tonight.'' His English got better all the time, but he never did get to manage the *l*s.

Marvelle brushed the boy aside.

''No kidding, GI,'' said Taki, running after him. ''You will draw to inside straight. Win big. You see.''

''What you say, boy? What kinda fool do you take me for, drawin' to an inside straight?''

''You see. You be lucky.''

Marvelle pushed him away and went into the game. Taki waited outside, stamping his feet to keep warm. He had worked this same routine many times before. When the game broke up, Taki would be standing thirty feet from the door of the Quonset hut. When the soldier he had told to draw to the inside straight appeared, Taki would yell, ''Hey, GI! What you say now?''

There were three possible outcomes. Most often the soldier just looked back blankly or shot Taki the finger, meaning that he had ignored the advice totally. On a few occasions, GIs who had lost money drawing to inside straights charged after him. This is why Taki stood thirty feet from the door; it gave him a good head start.

Every so often, however, the soldier won a big pot. Taki might then get a few bucks for bringing the man luck. He could eat for a week on a few bucks.

This night Marvelle came out of the game with a big smile on his face.

''GI smart, win big, yes?'' Taki yelled happily.

''Yo, kid. Come here.''

Taki ran over for his reward. Marvelle smiled until Taki was a foot away, then grabbed the boy by the lapels of his dilapidated coat and held him three inches off the ground.

''Uh-oh,'' said Taki, his feet pedaling uselessly in the air. ''I not so clever as I thought.''

''I oughta kill you!'' hollered Marvelle.

''You let me live, I help you,'' Taki sputtered.

"Help me lose another hundred bucks, you little Jap bastard?"

"Please, please, GI!" hollered Taki. "I worth more alive than dead."

"How you figure that, boy?"

"Please, I get you samurai sword. Good price."

American soldiers prized samurai swords over all other souvenirs. To afford food, many Japanese were forced to sell swords that had been in their families for generations. Taki knew a black market for swords in the Ginza; he had been chased away from it often.

"Okay, let's go," said the sergeant.

"No like Americans. You give me money, I bring back sword," said Taki optimistically. It was worth a try.

Marvelle laughed and put Taki back on the ground, but didn't let go of him. "You a real character, you know that? What's yo' name?"

"Tak Wing."

"Tak Wing, huh? Well, you and me's gonna take wing over to this place with the swords, but if you're dickin' me around I'm gonna cut your throat, you unnerstan'?"

"Sure, GI," Taki gulped with a smile.

Marvelle bought eight antique swords with the $300 he had won at the poker game by drawing to an inside straight. He sold the swords for $1,500.

Taki became Marvelle's assistant. Together they traded in food, currency, and defective army equipment, which Taki, who had an uncanny knack with machinery, was always able to fix. By the time Marvelle returned to the States a few years later, Taki was a successful dealer in contraband in his own right.

The authorities had begun to crack down on the black market, however. Without the protection of the Americans, Taki was at the mercy of the *yakuza*, or Japanese gangsters. He was persuaded to retire by a man missing several finger joints with tattoos running up his neck and spilling out of his cuffs onto his wrists.

It was 1951, the Japanese economy was in shambles, and Taki was Chinese, a nonperson. Within a few years he was reduced to sweeping the floors of a Tokyo fish market. He did his job and waited for things to change.

It took a decade for Taki to save enough to open his own stall in the fish market. The humorless Japanese men for whom he had mopped, cleaned fish, and repaired equipment congratulated Taki on his industry, then forced him out of business in a matter of months.

Taki was thirty-two years old and had nothing to show for a lifetime of work. One night, after drinking sake until two in the morning, he dreamed he was sitting in the middle of a busy crossroads when a bull walked up and pissed on his head. Taki awoke enlightened. He had been sitting at the fish market, waiting for the Tao to stop for him. All the while the world had been moving, passing him by.

Through friends Taki was able to get a berth on a commercial tuna boat. In less than a week he was on his way to the Philippines, as happy as his seasickness allowed, all his belongings stuffed in a canvas sack. He would go where the winds took him.

Tak Wing sailed around the China Sea for a few years. It was a busy life, full of hard work and a certain wary camaraderie. Taki was happy and could have done it forever, but then one day the boat was impounded in the harbor at Sydney—the Korean owners had gone bankrupt. Taki was stranded in Australia.

Taki had no incentive to make his way back to Japan, but to remain in Australia he needed someone to sponsor him. After being thrown out of a dozen offices, Taki found Bartlett Hewby, the flamboyant president of an Australian development company.

"Come, come, my little slant-eyed friend," said the big man, sipping tea behind a long desk. "What on earth do I need a translator for?"

"Much Asian money shopping in Australia. I fluent in all Oriental languages," said Taki, though he was barely understandable in anything but Japanese. "You need clever fella. Keep Japs honest in dealings with you."

Hewby smoothed his patrician head with a manicured hand. "My dear boy, why would I trust one Wog over another?"

"I bring you luck," said Tak Wing. "You engaged in big deal right now, yes?"

"I'm always engaged in big deals," sniffed Hewby.

"No, no. One in particular."

"Well, yes, I suppose. There is the Owens Flats contract. What are you leading to?"

Taki nodded happily. "I study this carefully. They bluffing."

"Really?"

"You can do twice as well as you think," said Taki confidently, not knowing whether Hewby was the buyer or seller, but recognizing an inside straight when he saw one.

Taki called a week later (a phone call was even safer than thirty feet). Hewby had been able to purchase the Owens Flats property for half the original asking price and wanted Taki to be his new assistant.

Things had changed. Taki had a new career, a new country, a new life.

By the time Hewby decided to retire to London a few years later, Taki had learned the real-estate business inside out. He wasn't rich, but he was able to offer Hewby a complex leveraged buyout for the company: an Australian bank would advance Hewby half the purchase price and Taki would pay out the balance over ten years.

For a while Taki prospered, developing properties. Then he got involved in the Adelaide water deal. Adelaide was a friendly little town in South Australia cursed with some of the worst-tasting tap water on earth. Always a tinkerer, Taki designed a new type of water desalinization plant. It was a golden opportunity, his chance to make some money as well as a real contribution to the country. If his ideas could bring good water to Adelaide, the government might let him become a citizen!

To finance the huge project, Taki leveraged his Sydney real estate and raised the remainder by private subscription. Within a year, however, cost overruns, technical problems, and underestimated graft had doubled the initial estimate. While Tak Wing frantically cut corners and scrambled to find additional backing, Bartlett Hewby was having trouble maintaining his standard of living in London and chose this moment to sell Taki's note. The buyers, a real-estate syndicate, found a loophole in the legal work and demanded payment in full.

Tak Wing was woefully overextended. His financing collapsed, millions of investor dollars were lost, and Taki was forced into bankruptcy. He was virtually destitute, his visa was revoked, and he barely avoided criminal prosecution.

Bartlett Hewby was distressed to learn of his protégé's troubles. Feeling partly responsible, Hewby sent Taki a plane ticket to London and put him up in his Mayfair flat.

Taki took the only job he could find, sweeping out a pub in Kensington. He began coming home increasingly late and increasingly drunk. Finally Hewby couldn't stand it anymore. He called in all his favors and helped his poor friend emigrate to the United States. Anything to be rid of him!

When Tak Wing arrived in New York he was forty-four years old. He had $100 in his pocket and a few belongings in a canvas bag.

Taki took a room at the YMCA and went through a lunatic series of jobs to support his drinking: making hats, modeling shoes, driving a fish truck for the Fulton Street market.

One day Taki was dispatched to New Jersey in his fish truck. As he exited the Lincoln Tunnel, he looked up and saw a sign for Weehawken.

Shivering with awe, Taki nearly ran off the road. Weehawken! The very name was magical. Weehawken was the place his friend, Sgt. Caesar St. Vincent Marvelle, had always talked about so many years before.

He pulled off the highway and found a phone book at a grocery store. The only listing under Marvelle was for a Cassandra. A few minutes later Taki was standing in front of the address, a decaying mansion on a cliff overlooking Manhattan. The sign in front of the building read LORD GOD ALMIGHTY SALVATION CHAPEL AND FUNERAL PARLOR.

Taki was shown a seat next to an open coffin with a thin black man inside, very dead. After ten minutes an enormous and elderly black woman entered. Her bearing was regal. She was dressed in a black silk dress and held her head like a queen.

"I looking for Sergeant Marvelle," said Taki, rising.

"Who wants to see him?"

"I old friend. Army buddy."

"You don't look like no army buddy I ever saw."

"We friends in Japan. Nineteen hundred forty-six. Best buddies."

"My brother been dead for six years. High blood pressure. I laid him out myse'f."

Taki sat down and began to cry.

Miss Marvelle couldn't believe her eyes. She finally calmed Taki down, took him upstairs to her living quarters, and had her cook, a feebleminded woman known only as Aunt Sally, fix him lunch.

They talked about Caesar and the funeral business through the afternoon and into the evening. Miss Marvelle was getting on in years. Lately she had been seriously thinking about finding someone young and energetic to help her out.

"You bein' a friend of Caesar an' all, mebbe I can trust you. You interested in learning the funeral business from the ground up? Can't pay you much, but the job comes with room and board."

The next day Miss Marvelle paid the Bonaducci brothers for the truckload of spoiled fish, and Taki moved his few belongings from the YMCA. Miss Marvelle was true to her word; Taki learned the business from the ground up—she started him out sweeping the floors.

EIGHT

"It's a what?" gasped Lucy, holding a limp hand to her throat.

"Funeral parlor," beamed Tak Wing.

"Neat 'n' Tidy?"

The little man nodded vigorously, his white teeth gleaming.

"New concept. No more embarrassing looking at dead body. No more big, expensive funeral. Cremation only. Cremation now fifteen percent of all funerals, up from three percent when I start. Be twenty-five percent within ten year. Growth industry."

"Think of that," said Lucy. But she wasn't thinking of that. She was thinking of the chimney belching white smoke atop the gingerbread house. And her hotel bill.

"Neat 'n' Tidy," Wing continued enthusiastically. "One phone call, no worry."

"For those who care but can't be bothered?" said Lucy.

"That good," beamed the little man. "You have talent for this."

"Please don't say that."

"I inherit," Wing continued, ignoring her. "Miz Marvelle. Kind lady, dear friend. She die five year ago."

His broad smile suddenly disappeared and Lucy watched, astonished, as he wiped away a tear.

"Funeral used to be biggest expense in most people's lifetime after house and car," said Wing, wistfully. "But things change. Young people not want spend fortune on making corpse happy anymore, yes? Want everything fast. Fast, fast, fast. Cheap, also. Cheap, cheap, cheap.

"So I make business fast and cheap. I make like Mc-

Donald's. 'You deserve a funeral today.' Call up Wing: station wagon come, take loved one away. Four hundred dollars, soup to nuts. Family have plenty of cash left to put new deck on house.''

"That's really…fascinating," said Lucy politely. Wing grinned cockily, adjusted his top hat, and folded his arms in front of him.

"Wing have the experience," he said confidently. "Wing have the technology. Wing have the vision.''

Lucy herself had the distinct feeling that things were getting out of hand. Over and over she asked herself, "Do I really need a job this much?" The answer kept coming back—yes.

"Show facilities now," said Wing, standing suddenly. "Come!" Lucy's résumé fluttered from his lap to the floor. He had barely glanced at it, just marveled over and over, saying, "To think Harvard woman working for Wing." Lucy felt like a snail about lying to him, but what choice did she have?

"Wing give tour," the little man squealed, motioning wildly with his pudgy hands. "You see. Humble place of business. Very modern stuff.''

"No, really, you don't have to.…"

"Come come!"

Reluctantly Lucy rose. Wing bowed at her. She bowed back. He bowed again. Lucy bowed. Wing bowed again. Lucy left it at that and followed him past the smiling punk receptionist and into the house.

After passing several empty offices they came to a large, homey room, lined with organ pipes and paneled in dark wood, where half a dozen women typed on computer keyboards.

"First floor used to be big profit center." Wing sighed. "Four viewing rooms. Fond Farewell Chapel. Heavenly Rest casket showroom. All gone now. Administration only.''

"It looks very advanced."

"Everything computerized." He brightened, punching buttons on a vacant terminal. "Handle paperwork for all of chain here."

"Chain?"

"Twenty Neat 'n' Tidies in tri-state area," he said, walking to the door. "Big expansion going on, you be very impressed."

Lucy followed speechlessly.

Wing poked his head into several other offices, some empty, some full of efficient-looking men and women. All the rooms were wood-paneled and nicely carpeted. The house was the sort of place where one would expect to find an elderly aunt.

"Not that I really want to know," Lucy finally said, unable to contain her curiosity, "but where are the bodies? This seems like just a nice old house."

"Funeral operation totally separate. In basement. Customers brought down ramp, side of house," said Wing proudly, his eyes twinkling. "Let's go see."

They proceeded down the center hall until they came to what looked like a closet. Wing opened the door and Lucy followed him into a tiny elevator, vaguely relieved that she didn't have to go down a ramp.

"I live on second floor," said Wing, pressing the button marked B. "Your room third floor. Private staircase. Very cheery."

The elevator hummed noisily. In a minute a gentle clunk indicated that it had come to rest. Wing opened the door into another world: stark, white, antiseptic.

They were in a cavernous basement hall. It looked and smelled like a hospital. The lighting was fluorescent. Against the low ceiling were bundles of pipes, each a different size and color.

"This is more like what I expected," said Lucy, looking at the pipes.

"Formaldehyde on tap," said Wing, leaning over conspiratorily. Then he darted into a door to their right. Lucy shuddered and hastened after him. She found herself in a room with two stainless steel gurneys supporting man-sized black vinyl bags.

"Wing meet all state requirements," he said, motioning at an empty table in the center of the room, proud as any owner of a modern noodle factory. Lucy's eyes wandered to the drain in the middle of the floor and the curled-up garden hose. She wasn't about to ask what the state requirements were. Wing was pointing to what looked like built-in file cabinets.

"Cold storage."

Lucy nodded.

"New, high-efficiency, electric crematory ovens," said Wing in the next room, motioning at two rows of small iron doors set into the wall. Lucy tried to look interested, or at least not sick.

"I call them 'snappy retorts,'" he chortled. "A little funeral parlor humor. Ha ha?"

"Ha ha," agreed Lucy.

They pushed through three more rooms. Wing introduced her to several nearly normal-looking people in white coats, held up shiny tools of his trade, poked into cupboards and cabinets, cracked what he obviously thought were jokes.

"Well," said Lucy finally, "that was very impressive, Mr. Wing. About my cab fare..."

"Please, please, Ms. Trelaine," said the little man, leading her to another door, this one steel, which he unlocked with a key from his ring. "My triumph. Will change course of funeral industry. Please, please," he begged, bouncing up and down, holding on to his top hat, which he apparently never took off.

"I don't think I really need to see..."

Whatever argument Lucy intended to muster instantly became moot. Tak Wing had opened the door and was urging her in.

Beyond the metal door was a gray room dominated by a machine, a monstrous iron contraption covered with intricate wiring, intimidating valve mechanisms, several chambers of varying sizes, and four polished hydraulic arms leading to gigantic pistons.

"Latest invention," said Wing, rubbing his hands together. He pulled a long lever. Lucy involuntarily took a step back.

Steam hissed out of a chamber, an engine revved up, governors spun. Slowly the piston arms began to move, then picked up speed, until finally it seemed like they were standing in a locomotive. Wing pressed a button and Lucy could hear the sounds of gears engaging. It was like a Frankenstein movie.

"What's in here?" Lucy shouted above the din, pointing at a chamber the size of a small garbage can that had begun to rotate in front of them.

"Mrs. Hernandez!" hollered Tak Wing as he pulled another lever.

Without another word Lucy ran for the door. Wing ran after her, grabbing her arm.

"No worry! No worry! She already dead. Just ashes, no sweat. Come, come, come."

He ran back to his machine. Lucy stood frozen at the door. She wanted out of here, out of Weehawken, out of the state. She also wanted to be reimbursed for her cab fare. Resignedly she walked back to Wing, who was fooling with levers. The noise was deafening. Suddenly he pressed a red button and the racket stopped, the engine ground to a halt, the pistons hissed and died.

"Come, I show you," said Wing merrily and led her around the machine. There was a small chamber at the back, directly in line with the larger chamber, which had now stopped turning. This he opened and took out a polished gray cylinder a little longer than a flashlight battery, a little shorter than a stick of dynamite. He handed it to her.

Lucy examined the artifact cautiously. It was heavier

than it looked, some kind of stone, almost like the granite or limestone facing on an office building.

"Mrs. Hernandez," announced Tak Wing with obvious pride. "Final version."

Lucy dropped the cylinder in shock. Mrs. Hernandez didn't break.

"Compression is key," Tak Wing said, picking up the cylinder. "Plus a little epoxy. No more messy ashes to spill on living-room rug. Beloved relative now rest peacefully on desk or coffee table."

"Seems a little callous," Lucy sputtered, "turning your family into paperweights."

"Better turning them into flower beds?" Wing shrugged and walked to the other side of the room. He deposited the cylinder in a small lathe-like device, then tapped on a nearby computer keyboard. "Now for icing on cake."

"There's icing?"

Wing grinned. The contraption spun for barely a minute. When it stopped, Wing opened the hatch and took out the gray cylinder. There was now an inscription lettered on its side in gold:

Mrs. Maria Hernandez
Rest in Peace

"Neat and tidy, you see?"

"I see," said Lucy.

"So you want assistant to entrepreneur job?"

"Well, this…" said Lucy, nodding at the machinery, "…this isn't exactly what I look for in an entrepreneur."

"Not waste you here. Job upstairs with me."

"What exactly is this job?" she asked suspiciously.

"Thirty thousand dollars, plus good benefits. Medical plan with dental. Room and board. Growth opportunity."

"I really don't think—"

"Okay, thirty-one thousand dollars. You very persuasive. Harvard do good job."

"Really, Mr. Wing..."

"Come, come. You see room now."

Wing popped Mrs. Hernandez in his pocket and bowed.

"Your predecessor," he said absentmindedly, patting his pocket and walking out the door. Lucy followed at a run.

NINE

LUCY SAT next to Neal Bell, Tak Wing's driver, in the front
seat of the white Cadillac limousine—white being the funeral color in Japan. Neal was an older black man with a
pencil-thin moustache and a voice like a pipe organ.

Lucy looked at her watch. It was 12:30. At least they
were out of that horrible tunnel. It had seemed like all New
Jersey was trying to get into Manhattan for lunch.

"It's not much further," said Neal.

"That's good."

He had been talking the whole trip, pointing out land-
marks, editorializing about the good old days. Lucy didn't
feel too much like talking.

"You'll like Weehawken. It's a real nice place."

"I'm sure."

"You know I worked for Miss Marvelle for ten years.
That was the lady that owned the place before Taki. That's
what we call Mr. Wing. Taki. I used to drive the families
to the cemeteries. No call for that anymore. Now we just
send the ashes. COD."

Lucy grunted, totally confused about what to do. At least
Wing had given her a couple days to think it over.

The best thing about the offer, ironically, had nothing to
do with the work. It was the suite of rooms she would be
able to live in.

After the tour of the basement, Wing had taken her up
a narrow, poorly lit staircase from the kitchen at the back
of the house. The door at the top was a dark slab, like the
entrance to a tomb. Wing opened the ancient lock with a
key from his ring. Lucy was expecting a dusty garret at

best. Instead she found a huge, clean space that the morning sun lit up like a lantern.

There were windows on all sides. The ceilings were the insides of the gabled roof—a maze of right angles, a three-dimensional crazy quilt. Every wall was a different size, the floor of each room a unique geometric shape. The pale patterned wallpaper might originally have been deep red. Washed with light, it was now the faintest pink, the tiny flowers barely visible.

There were four rooms in all: a large sitting room with a fireplace, a bedroom, a smaller room that had been fixed up as a study, and a huge bathroom with old-fashioned brass fixtures. It took Lucy a moment to realize that the blue picture on the ceiling above the tub was a portrait of the morning, framed in a skylight.

"When you start?" Wing had asked, bouncing up and down on the bed.

"I still don't understand what the job is."

"See? Lots of room for creativity. You help me run business. We team, like Yankees."

"Don't you want to interview anyone else?" Lucy was still too stunned to think straight.

"Why? Wing decisive guy. You Harvard woman. You enthusiastic—phone on Sunday. Have good sense of humor—laugh at my jokes. You pretty. I like you."

"Look, Mr. Wing if you think…"

Wing hung his head.

"Please accept apologies. Wing no sexist pig. Meant only compliment. No funny stuff. Promise."

He held up his right hand and made a crossing motion over his chest with his left.

"No dead bodies?" asked Lucy warily.

"Strictly management."

"I might need to get into the city during the week sometimes…."

"Hours flexible. Neat 'n' Tidy never sleep."

"Well, I'm used to working for more money…."

"Profit-sharing plan. Three weeks' vacation. Room and board. Free cremation if you croak...."

Lucy was surprised at how tempted she was. It would be great to have the sunny apartment and a salary while she looked for clues to her past. Wing had even reimbursed her for the cab. He seemed on the level and her hotel bill was only going to get higher. Still...

"What happened to Mrs. Hernandez?" Lucy asking as the car turned onto Fifty-seventh Street. Bell shrugged.

"Natural causes," he said melodiously. "I guess."

The limo was pulling up behind a parked tour bus in front of the hotel.

"What would you do if you were me, Mr. Bell?" Lucy asked sincerely.

The man raised an eyebrow and studied her for several seconds.

"Well, honey," he said kindly, "I think I'd start by wiping the lipstick off my teeth."

Lucy shrank an inch. Bell laughed. She got out and stood at the curb as he drove away, acknowledging his wave half-heartedly.

"God, give me a sign," she murmured at the sky.

God didn't answer, but the doorman gave her a strange look. Lucy turned and walked into the hotel, feeling uneasy, worried, confused.

The lobby was full of loud women who smelled like gardenias and men in peach-colored pants and white shoes. Lucy's thoughts wandered involuntarily toward Neat 'n' Tidy. The marketing possibilities were endless.

"Why only gray paperweights?" she asked the empty elevator. "Why not pastel paperweights? Why not paperweights with holograms? Paperweights with American flags?"

The door opened on the seventh floor and Lucy got out.

"Don't tell me I have a talent for the funeral business!" she muttered at the dimly lit hall as she walked toward her room. "I can't lose my perspective about this. It's just a job, just a way to earn money while I wait for Theresa Iatoni to come back.''

Lucy noticed that her door seemed to be ajar, but she automatically pushed it open. The scene didn't register at first. Drawers were open, clothes littered the floor, the mattress was askew on the bed. Was she in the right room? No, those were her suitcases lying open on the floor, and that was her underwear scattered on the bed.

Suddenly Lucy understood. God had given her a sign all right. She'd been robbed.

"ANY BREAK-INS BEFORE?" said the cop, one of a pair of matching blue walruses Lucy mentally had tagged Tweedle Dee and Tweedle Dum.

"Not for weeks," said the hotel assistant-manager unhappily. He stood looking out the window into the air shaft, a thin man in a shiny blue suit.

Lucy sat on the bed, still not believing what had happened.

"One laptop computer, one pair of gold earrings, one pearl necklace," read Tweedle Dee from his notebook. "Anything else?"

Lucy winced. It had taken her three months to save up for those earrings.

"They were looking for cash, no doubt," said Tweedle Dum, playing with his walkie-talkie.

"Why didn't they take my printer?" she murmured.

"Probably needed letter quality," said Tweedle Dee, examining the Diconix. "Is this little thing any good?"

"It's fine if you have a computer."

Lucy mentally kicked herself again for not making backups of her hard disk. Her whole MacAlpin database, ten years' worth of information, was irretrievably gone.

"I got a IBM," said Dee proudly. "I got my wine cellar on disk. It also is useful for managing my finances."

"He's a regular hobbyist, he is," said Dum.

Lucy suddenly thought of something else. She rose shakily and crossed the room to one of the plundered suitcases.

"They took my Walkman," she groaned.

"One Sony Walkman. Tape player or radio?" said Dee, making a note.

"Tape player. They've stolen *Pride and Prejudice!*"

"It's pathetic what drugs can do to da human brain," deadpanned Dum.

"When am I going to get a break?" she demanded, whirling to face the assistant manager. "I mean, I've been good. I eat my vegetables. What did I do to deserve this?"

"Are you sure you locked your door?" the man replied lamely.

"They opened it with a crowbar!"

"I have to ask these questions, you understand. Our insurance company…"

"You mean you'll reimburse me for my losses?" Lucy asked skeptically, looking up.

"I'm sure we can work something out.…"

"I'll give you fifty bucks for the printer," said Tweedle Dee. From the air shaft came a faint "I can do it, I can do it," and the sounds of a headboard clapping against the wall. The hotel manager nervously rubbed his hands together.

"Perhaps if we simply canceled your bill…that is if you have another place that you can go…Miss Trelaine? Would that be satisfactory, Miss Trelaine?"

"PLEASE PASS BROCCOLI," said Wing happily.

The last time Lucy had eaten with so many people had been in Atlanta with a family of McAlpens. That was nearly a year ago. It felt nice not to be eating alone for a change.

Before Neal had returned in the limo for her, Lucy had gotten a free lunch—two shrimp cocktails—courtesy of TownLodge, and had bargained Tweedle Dee up to $75 for her printer. Just getting out from under her bill, however, was enough to make up her mind about the job with Neat 'n' Tidy. Wing had welcomed her with open arms. Literally.

"Glad to have you with us," he had said, squeezing her like she was some kind of melon. "You not be sorry. Welcome aboard."

The bookkeepers and typists had all departed at 5:30, leaving only the residents. Wing sat at the head of the table in the big dining room—once the Fond Farewell Chapel—shoveling rice into his mouth with chopsticks. An obese basset hound named Bartlett Hewby sat mournfully at his feet.

The rest of the group consisted of Neal, Tina Snicowski (the little receptionist with the thick glasses and the earrings), and Aunt Sally, a silent hulk of a woman with bad teeth and a vacuous stare.

Aunt Sally frightened Lucy. She was some kind of culinary idiot savant and had joined them after bringing their food out from the kitchen. Lucy was having second thoughts now, but all her bridges seemed to have caught fire behind her.

Every so often the sounds of station wagons in the driveway reminded Lucy of what went on in the basement twenty-four hours a day. Apparently institutions such as hospitals and nursing homes favored nighttime for pickups, so as not to alarm their living patrons.

"What's the best way into the city?" Lucy asked, looking up from her meal, delicate morsels of chicken and various vegetables.

"There's a van that leaves from across from Port Authority," said Tina breathlessly. "There's a really neat ferry to the Westside piers."

"You can always hitch a ride in with one of the station wagons," rumbled Neal Bell. "We make pickups in the city all the time.

Lucy tried to smile politely.

"You have business in city?" said Wing abruptly. At

least he had taken off his top hat for dinner. His hair was gray like his beard, and thinning.

"Yes," said Lucy, buttering a roll.

"What, what, what?" persisted Wing. "You go to Harvard Club? Disco? Hot date?"

Lucy didn't know what to say. She didn't want to burden everyone with her problems. Wing was probably just trying to be friendly, she supposed.

"I'm looking for someone," she said quietly, not meeting his gaze.

Wing placed his fingers to his lips and stared at her for a moment. "You not want to tell?"

"It's just…"

"You no have to tell. It's okay." He clapped his hands. "Tina, Tina," he said. "Now, please."

"Yes sir, Mr. Wing," said Tina, getting up from the table and going to the kitchen.

Lucy didn't know what was coming, but she didn't like the way everyone was grinning. Her nerves were still shot from the burglary.

Tina returned with a bottle of champagne in a silver ice bucket and five glasses. She placed one glass in front of each of them, while Wing slowly and professionally opened the bottle.

"We drink toast now," said Wing, walking around the table, pouring. He stopped at his own glass, which he filled with another small bottle from the ice bucket, a bottle with a twist-off cap.

"I think I have club soda today," he said quietly, then raised his glass. The others stood and raised their glasses, too.

"To Rucy Trelaine," he said solemnly, still unable to pronounce her name. "May she find everything she is looking for."

Lucy was so touched she nearly dunked her sleeve into the applesauce as she reached for her glass.

After dinner Lucy climbed the narrow stairs to her room

and lay on the bed, staring at the cookie-cutter ceiling. Unfamiliar shadows played across the walls. Although she had opened the windows, the room retained a faint musty smell. Maybe she would put some lemon oil on the chair rail tomorrow. She could even contact-paper the drawers. It was strange to have a room all her own.

"Maybe my luck is finally changing," she said softly to the stuffed teddy bear Aunt Sally had pressed into her arms after dinner. "What did I need all those MacAlpins in the computer for, anyway? None of them knew anything. Now I have new friends, a place to stay. What do I want to hang on to the past for?"

The teddy bear didn't feel the need to answer.

It would be strange to sleep in the same bed for longer than a week, Lucy realized, putting her hands behind her head. She could even unpack all four of her suitcases. She had never done that before.

Lucy tried to picture her mother, but all she could see was the little grave marker at the church cemetery. Lucy fought the image out of her mind. Somewhere across the river might be her past. And her future.

It was a long time before she fell asleep.

TEN

"I'm sorry, Mr. Wing," sniffed the chinless person who a plaque proclaimed was Edward M. Leach. "We've done a discounted cash-flow analysis on your new branches and calculated the weighted average cost of your capital. Your net present value is substantially negative and…"

"Woa," muttered Wing, obviously confused. "Translate into English, please."

Lucy looked around the ornate Manhattan bank. Walnut paneling rose thirty feet up the walls to a gilded ceiling. The tellers stood like exotic zoo animals behind carved steel bars. Leach rocked back smugly in his leather arm-chair. They had been here ten minutes, seven of which Leach had spent on the phone with his stockbroker.

"I'm telling you that acquiring all these new branches made no sense," said the goony-looking banker, examining his knuckles, perhaps for signs of hair. "Your current re-turns aren't enough to justify the carrying costs."

"Numbers not tell whole story," protested Wing. "Wing buy not what is, but what might be."

"Well, it might be, Mr. Wing, but not with our money."

Wing stood, bowed, and walked out, head high. Lucy rose and glared at Leach, who was stifling a smirk. She had half a mind to throw a wastebasket at him, but hurried after her employer instead, catching up with him at the car.

"So how'd it go?" asked Neal Bell, opening the back door for them.

"Big man, little mind."

"Didn't get the loan, huh?"

"There are plenty more banks. Cannot all be run by dopes. We work up new business plan, Rucy, yes?"

"Yes, Mr. Wing," she said, trying not to sound worried. Neal got behind the wheel and started the car. In twenty minutes they were out of midtown Manhattan and on the road to Connecticut to inspect the Bridgeport Neat 'n' Tidy. Wing made it a point to visit at least one branch each day.

This was the ninth loan application Lucy had seen turned down in the three weeks she had worked for Wing. It hadn't taken her long to understand how grim the situation was: Wing was leveraged to his eyeballs and needed at least $3 million to keep operating.

It was a shame, Lucy thought. Wing was the best boss she'd ever had. He came up with new ideas as easily as lesser men percolated coffee. He was on top of every problem, understood each opportunity, knew every one of his many employees by name. His innovations had transformed one nearly bankrupt funeral home into a money machine. Although Lucy still had reservations about his "product," she had to admire the boldness of his vision.

"Soon have Neat 'n' Tidy everywhere," Wing had proclaimed during her first day on the job. "People no more waste money on big funerals for dead relatives. Wing set up branches in inner cities. Pay less rent. Give jobs to poor people. Give them hope."

The only problem in the scenario was the fact that Wing's dreams were bigger than his financing. A new branch took only a year to begin making money, but Wing's balance sheets were drowning in red ink from the start-up costs for so many new branches. If he had slowed down, digested his gains, everything would have been fine, but Wing couldn't wait. He plunged ahead, blindly optimistic, using his genius to increase sales rather than reduce expenses, buying new branches with his profits rather than covering his debt.

They drove in silence into the tangle of roads that had so frightened Lucy that first night. Even in daylight the tenements below looked menacing, but Neal navigated con-

fidently through the devastation and finally into the sunny
greenery of the Connecticut Turnpike.

Of the people in the big house in Weehawken, Neal was
Lucy's favorite after Wing. Over the past three weeks he
had gone out of his way to make her feel at home, driving
her to a mall in Passaic to pick up some new clothes, giving
her knickknacks for her mantlepiece and plants for her win-
dowsill. The little apartment on the third floor was beginning to feel really cozy.

Lucy had also struck up a friendship with Tina Snicowski, the little receptionist. Tina was a runaway whom
Wing had taken in and was sending to night school. Despite
her five earrings and the occasional patch of orange she put
in her hair, Tina turned out to be painfully shy. She blushed
crimson when Lucy offered to help with her homework,
but finally accepted.

Even Aunt Sally seemed less menacing once Lucy figured out that the verses she constantly muttered were not
incantations, but nursery rhymes.

"Stop the car! Stop the car!"

"What's the matter, Mr. Wing?" said Lucy as Neal
pulled the Cadillac onto the berm.

"Look! Look at beautiful tree!"

"It's very beautiful, Mr. Wing, but why have we
stopped?"

In addition to taking notes, helping with loan applica-
tions, and managing his correspondence, Lucy was also responsible for keeping Wing on schedule. They were due in
Bridgeport in ten minutes.

"How many people have beautiful tree in backyard?
People cherish beautiful tree, but loved ones end up in urn
on TV set. Rucy, make note for new ad campaign. 'Have
your ashes planted under your favorite tree. Do-it-yourself
perpetual peace.'"

Lucy wrote down the suggestion, amazed again. She
wished her own life were so simple, that like Wing she

could forget about all her problems just because she saw a
beautiful tree.

But that was impossible. It was May 1. Theresa Iatoni
would return from California today.

AS USUAL Wing was oblivious to the seriousness of his
financial situation at dinner that night, recounting over a
roast chicken wild, obviously fictional tales of fishing in
the China Sea.

After dessert—a peach cobbler that Aunt Sally delivered
from the kitchen with as much pride as other women delivered children—Lucy went up to her room and closed the
door. She had purposely waited until evening to make her
call, wanting Theresa Iatoni to be settled in and comfortable
when the phone rang.

For moral support Lucy had brought hang-jowled,
floppy-eared Hewby upstairs with her. The basset hound
sprawled on the rug at her feet, looking up with mournful
eyes. Lucy had never had a pet before and was surprised
at the deep rapport she and Hewby had quickly established.
The dog shared her enthusiasm for both junk food and
Gershwin, and they often listened to the stereo, sprawled
on the living-room sofa together, munching potato chips.

"Okay, are you ready?" Lucy asked the dog. She was
seated on the edge of the bed, holding the phone in her lap
with one hand, the teddy bear with the other.

Hewby adjusted his chins.

"I'm glad you're here," confided Lucy. "I used to talk
to inanimate objects."

"Woof," said Hewby sadly.

"Okay, now, be quiet while I make my call."

The dog stared at her, licked his face, went back to sleep.
Lucy dialed.

"Yes?" answered a small voice after three rings.

"Theresa Iatoni, please," said Lucy, half confident, half
terrified.

"Speaking," the voice cracked.

"Miss Iatoni, my name is Lucy Trelaine. I was the baby who survived the crash that killed your brother. I'd like to talk with you."

The line was silent for several seconds. Finally the little voice spoke again.

"What about?"

"I'm trying to find my family, Mrs. Iatoni."

"Oh. I don't know how I can help you."

"I don't know, either," Lucy said, trying to put a chuckle in her voice, to sound disarming.

"So why are you calling me?"

"I only found out about your brother a few weeks ago and there are a million things I don't understand."

Hewby sniffled audibly. Lucy knew she was blowing it.

"It was all such a long time ago," said the voice in her ear unhappily.

"Yes, I know, but I'm not trying to make trouble or anything, Mrs. Iatoni," Lucy said desperately. "I grew up in foster homes. Nobody knew where I came from. A few weeks ago I found out about the car crash that killed my mother. I just want to know the truth, whatever it is."

There was a pause.

"What do you want to know?" said the voice finally.

"It's hard for me to do this over the phone. Can I come and see you?"

"Oh, I don't know...."

"Please, Mrs. Iatoni. It can't matter that much to you anymore, but it means a great deal to me. Please."

"Well..." said the voice. Lucy held her breath. "All right, honey. Can you come out tomorrow?"

When Lucy put down the phone, her hand was trembling. Hewby roused himself from his lethargy and waddled over to lick it. Lucy scratched his raggedy ears.

What was she going to say to this woman? And, more important, what was Theresa Iatoni going to say to her?

ELEVEN

The Audubon Park Condominiums in Amityville looked like books on a shelf from a distance. Closer up, you could discern the six different styles, the eight available colors, and various other options that differentiated the abutting townhouses. Interconnecting streets of them radiated off a main drive. In the center of the development was a manicured lawn and a shallow pool surrounded by a waist-high chain-link fence—a precaution against grandchildren and other unenlightened visitors who might mistake the pool's symbolism for an invitation to wade.

Lucy steered the big Cadillac down Blue Jay Cove and onto Turtle Dove Lane. When she had asked for the day off, everybody had been pointedly discreet. Wing had even insisted she take the car, and Lucy had been too embarrassed to refuse. It was like driving a boat.

There wasn't a living soul to direct her through the maze of streets, so the only way to find 1451 Bobolink Place was trial and error. After several wrong turns and cul-de-sacs, Lucy found the address she was looking for. She parked the car at the end of a row of townhouses and walked to the door of the only one painted green.

She pressed the doorbell. Nothing happened at first. Then the door opened and Lucy found herself facing a squat, blue-haired woman. Was this her aunt?

"Hi," said Lucy, nervously manufacturing a smile. "I'm Lucy Trelaine."

The little woman looked her up and down, then nodded.

"Come in please," Theresa Iatoni said stiffly, and led Lucy into the living room, a narrow white box.

"Can I get you anything?" said the woman.

"No, thanks."

"Coffee? Soda? I have some iced tea."

"No, really, I'm fine."

Lucy sat down on the orange sofa. Mrs. Iatoni sank into a paisley chair. There were two white table lamps in the shape of poodles. The rest of the furniture was the sort of thing Lucy would expect to find on top of a wedding cake.

"This is very…homey," Lucy said brightly.

"We like it," said Mrs. Iatoni, primly straightening her dress.

"Well," said Lucy. "So here we are."

"So here we are," repeated the little woman, and she smiled for the first time.

"Thanks for seeing me, Mrs. Iatoni."

"Well, like I told you on the phone, Lucy…may I call you Lucy?"

"Please."

"Well, I really don't know anything. Look, I'm sorry about what happened, but it was such a long time ago."

Lucy nodded. "If you could just help me understand what your brother was doing with…with my mother…."

Mrs. Iatoni crossed her arms in front of her defensively. "There was nothing between them, if that's what you mean."

"Maybe I will have some coffee," said Lucy, hoping to head off any confrontation.

"Certainly," said Mrs. Iatoni, her features frozen into a mask, and left for the kitchen.

Lucy stood and tried to admire the black velvet painting of a matador that hung over the fireplace. The woman obviously still felt guilty after all this time. How could Lucy get through to her? After a moment Theresa Iatoni returned with a coffeepot and two plastic cups on a tray. She sat on the sofa and placed the tray on a low table.

"I'm sorry, Mrs. Iatoni," said Lucy, easing down onto the sofa next to her. "You didn't have to see me, I know. It must have been hard for you—your brother dead, a strange woman, a baby. I want you to know that I'm not mad or anything. I just want to find out who I am.''

The hard face softened.

"Look, honey," said Mrs. Iatoni, pouring them each a cup of coffee. "The police called from Massachusetts and said that Alex was dead. This was such a long time ago."

Lucy didn't say anything. Finally the woman continued.

"My brother and I had had a falling out long before that. I hadn't seen him for months. The police wanted to know who he might have been with, but how should I know?"

Lucy nodded.

"My husband and I went up there to identify the body," said Mrs. Iatoni, making a face. "It was horrible. Stephen didn't want me to go in, but I had to see. My brother was all burned up, like a piece of meat. Cream?"

"I take it black."

"I recognized him by his teeth, really. We had been brought up in the depression, so we couldn't afford orthodontists like the kids today. Alex's teeth always looked like a train wreck. Really awful. We were amazed he could chew."

"I'm sorry."

"Well, that was a long time ago. All my grandchildren wear braces, you know," said Mrs. Iatoni, brightening.

"I take it he wasn't married," said Lucy, bringing the cup to her lips. The coffee was still too hot to drink.

"That was the point, Lucy. And it wasn't because of his teeth, if you understand my meaning."

Lucy didn't. Mrs. Iatoni saw it on her face. She smiled and spoke softly.

"My brother was a homosexual, dear. It wasn't fashionable to be a homosexual back then, especially in an Italian neighborhood in Brooklyn. But that's what he was. That's why I knew he couldn't have been involved with that wo…your mother…like they suggested. I couldn't say so at the time, but there you are."

Lucy sat back, stunned.

"Oh, look, honey. I wish I could help you. At the time I was pretty ashamed of my brother. And not just for…you know. Alex had also been arrested a few times for taking tourists for rides."

"He hired out his car, right?"

"When I say he took tourists for rides, I mean he took them for rides. He could somehow persuade foreigners that America had no dependable trains or buses. He would drive them to Cleveland or Nashville or wherever. They'd pay his expenses plus who knows how much? The only reason I know is because he kept hitting me for bail when he got caught. That's why we had the falling out, in fact."

"The police in Pittsfield never mentioned any of this," said Lucy.

Mrs. Iatoni shrugged. "The charges were always dropped. When he was caught Alex would plead 'simple misunderstanding' and return the money. No tourist was going to wait around months for a jury trial when they could just take their money and run."

"So you're saying that my mother could have been a tourist. Your brother could have picked us up at the airport and been taking us practically anywhere."

"That's right. My guess would be that they were heading for Boston—the scenic route—but who knows?"

Lucy's heart sank. Boston, of course, was the first place she had looked for Trelaines, paging through the phone books at the orphanage when she was seven years old. If there was one thing in the world she was sure of, it was that there weren't any Trelaines in Boston.

Theresa Iatoni smiled sweetly, her conscience cleared at last. Lucy tried to smile back. She had come a long way to find such a dead end.

"YOU GOT SOME MAIL, Lucy," said Tina as Lucy dragged herself through the front door feeling like a sack of over-cooked pasta.

"I did?" said Lucy absently, taking the large manila envelope with a New Hampshire postmark.

"You have fun cruisin' in the Neal-mobile?"

"Huh? Oh, sure. Anybody asking for me?"

"Nope. Mr. Wing's in the basement, inventing. Neal is out with Hewby."

"Thanks, Tina," said Lucy and headed for the back stairs, trying to fight the depression that had veiled her since her conversation with Theresa Iatoni. If her mother was just a tourist passing through, then searching for birth records in New York City was pointless. She could have been born anywhere.

"At least I won't pass along the tacky furniture gene," Lucy advised the door to the rear of the house as she opened it. Aunt Sally was in the kitchen.

"I made you a sammich, Lucy," said Aunt Sally in her frightened child's voice. Lucy wasn't really hungry but couldn't bear to hurt the woman's feelings.

"Thank you, Aunt Sally. I'll take it upstairs with me."

"Would you like a glass of milk?"

"No, just the sandwich will be fine."

Aunt Sally padded over to the refrigerator and handed Lucy a plate draped in wax paper.

"Thanks very much," said Lucy, bounding up the stairs, feeling guilty. Not only was she not helping Mr. Wing raise money, she was eating him out of house and home as well.

Flopping listlessly on the bed, Lucy unwrapped the sandwich and took a bite. Tuna fish. Her least favorite. Chewing unhappily she tore open the manila envelope. It was her mail that Billy Rosenberg had forwarded, of course. Lucy had finally called to touch base with him last week.

The envelope included the usual bank and credit-card statements, some junk mail, a tax form. One letter, however, caught her eye. The return address was from a Robert MacAlpin in New York City. Lucy liked to hear from MacAlpins, but couldn't place the name at first. Then she remembered. The insurance man. This really was her lucky day.

She sighed and opened the letter. It contained a single sheet of Home Trust stationery and was dated three weeks ago.

Dear Miss Trelaine,

I've been doing some thinking since our conversation and realize now that I do know something about you. In fact I think I can clear up the whole mystery.

I tried to reach you at the TownLodge, but you had already checked out. With your experience in hotels I would have thought you might have left a forwarding address, but I'm writing to the address in New Hampshire you gave me in the hopes that you will receive it before too long.

Please call me at the telephone number above as soon as you receive this. I am very eager to meet with you and explain everything.

Yours truly,
Robert MacAlpin

Lucy had dropped the sandwich and was sitting straight up on the bed, her depression not even a memory. She read the letter again with growing excitement.

After losing her computer she had tried to forget about MacAlpins altogether. Wouldn't it be something if a MacAlpin solved the puzzle now, after all these years?

"Can I ask for another day off this week or is that too much?" she asked the remains of the sandwich.

The sandwich didn't answer. Lucy took another bite.

"All right," she said with her mouth full. "But there's no reason I can't meet with Robert MacAlpin on Saturday, is there?"

What could the sandwich say?

Still, there was something about this that bothered Lucy, something that seemed out of place, out of joint, though what it was she could not say.

TWELVE

LUCY WALKED INTO Trump Tower stifling the impulse to giggle at the doorman. He was decked out in red military splendor like one of the guards at Buckingham Palace, his awesome height and jet-black face topped off by what looked like a gigantic black rabbit's foot on his head.

Inside, the lobby was done in veined red marble—floors, walls, and ceiling—giving Lucy the distinct feeling of being in a huge and ostentatious bathroom. In the center of the concourse a man in a tuxedo was playing Cole Porter on a grand piano. Behind him the space opened to a ten-story atrium with a waterfall cascading down one marble wall. Weekend shoppers nibbled cream puffs in the café, a floor below ground level. Gawking tourists admired their reflections in the polished brass. Crudely accented conversation swirled all around.

"Ain't it the most beauty-ful thing you ever seen?"

"Can you imagine what they paid for all this?"

A goggle-eyed fellow in a baseball cap and T-shirt strained what he used for a neck. "Now this is the kind of place I should live in," he said to the creature in a lavender pantsuit by his side.

Lucy made her way up the escalator. She couldn't resist taking a spin around the second floor, a subway tunnel of red marble. She passed several tiny stores featuring merchandise like $600 belts and $1,500 purses before coming out where she started. Each of the next six floors had similar shopping tunnels, but Lucy wasn't interested in shopping. At least not at these prices.

She rode the escalator to the top level of the atrium and walked down the marble hall. This floor followed the same plan as those beneath, but at the back instead of another store there was a miniature restaurant with tables set with white linen and gleaming crystal. A man at one of the tables—there were only eight and all were against windows—stood and waved her in.

"Mr. MacAlpin?" asked Lucy nervously.

"I am. An' you moost be Lucy Trelaine. Pleased to make your acquaintance at last."

MacAlpin held out the chair as she sat down. He was a wiry man of average height with soft gray eyes. There were still some flecks of brown in his graying hair. He was wearing an elegant charcoal gray suit with a faint pinstripe. His shoes shone like mirrors.

"This is quite a place," said Lucy, bursting with excitement, exhilarated by the view down Fifth Avenue.

"Indeed it is," he grinned. "We hae castles in Scotland, but naught the likes of this."

A white-jacketed waiter swooped over Lucy's shoulder and handed her a menu.

"The fish is very good here," said MacAlpin, studying her with a kind face. "An' I've ordered a wee bottle, if tha's all right with you."

"Sure," said Lucy.

As if on cue, another waiter brought over an ice bucket and unobtrusively opened a bottle of Pouilly-Fuissé, then passed MacAlpin the cork. MacAlpin absently rolled it between his fingers and nodded. The waiter filled Lucy's glass, then MacAlpin's, and departed. Lucy took a sip of her wine.

"It's delicious," she exclaimed.

"Ye should try the trout," said MacAlpin with a smile. "I'm sairtain ye willna be disappointed."

"Can I have a shrimp cocktail, too?"

"Absolutely."

Lucy grinned. She had to admit that this Robert MacAlpin had a lot of style—for an insurance agent.

"Two trout, please," said MacAlpin when the first

young waiter returned. "And a shrimp cocktail for the lady to start."

"You really didn't have to go to all this trouble...." Lucy began as the waiter departed, but the little Scot held up his hand.

"Wha' man in his right mind would consider it trouble to have lunch wi' a bonnie yoong lass, I ask ye?"

"Well, I'm flattered," said Lucy, flattered.

MacAlpin pushed himself back from the table and studied her for a moment, grinning.

"Lucy MacAlpin Trelaine," he said finally.

"Mr. MacAlpin," Lucy replied, grinning right back. "So. Can you really tell me who I am?"

"I hope so. You've brought your brooch like I asked?"

Lucy nodded eagerly.

"May I see it?"

Lucy took the monstrosity out of the pocket of her jacket—she hated to carry a purse—and put it on the table between them. MacAlpin picked it up as gently as one might pick up a robin's egg and stared at it. When he turned it over and studied the inscriptions on the back, Lucy saw that his hands were trembling.

Finally, as a silent man in a white coat delivered four of the most gigantic shrimp Lucy had ever seen, MacAlpin placed the brooch carefully back on the table between them.

"Well?" said Lucy, practically jumping out of her skin.

"I dinna want to say anything until I'm sure. Please now, go ahead and eat."

Lucy speared a shrimp and impatiently took a bite.

"Very good," she said, chewing. "When will you be sure? Sure about what?"

"Well, I've asked someone to join us here if ye dinna mind. I think he'll be able to tell us if your brooch is genuine."

"Oh?"

"Yes. His name's Fraser. He's sairt of a low-life character, wha' they call a 'fence' on the telly, actually, but an expert on this type of jewelry.''

"You have some peculiar friends," said Lucy, putting down her fork, suddenly very uncomfortable.

"In the insurance business ye meet all kinds." MacAlpin grinned. "He knows me by the name of 'Scott' by the way, so I'd like you to play along."

"Why?" She didn't like the sound of this at all.

"I dinna want to get too involved with the man, if ye catch my meanin'. Nor should you."

"Look, Mr. MacAlpin," said Lucy, feeling like a first-class chump, "I'm here because you said you could tell me something about my family. All of a sudden you want some…criminal…to look at my brooch. You want me to accept some phony name. Maybe I should just finish my appetizer and say *adiós*."

"I do ha' a good reason for askin' this man here, Lucy," said MacAlpin sincerely.

"Like what, for instance?"

"Like if the man says that the brooch is genuine, then I think I'm your faether."

LUCY SIPPED HER COFFEE and tried to think. The trout had looked wonderful, but Lucy couldn't even remember what it tasted like.

MacAlpin's story had been simplicity itself. Thirty years ago back in Glasgow, he had been engaged to marry a girl named Bethoc Trelaine. Bethoc Trelaine worked at Glasgow's Celtic Museum of Antiquities. One day Bethoc disappeared. So did a valuable brooch from the Celtic museum. MacAlpin never suspected that Bethoc might be pregnant, but when he thought about what Lucy had told him, suddenly it had all made sense.

"Dinna ye see, lass?" he was saying now in a soothing voice. "She couldna face the shame. She needed money to get away, so she stole the brooch."

Lucy felt dizzy. This man was her father. Her mother

was a thief. Lucy tried to take a breath, but her lungs wouldn't work. Everything was happening too fast. She couldn't get her bearings. Her perspective, her distance from the action, was gone. She had been plucked out of the audience and dumped onto the stage.

"Why does the brooch have this writing on the back?" Lucy finally stammered, picking up the silver ring and turning it over in her hand.

"Bethoc must have had it engraved," said MacAlpin softly.

"But why would she do that if she only stole it to sell it?"

MacAlpin shrugged.

"Who can say wha' went through the poor lassie's mind? Maybe the brooch reminded her too much of the past to pairt with."

"I read you the inscription when we first talked," said Lucy. "Why didn't you know right away?"

"Your pronunciation left somethin' to be desired, lass." MacAlpin smiled and patted her hand. "And remember, this was thairty years ago and a world away. I dinna put two and two together until afterwards."

"Is that the piece?" said a voice from behind Lucy's shoulder. A tall, red-haired man with horn-rimmed glasses and a square jaw pulled out the chair next to her and sat down.

"Fraser," MacAlpin said evenly, releasing Lucy's hand and rising. "I'd like ye to meet my daughter, Lucy...Scott."

"Michael Fraser," said the man, cracking a smile.

"Pleased to meet you," Lucy said coldly.

Fraser's knees accidentally touched hers under the tiny table as he sat. His grin widened. Lucy pulled away, feeling a blush race across her face. Fraser was pretty good-looking. For a crook. But why did she care? This was certainly no time to think about her sex life. It hadn't been the time to think about her sex life for years.

"You can call me—" Fraser began, but MacAlpin interrupted with a noticeable touch of impatience.

"We chust need to know if this brooch is genuine."

"All right. May I?" said Fraser, plucking the heavy silver ring out of Lucy's hand and taking off his glasses to study it close up.

"What do you think, Fraser?" said MacAlpin finally.

"I'd have to study it further to be sure," the redhead answered, putting his glasses and his grin back on, "but it looks Pictish to me."

"Pictish?' asked Lucy.

"The Picts were the Celtic inhabitants of the area we now call Scotland," said Fraser breezily. "They vanished in the ninth century. The brooch might even be as old as that. If it is, certainly things have been added on the back."

"We're not interested in—" began MacAlpin, but Lucy cut him off.

"Like 'Lucy MacAlpin Trelaine'," she said.

Fraser turned the brooch over. "Yes, that. But this other inscription is intriguing. 'Dumlagchtat mac Alpin Bethoc.' Kenneth mac—or 'son of'—Alpin was the king who united the Picts and the Scots, of course, and Bethoc was a traditional woman's name in the house of Alpin. I'm not sure what Dumlag…"

"But it is genuine?" asked MacAlpin.

"Yes, it appears to be. But as I said, I have to study it further, do some tests…"

"Well, I dinna think that will be necessary right away." MacAlpin's voice was soft, measured. "I think Lucy and I need to talk privately now, if ye dinna mind."

Fraser shrugged, handed the brooch back to Lucy.

"What do you think it's worth?" she said.

"I dinna think this is the time to…" began MacAlpin.

"I want to know," said Lucy. MacAlpin started to protest, then apparently thought better of it.

"It's not really museum quality," said Fraser with a shrug. "I'd say it might bring anywhere from a few hundred to a few thousand at auction. There's not a large market for this sort of thing.''

"I hope cooming here wasn't too inconvenient for ye," said MacAlpin, standing up—clearly a dismissal. "I'll ring ye oop later."

"Sure," said Fraser, a little unhappily. He stood, grinning at Lucy. "It was a pleasure meeting you, Lucy. I hope I'll have the pleasure again. You'll call me, Mr. Scott?"

"I'll be in touch."

"Yes, well. Good-bye." Fraser turned and walked out of the tiny restaurant and down the red marble hallway, glancing back over his shoulder periodically.

"He said the brooch wasn't museum quality," said Lucy when Fraser was out of sight.

"Chust a negotiating tactic." MacAlpin smiled knowingly, then caught the waiter's eye and motioned for a check. Lucy looked into a mirrored panel and tried to see Robert MacAlpin's likeness in her sharp features. There was some slight resemblance, she supposed. Neither of them was particularly tall. His hair might have been black once.

"I still don't understand about the inscription."

"Wha' dinna ye understand? Your mother's name was Bethoc Trelaine. My name is MacAlpin."

The waiter appeared with a leather folder with the bill. MacAlpin didn't even bother to look at it, just handed the man a gold American Express card.

"I've been in hundreds of cities," said Lucy, "and I've never found a single Trelaine."

"It's a common enough name in Glasgow," shrugged MacAlpin.

"Who's Lucy?" asked Lucy. "As in 'Lucy MacAlpin Trelaine'.''

"Why, tha' must be you. Tha' must be wha' poor Bethoc named you, with her surname and mine. And to answer your next question, *Dumlagchtat* means 'I love you' in Gaelic. Now, aire ye satisfied?"

Lucy nodded. The man seemed to have all the answers.

The waiter returned with the credit-card slip. MacAlpin signed it, then came around the table to pull her chair out. Lucy stood shakily. MacAlpin put his arm around her shoulder and they walked in silence down the snaking marble tunnel.

Why didn't she feel anything? Lucy wondered. After all these years, she expected to feel something, some burst of recognition, of relief, of love. She glanced over at MacAlpin. He smiled. Lucy had always harbored a secret belief that when she finally found her family, they would turn out to be royalty or at least movie stars, not insurance salesmen. Was this how dreams ended? Stomped to death by the mundane?

"I wasna there when you needed me, Lucy," MacAlpin was saying at they came out into the top level of the atrium. "I couldna even gi' you my name. But now I can make it oop to you. I hope you'll let me."

They ambled the long way back toward the escalator, along the side of the building, then across a kind of skybridge stretching across the chasm of the atrium. When they got to the middle, Lucy stopped.

"I don't believe you," Lucy said, her lip quivering. "You're not my father."

The skylight ceiling was only twenty feet overhead from here. The illuminated waterfall began a few feet above them. Water trickled down the marble wall to the ground eighty feet below. There was no one else around.

"Why would I lie to you, lass?" MacAlpin replied soberly.

It was true. What reason could he possibly have to lie? Lucy knew she was being childish. Why couldn't she accept the truth?

"Canna we be friends?" MacAlpin said gently.

Lucy bit her lip, fighting back tears.

"I know this has been a frichtful shock t'ye, lass," MacAlpin continued soothingly. "I dinna expect after all this time for ye suddenly to accept me as a faether. We can go as slow as you like. I chust want to do something for you, now that I'm able to. Why don't I stairt by returning the brooch to the museum in Glasgow? I think Bethoc would like that.''

Lucy looked over the guardrail. The tables in the basement level far beneath looked like chocolates in a box. The waterfall was right next to them, water dripping down the red marble face like blood.

''You'd give away my brooch?'' she said, reaching into her jacket pocket and clenching it in her fist.

''It doesna' belong to us. Besides, wha' importance does it have now? It's done its job. It's brought us together.''

He clasped her shoulders. His hands were remarkably strong.

''Your luck has changed, Lucy MacAlpin Trelaine,'' MacAlpin said, beaming. ''Yes sir. We'll find a good job for you here. Harvard women are like gold in this town. I can get you into Home Trust. It's a good living. Come on. Why dinna ye let me hang on to the brooch now, for safe-keeping? You canna be too careful in New York, you know.''

Lucy took the brooch out of her pocket and started to hand it to him, then pulled back.

''How did you know that I went to Harvard?''

MacAlpin shrugged. ''You said so.''

''No I didn't.''

''When we talked that first time,'' he said with the most benign of smiles. ''You told me.''

''I never tell people I went to Harvard,'' Lucy said, staring at him unbelievingly. ''I failed out. And you knew about my working in hotels. You said something about it in your letter. How did you know that? How could you have known, unless...''

''I swear you mentioned it. What difference does it make?''

"Unless you read the résumé in my computer! You were the one who broke into my hotel room."

"Ye dinna know what yer sayin', Lucy."

"It must have been you. I told you where I was staying. You knew I would be out that morning. You wanted to steal my brooch, didn't you? When you couldn't find it you took my computer and earrings to make it look like junkies broke in. Didn't you?"

MacAlpin's smile evaporated. His face turned hard, ugly. He reached out and grabbed her hand.

"Gi' me the brooch, lass," he said quietly.

"What kind of father steals from his own daughter?" she hissed.

"I dinna want to hurt you. You couldna make it easy, could you? You Fingons aire all alike."

"Fingons? Who are…"

MacAlpin grabbed her hand and wrenched the brooch out of it. Lucy tried to pull away. The waterfall roared in her ears. She started to scream, but MacAlpin clasped one hand over her mouth and spun her around, pinning both her hands behind her back with the other. Lucy could feel her brooch still in his hand as he pushed her onto the railing.

Lucy looked over her shoulder in helpless panic. MacAlpin's teeth were clenched, his face grim, determined. He was going to pitch her into the atrium!

All Lucy could think of was getting away. She struggled, squirmed furiously, but MacAlpin was too strong. He pushed her further up the railing. Without thinking, Lucy unlocked her trick shoulders, threw both arms up over her head, and sat down. MacAlpin stumbled off balance above her, still holding on to her hands until it was too late.

He seemed to hover above her for a single moment, poised between heaven and earth, then sailed out over the rail upside down. Lucy lay on the floor of the skybridge and listened to the endless, fading scream until he finally crashed onto a table of snacking tourists a million miles below.

THIRTEEN

LUCY SAT IN DISBELIEF on the red marble floor for a moment, dazed by what she had done. Then she struggled shakily to her feet and looked over the rail. A charcoal gray ant lay broken on a miniature table in the café far below.

"This can't be happening," Lucy whispered in a state of shock. The screams from the bottom of the atrium gradually subsided.

MacAlpin had ransacked her hotel room. He had stolen her earrings. He had tried to kill her! She had not imagined his hands at her throat, the atrium swirling beneath her head. Had she really hurled him to his death?

Lucy straightened her dress, ran a hand through her thick, black hair, and walked slowly to the escalator so as not to arouse attention. She fought the temptation to run down the moving metal stairs, and just stood statuelike while people beneath strained over the rails to catch a glimpse at what was causing the commotion.

Lucy had to change escalators at each level before finally stepping off into the buzz of stunned shoppers in the basement café. A ring of people blocked the center of the little court. Lucy eased her way through the crowd, feeling strangely calm, almost as if in a dream.

The Scot had smashed onto one of the tiny tables, collapsing it like an accordion. The floor around him was slick with spilled cappuccino. Two well-dressed women were lying several feet away, dazed but apparently all right.

Suddenly there was only one thought in Lucy's mind—she must retrieve her brooch. It had been in MacAlpin's hand when he went over the railing. She had to get it back before the police came. It had her name on it!

Lucy edged closer. MacAlpin was bent into a strange shape, like a member of the Phoenician alphabet or a paramecium. He was obviously dead, his eyes open and unfocused, a pool of blood melting into the red floor beneath his head. A tall, red-haired man knelt next to him. As Lucy broke from the crowd toward them, the man turned. It was Fraser. In his hand was her brooch.

They stared at one another for a split second, then Lucy turned and ran, pushing her way back through the gawking shoppers.

"Wait!" she heard him shout behind her. She looked over her shoulder. Fraser was fighting through the crowd toward her. Lucy wasn't about to wait. Terrified, she tore down the marble hall, past the chocolatier and the newsstand.

Instantly she realized her mistake. If this corridor was like the ones on the floors above, it would simply come around in a circle and deliver her right back to the escalators. Fraser could be waiting for her. If he wasn't hot on her heels. She had killed his partner. He had her brooch!

Lucy tried to choke back panic. She had to get away. She wanted to scream, but didn't dare. If someone saved her from Fraser, how would she explain why he had been chasing her? She kept running. There was a sign for the rest rooms ahead of her. Was this a dead end? Had anyone seen her struggling with MacAlpin on the bridge? What would Fraser tell the police?

To her left was a fancy antique store. Inside Lucy could see a staircase leading up. There might be only seconds before Fraser caught her. Lucy opened the door and swept past the startled saleslady. At the top of the stairs she found herself amidst posh jewelry and antiques. Through the glass doors she could see the crowds on Fifth Avenue.

"May I be of help, madam?" asked a slim man in a three-piece suit, looking down his nose at her.

Lucy didn't even slow down. No one could help her now. She had killed her own father. The awful destiny that had foreshadowed her life with failure had finally caught up with her, full force. Everything was clear now. God wasn't merely angry at her—He was Irate. Heart pounding, eyes full of tears, Lucy opened the door to the street and vanished into the moving carpet of people.

LUCY TRIED TO ACT NORMAL at dinner that night, but had no appetite and couldn't find much to say. After all the years of looking for her family, she had finally found her father and promptly tossed him down the Trump Tower atrium. If MacAlpin weren't dead it would almost be funny.

Lucy had returned from the city, pale and shaken, to find that Wing was throwing a little celebration for Tina. Tina, the shy little receptionist with the five earrings, had just been awarded a full scholarship by the Computer Science Department at NYU and would start classes in the fall.

Wing rapped his spoon on his club soda, pulling Lucy back from her jumbled thoughts. He raised his glass in a toast. Lucy held up her champagne with the others and tried to smile.

"Little Tina Snicowski. Remember when you first come to live here. Poor little runaway. No home. Play rock and roll all the time. Nothing but rock and roll. Talk about piercing ears, oy!"

Everyone laughed. Tina blushed.

"Now you have home," continued Wing. "You work hard, study hard. No time for rock and roll, thank goodness. Make us very proud."

"Speech, speech," demanded Neal.

Aunt Sally poured herself another glass of champagne, smiled, and said, "Hurray for Tina."

Wing motioned with his glass. "Tina? You say few words, yes?"

Tina stood up, looking around the table. Her eyes fell back modestly to her plate.

"I want to thank all of you for treating me so fantastic, for making me, like, feel so welcome, so at home. Especially you, Mr. Wing. I know you have problems of your own, but I mean here you're going out of your way to do all this. I just want you to know that I, like, really appreciate everything, you know? You're all so great.''

Wing beamed. The Trenton bank had turned down their loan application yesterday. Lucy knew Wing was running out of time, but his face showed only happiness.

"You're my family," continued Tina, getting misty. "I'm gonna work my buns off, I promise. I mean, I don't know why you're doing this for me. Everybody always said I was never going to amount to anything."

"Don't you believe that, Tina," said Lucy, surprising everyone with her vehemence, including herself. "Don't ever let anyone tell you you're not terrific, because you are."

Everyone stared. Lucy put down her champagne, threw her napkin onto the table, and ran upstairs to her room.

THE NEXT MORNING, after a sleepless night, Lucy took Hewby for his walk. She couldn't get MacAlpin's last words out of her mind. "You Fingons are all alike," he had said. What did people named Fingon have to do with this? Could it be possible that she wasn't a Trelaine or a MacAlpin at all, but a Fingon? It sounded like a little German sausage.

A less hypothetical sausage was tugging at his leash. Lucy returned to the matter at hand. The sad basset hound marched regally up and down the sidewalks and through the grassy park. He finally peed on a war memorial, the monument to Hamilton being safely out of range behind iron bars.

Satisfied that Hewby had discharged all his professional duties as a dog, Lucy picked up the fat weekend papers from the machines outside the little Spanish coffee shop at the top of the Weehawken Cliffs and went inside. The waitress automatically brought coffee. They were beginning to understand one another, language notwithstanding.

The *Daily News* had a story on the second page.

MAN IN DEATH PLUNGE AT TRUMP TOWER

A man mysteriously fell to his death from the sixth floor of the Trump Tower Atrium yesterday, narrowly missing diners in the basement cafe.

Robert MacAlpin, a Manhattan insurance executive, apparently was standing on the bridge across the atrium space in the midtown luxury shopping area, when he fell over the side. Two startled shoppers were treated for minor cuts.

Police are investigating the incident, but the possibility of suicide has not been ruled out. It was the first such incident since Trump Tower opened. A spokesman regretted the incident and the bridge has been closed until a full safety check has been completed.

Lucy took a sip of coffee and tried to think, but the image of MacAlpin's crushed skull and empty eyes kept swirling through her brain.

Nothing made sense. Fraser had said her brooch wasn't worth more than a few thousand dollars. Why would MacAlpin be ready to kill his own daughter for such a paltry sum? He'd just spent a hundred dollars on lunch, for crissakes.

Lucy put down the first paper and glanced through the *Times*. It, too, had a small story about the incident, but it was buried in the second section. To her surprise there was also an article about MacAlpin on the obituary page, along with a photograph, the kind of posed shot businessmen favored for press releases. MacAlpin stared out smugly, his tie perfect, the faintest of smiles across his thin lips.

To rate an obit in the *Times,* Lucy realized, MacAlpin must have been a substantial citizen. That meant the police wouldn't just let the case slide, the way they did when the person was unimportant. The way they had for her mother. Lucy fought down a wave of nausea and read the story.

ROBERT MACALPIN, INSURANCE MAN

Robert J. MacAlpin, 56, of Guttenberg, New Jersey, died yesterday in a fall in New York.

Mr. MacAlpin had been with Home Trust Life Insurance for 26 years and was a member of its "Golden Circle."

He was born in Dumlagchtat on the Scottish island of Lis in the Inner Hebrides, but emigrated as a young man and eventually received U.S. citizenship. He is survived by his wife, Margaret.

Lucy read the story again, unable to believe her eyes. Dumlagchtat! MacAlpin had been born in a place named Dumlagchtat—the word written on the back of her brooch, the word MacAlpin had told her meant I love you in Gaelic. He had lied! What else had he lied about?

"Oh, God, please," she muttered to her coffee, "please let him have been lying about being my father."

The coffee steamed encouragingly. Lucy tore Mac-Alpin's picture and the obit out of the *Times* and put them in her wallet. Then she went into the little phone booth across from the *Hombres* room and closed the door.

"Glasgow information," said a pleasant voice a few minutes after the international operator had patched Lucy through.

"Yes," said Lucy, taking a deep breath. "I'd like the number for the Celtic Museum of Antiquities."

"I'm sorry, but there is no listing under that name," said the voice a moment later.

"There's no Celtic museum? Are you sure? Maybe you could try it under Celtic Art Museum or Museum of Antiquities or something like that."

There was another, longer pause.

"I'm sorry. There doesn't seem to be anything like that."

"Would you check and see how many listings there are in Glasgow under the name Trelaine, T-R-E-L-A-I-N-E."

After a moment the operator returned again.

"Nothing under Trelaine as you spelt it. I do have several listings under Trelevens and Trelegens."

"Thanks," said Lucy. She hung up the phone and returned to her seat at the counter. It was a good thing MacAlpin hadn't thought to sell her the Brooklyn Bridge.

"Carmen," said Lucy earnestly to the little Spanish waitress. "Take a look at a girl who just fell off the turnip truck."

"Ah." Carmen nodded, reached into the refrigerator, and handed Lucy a chocolate doughnut.

FOR THE NEXT TWO DAYS Lucy walked around in a fog, unable to decide what to do.

MacAlpin had obviously made up the entire story just to get her brooch. There was no Celtic museum. There was no Bethoc Trelaine. Lucy desperately hoped that the man had been lying about being her father, too, but how could she be sure? Why had he wanted the brooch so badly? And if he wasn't her father, then who was he?

There was nothing further in the papers about the incident at Trump Tower, but that gave Lucy little solace. She had killed MacAlpin and fled the scene. A professional criminal was a witness. If Fraser hadn't gone to the police with the brooch, it probably only meant that he wanted to blackmail her with it.

For a moment Lucy had thought that since Dumlagchtat was really a place, then Trelaine might be, too. But there were no Trelaines in the atlas. There were no Bethocs. Nor could she believe that either Lucy, Louisiana, or Lucy, Tennessee, had anything to do with her.

"Why you so sad, Rucy?" said Wing, finally confronting her about her muddled state on their way to inspect the

White Plains Neat 'n' Tidy. "By Friday all worries will be over. First Connecticut Savings give loans to anybody. That why they in so much trouble."

"Nobody is going to give you a loan unless you cut expenses and sell off some of the branches," answered Lucy unhappily. Somehow watching Wing founder made her own situation seem all the more hopeless.

"Cannot sell. Wing buy branches for cheap because no one want them. Who buy now?"

"Well, you have to find somebody," she said angrily. "Or find a miracle."

"Okay. Wing look for miracle. Always look for miracle, Rucy. No look, no find, yes?"

Lucy didn't answer.

"Why you so unhappy, Rucy? Something bother you?"

"No. Everything's great. Just great."

"Okay. You no want to talk, okay. Have to do with your business in city, maybe?"

"Actually it would help if I could have another day off."

"Sure. You take tomorrow. See, Wing your friend. Care about you. Look out for your interests, yes?"

"Thank you, Mr. Wing. You're very generous."

"You work next Saturday instead," Wing announced happily. "By then First Connecticut give us loan and we have new money to spend, yes?"

"Sure," she said, patting his arm. Saturday was a hundred years away. She could be anywhere by Saturday. Probably in jail.

FOURTEEN

THE NEXT MORNING Lucy hitched a ride into the city with one of the Neat 'n' Tidy station wagons. She didn't really believe that the police would be staking out the ferry and the commuter van the way they did on old TV shows, but why take chances? She nervously looked over her shoulder the whole way. Mercifully the gurney in the back was empty.

The van driver, Jesus Esteban, rattled on incomprehensibly about cars and music. Lucy pretended to be interested, but was relieved when he dropped her off in the West Eighties before making his pickup.

Jesus said she could just walk across Central Park to the East Side. Lucy had heard how dangerous the park was and didn't want to take any chances. She might be wanted for murder, but God forbid she should risk a walk in the park on a flawless spring day. She knew how silly it sounded, but she still took the crosstown bus.

Twenty minutes later Lucy was climbing the stairs to the Metropolitan Museum of Art.

Even if it wasn't in her possession, the brooch was her only clue to this mess. All the information she had about it had come from Fraser, who was hardly a reliable expert. The more she thought about it, the more likely it seemed that Fraser might have colluded with MacAlpin to trick her. Perhaps someone here at the museum could tell her what kind of brooch men might be willing to kill for. It was a long shot, she knew, but she couldn't think of anything else to do.

The Metropolitan's entry hall was even larger than the library's. There were fresh flowers everywhere and hundreds of people. Lucy had never seen so many people in a museum before, and it was only a weekday.

She wandered around for forty minutes, through the caverns of furniture, paintings, treasures of the past. She hated to ask for help, but the museum was just too big for her to find what she was looking for. She finally approached a dark-complected guard in a blue uniform.

"Where is the Pictish art?"

The man stared at her blankly.

"Pickish? No pickish."

"Pict-ish. Old Scottish. Old British."

"Try the passage to left of main stairs. Where you first come in," he said pointing.

Lucy eventually found the little passageway. It was a narrow hall, not more than fifty feet long. Glass cases filled with a miscellany of ancient jewelry, beads, carved ivory, and other small objects lined both walls.

Lucy walked the hall twice before she found the Celtic items. There were a few carvings, some rings, a coin. Then she saw it: a C-shaped brooch like hers, but smaller and less ornate. The piece was numbered and Lucy found a description on the wall.

PENANNULAR BROOCH
Silver, Amber
Pictish, second half 8th century

"Is there anybody around here who knows about this Celtic art?" she asked another guard, a tiny black woman in a uniform two sizes too big.

"You might try Medieval," said the woman after thinking for a second. "Do you have an appointment?"

"No."

She clucked and shook her head. "You gotta have an appointment."

"Can't I just talk to someone..."

"No way. You gotta have an appointment. Go call from the desk in entrance hall."

Lucy walked out into the vast entry hall again. In the center of the room was a round information desk, big enough to hold a dozen volunteers distributing maps and giving directions. It was a moment before one was free to speak with Lucy.

"I'd like to talk with someone in the Medieval Department, please."

The volunteer, a pale man with a beard, dialed an extension on a telephone on the desk and handed it to Lucy. She took the receiver.

"Medieval," said a metallic voice.

"I need some information about the Pictish penannular brooch you have on display."

"One moment."

Lucy waited. In a moment another voice answered.

"Dr. Brickwall."

The name wasn't particularly encouraging. Lucy put a finger in her ear against the din.

"Yes, I'd like to talk to you about the Pictish brooch you have on display," said Lucy and gave its number.

"Well, let's see," said Dr. Brickwall after a pause. "I can give you an appointment sometime in July."

"I can't wait that long. Can you just tell me how expensive a brooch like that is?"

"I'm sorry," said the voice. "We don't go into that sort of thing here. You should try one of the auction galleries."

"Please," said Lucy. "It's very important."

"I'm sorry."

"Are they very valuable? Can't you just tell me that?"

"We really..."

"Are any worth more than a few thousand dollars?"

"Not silver ones. Look, miss..."

Lucy's eyes had wandered back down the hallway behind the admission booth where she had seen the penannular brooch. Suddenly she saw something that made her knees lock and her pulse race. Coming through the arch at the end of the passageway was Fraser.

Lucy couldn't believe her eyes at first. How had he found her? Then she realized that Fraser hadn't found her at all. He needed more information about the brooch and had had the same idea about the museum. He was a step ahead of her!

Lucy wanted to sink into the ground. Brickwall's voice was still chirping from the receiver. Lucy replaced it in its cradle, trying not to make any jerky movements that might catch Fraser's eye.

She couldn't believe he would be able to see her from such a distance as she backed slowly away from the desk, but he did. Their eyes met. Both of them froze, then Fraser started down the hall toward her.

Lucy pushed through a group of carefree, laughing kids dressed in spring pastels and smiles. She ran out the entrance, tore down the long flight of stone steps, and headed south down Fifth Avenue, past the fountains and the neat rows of benches. A few heads turned, but no one really seemed to notice her.

She didn't look back until she was at the entrance to the underground parking lot on Eightieth Street. In the crowd she could make out a tall figure on the steps two blocks away. It was Fraser. He was running after her!

Lucy could see the tip of the Empire State Building rising out of the canopy of buds forty-five blocks away. To the right was an entrance to Central Park. The park was suddenly the safest place she could see, certainly safer than the long, straight avenue where Fraser could keep her in plain sight. Lucy made a sharp right turn onto an S-shaped asphalt path. It would be easier to lose him in the cover of trees.

Crisp sunshine bounced off the angled glass wall of the museum to her right. Old men with pipes lined the benches; girls in spring dresses sauntered dreamily; Lucy ran for her life.

She supposed she could scream for help, but then what? If the police came, it was she who would be in trouble. She was the murderer, Fraser was merely a witness. What did he want with her? He already had the brooch.

There was no time to think. Directly ahead were iron bars. Lucy despaired for an instant, thinking she had trapped herself in a dead end, then saw it was merely a playground—the bars were there to keep the squealing, happy children in.

The path continued to the right, around the playground, behind the museum. Lucy, however, made a hard left onto a path that crossed over the street. She didn't want to lose sight of Fifth Avenue or she might double back in an unintentional circle and collide with Fraser. As long as the limestone façades were on her left, she'd be okay.

Lucy didn't know whether Fraser had seen her turn, but she wasn't about to stop and look. She sped down the path, feeling ridiculous. She hadn't run anywhere for years—especially not in stretch pants and flats.

A boarded-up maintenance area loomed on her right. On her left was a small, grassy lawn full of people sunning themselves, tossing Frisbees, playing with their dogs. A few people looked up as she whizzed by, tucking the long ends of her yellow sweater into her fanny pack so they wouldn't slow her down, but no one appeared prepared to intrude on her privacy. She was just another New Yorker taking advantage of Central Park, enjoying May, running for her life.

The day was beautiful, the sky a bold, cloudless blue. The air smelled clean, perfumed with spring. Everything was sunshine, but Lucy had never felt so frightened, so alone. Already she was breathing hard.

Another lawn rose up a hill toward a crown of pine trees to her right. Lucy followed the path toward a little bridge. Two laughing boys hung over the rail, playfully pushing one another. Gray boulders rose out of the grass like giant mushrooms.

Lucy sped under the bridge, dodging children and dogs,

momentarily losing sight of Fifth Avenue. Her side was beginning to hurt and she was breathing heavily. Ahead of her the road forked. She took the right leg, afraid the left would take her out of the park onto Fifth.

A little girl with a ball ran after her. The mother ran after the child. Lucy looked over her shoulder. Coming out from under the bridge was Fraser. He was still a good ways back, but he was running at a good pace, his body seemed relaxed, his head turned, searching for her in the crowd. Suddenly he saw her and began to sprint. Fear gripped Lucy's throat. The man was gaining!

Lucy was nearing a large pond. She veered left toward a weeping willow, hoping it would conceal her course from Fraser. The little clearing teemed with children and she nearly collided with one. She jumped down a step and glanced back. A dozen little girls were sitting in the giant lap of a bronze Alice, the Mad Hatter and the March Hare by their sides, dogwood blooming all around them, Fraser coming up fast in the distance.

Boys with remote devices sailed boats on the pond ahead. Across the water kids were lining up for ice cream. Lucy dashed past a giant bronze statue of Hans Christian Andersen with a duckling looking up at him, its bill rubbed shiny by little hands.

Now she was running toward one of the park drives, where lines of city traffic coursed through the green like blood vessels through body tissue. Majestic spires of buildings jumped out of the trees far ahead of her. Had she turned around somehow? She started to panic, then realized it was not Fifth Avenue she was seeing but Central Park West, the street on the other side of the park.

Lucy followed the twisting path through a short, dark tunnel under the road and up the stairs on the other side. A black-jacketed kid on his bike with a pounding radio almost cut her off. She desperately ran onto a path leading up a short hill. In a moment she was at the top, huge boulders on either side of her. The pain in her side was sharper, nearly unbearable. She couldn't get her breath. From the cover of madly blooming magnolias she looked back, unable to go on.

Fraser was just coming out of the tunnel. He stopped, looked around, then took off down the path in the opposite direction. Lucy watched as he disappeared behind rowboats stacked like fish scales by a boathouse.

After a moment Lucy began running again, panting, exhausted. A horse-drawn hansom cab passed by on the park drive in front of her. The sun shouted through the greenery. Birds sang all around.

The traffic stopped for a moment and Lucy dashed across the road. She ran and she ran, oblivious to the beds of pale daffodils and bicyclists and trees thick with ivy all around. She saw only MacAlpin's empty, dead eyes. Guilt closed in around her as she trotted down the snaking path toward the Fifth Avenue buildings, holding her side, blinking the perspiration from her eyes. Her black hair was damp. Her muscles screamed. She had lost him. She was safe.

For now.

FIFTEEN

IT WAS TWO DAYS LATER. Wing was in his basement workshop. Hewby, the fat basset hound, was snoozing on the sofa. Lucy was sitting at Wing's desk at the end of her rope.

She stopped drumming her fingers for the first time in five minutes, then dug out the Manhattan phone book and looked under Fraser. She couldn't stand it anymore. Maybe he'd be willing to make some kind of deal.

There were half a dozen Michael Frasers in the book. Lucy wasn't even sure that was how he spelled his name. It was hopeless. Besides, she didn't even have anything to bargain with.

Lucy thought briefly about phoning MacAlpin's widow, then dismissed it. What could she say? "I'm sorry to have killed your husband, Mrs. MacAlpin, but did he ever mention having an illegitimate daughter?"

Lucy sat back into Wing's deep armchair. She hadn't gotten any work accomplished for days. Their loan meeting at First Connecticut was tomorrow morning, but Lucy's mind kept wandering to images of Fraser chasing after her and MacAlpin's crushed skull.

"What am I supposed to do now?" Lucy asked helplessly. Hewby didn't answer, being sound asleep.

Maybe she should just turn herself in. The cops might believe her story. Maybe they would go after Fraser and get her brooch back. Maybe Fraser would know what MacAlpin had been up to. Maybe, maybe, maybe. Maybe they would lock her up and throw away the key.

Lucy nibbled what was left of her thumbnail and tried

to think. She was an intelligent person. Surely there was some logical course of action. Why couldn't she see it?

"Because I'm a killer, what's why," she mumbled to the sleeping dog. "I'm being eaten alive by guilt. I'm 'Dostoyevskying' out. Next I'll be hearing hearts beating under the floorboards."

"You feel okay, Rucy?" said the voice, shattering her reverie. Lucy shook the cobwebs from her mind and bounced up.

"I'm sorry, Mr. Wing. I was just thinking."

"Sit, sit, sit," commanded Wing, motioning downward with his hands.

Lucy sank back, blushing, into his big chair. Wing walked to the door, closed it, then sat down facing her in the armchair she usually occupied. Hewby looked up briefly, then went back to sleep.

"We talk, Rucy Trelaine. Something bothering you. You tell me now."

Lucy felt the panic welling up in her chest. She wanted to tell him the truth, but how could she?

"I don't know what you're talking about, Mr. Wing," she said guiltily. "I'm fine. Really I am."

"Wing your friend. Can help, maybe."

"I don't…"

"You in trouble?"

"No."

"Need money?"

"No."

His eyes opened wide. "You pregnant?"

"No! There is something on my mind, but it's…there's…"

She tried to push some hardness into her face, but her lip kept quivering.

"You in trouble, Rucy Trelaine. Yes?"

"Yes," she answered, startled at how small her voice sounded.

"You tell now what's bothering you, please?"

"You wouldn't understand," she said desperately.

"I surprise you maybe."

"Why should you be interested in a poor little orphan girl? Why should anybody? I'm nobody, don't you understand? And I'm practically thirty years old. I don't have a thing to show for my life. Not a goddamned thing."

Lucy struggled not to cry. She had always prided herself on being so tough, on being able to deal with any situation that came her way. Now she wept at the drop of a hat. What was happening to her?

"Harvard graduate, yes? That something," Wing said gently.

Lucy stared at the desk top in front of her. She could barely breathe beneath the weight of accumulated shame. Wing was the only person in the world who seemed genuinely to care about her. And here she was, not even telling him the truth.

Lucy looked up. Wing sat with his hands in his lap, smiling expectantly. She might not be able to correct a lifetime of mistakes or bring Robert MacAlpin back to life, but at least she could level with Wing. She owed him that much.

"I didn't graduate from Harvard, Mr. Wing," she said miserably. "I flunked out. And I've been fired from nearly every job I ever had. I'm sorry."

Wing's eyes widened. He snorted, frowned, then spoke in a low voice.

"You trick me?"

"I'm sorry, Mr. Wing. I'll go upstairs and pack."

She started for the door, but Wing rose and held up his hand.

"Wait. Why you trick me?"

"I needed the job," she said simply.

"You say you orphan?"

"Yes."

"Wing orphan, too," he said, still frowning. "Family

killed by Japanese in World War II. Have many hard times. Now prospects dim again. Have friends, though.''

They stared at one another for a moment, then Wing stood and walked around the desk to her. Lucy was embarrassed, afraid that he would try to touch her, to give her sympathy. He did. He put his arm around her shoulder and hugged her gently.

''You have friends, too, Rucy. Not need Harvard degree to be big help to me. Everything okay. Okay?''

''Everything's not okay. How can you say everything's okay? You're about to go broke.''

He shrugged. ''Just money. You person. Wing live long time. Know what important in life. You important, Rucy.''

Lucy tried to keep her upper lip from pushing down and pressing her mouth into the smile she cried with. She couldn't. Tears began streaming down her face.

''I'm sorry, Mr. Wing,'' she sobbed.

''It's okay, Rucy. Wing understand.''

''I just bring bad luck everywhere I go.''

''No, no, no. You good luck. Help with management. Wing not so stupid with bankers anymore. You okay. Wing accept apology. Everything hunky-dunky.''

''Everything not hunky-dunky.''

''No? More problem? Okay, tell what other problem is, please.''

''I can't.''

''Yes, yes, yes.''

''I can't,'' she sobbed. Wing pushed her to arm's length so he could look into her eyes.

''You not alone anymore, Rucy Trelaine,'' said Wing, patting her gently on the back. ''Now please tell what is wrong.''

Suddenly Lucy was spilling the whole story—the orphanage, the foster homes, seeing the ad, the meeting with the lawyer in Pittsfield, the brooch. The more she talked, the more she cried. Shoulders heaving, Lucy described the crash that had killed her mother, Theresa Iatoni's story, and

finally the letter from MacAlpin, the meeting, his claim of
being her father, his ruined body splattered on the red marble floor, Fraser chasing her through the park.

Wing listened severely, interjecting guttural *oh*s or *ah*s,
patting her gently on the shoulder from time to time.

"Don't you see?" Lucy said finally, pounding the clut-
tered desk with her fists. "I killed a man. Maybe he was
my father, maybe not. It doesn't matter. He was a person
and I killed him. And my brooch is gone. And the police
are probably looking for me right now. And I don't even
have a birthday. God, I want to die."

"No die, no die," said Wing. "Man killed accidentally.
Police not look for you."

"Fraser will tell them."

"Not if he want to keep brooch. Yes?"

"I suppose," she sobbed, afraid to look at Wing,
ashamed of making such a fool of herself.

Wing stood silently for a few moments, letting her cry.
Then he went around the desk and took out Hewby's leash
from a drawer.

"Come, Hewby. We go for walk."

Hewby raised an eyebrow, then parked his chin back on
the sofa. Lucy blew her nose and wiped her eyes with a
Kleenex. Wing clapped his hands.

"Come, come, come."

Hewby sadly raised himself up and jumped to the floor
with a thud. Wing attached the leash and walked him to
the front door.

"You come, too," he said to Lucy. She followed, miserable.

In a moment they were out on the street. Hewby ambled
down the sidewalk, sniffing at favorite trees and hydrants.
Wing said nothing. He seemed lost in thought.

Lucy felt drained and empty, as if a plug had been pulled.
But while some of her guilt seemed to be gone, nothing
had replaced it.

After ten minutes Hewby had exhausted the neighborhood smells and was straining at the leash to get back into the house.

"You must go to Scotland," Wing abruptly announced as they walked up the driveway.

"What would I do there?" said Lucy, struggling out of her daze.

"Check out clues."

"I don't have any clues. I don't have anything."

"Yes, yes, yes," said Wing. "Two clues. One, name of unpronounceable town where MacAlpin was born and which appear on brooch. Two, name of Fingon—'You Fingons all alike.' So you go to unpronounceable town and look for people name Fingon."

"I can't," Lucy said after a moment.

"Why not? You need money? I lend money."

"Money's not the problem. I have money."

"So what stopping you?"

"Well, for one thing, I can't get a passport. You need a birth certificate to get a passport, and I don't have one. I'm not a real person. Everything about me is phony."

Wing opened the door, frowning. Lucy followed him into the hallway. She felt like a bundle of wet rags. Wing bent down to release Hewby from the leash, but suddenly stood up and thumped his head with the palm of his hand.

"There is way! I figure out!"

Hewby woofed indignantly. Wing danced a little jig on the welcome mat. Hewby escaped down the hall, dragging his leash behind him.

"Tina! Tina!"

"Yes, Mr. Wing?" said Tina, appearing from the kitchen, wiping her hands with a dish towel.

"Get travel agent on phone. Quickly. Chop-chop."

"Sure, Mr. Wing," she said, heading toward the phone, obviously impressed with his excited tone. Lucy grabbed the little man's arm and pulled him around to face her.

"What are you doing?" she exclaimed.

"Wing help you."

"I don't want to involve you in this mess," said Lucy, feeling tears well up again. "I should never have told you. We have to make the loan presentation tomorrow. We should be working."

"This more important. Must clear your name," said the little man, bouncing up and down. "Must go to Scotland."

"Didn't you understand?" said Lucy, exasperated. "I don't have a passport."

"No problem. You use Tina's."

Lucy's jaw worked for several seconds before she managed to produce sound.

"You're out of your mind," she sputtered finally.

"Yes. yes. You same height, same weight. With haircut and brown contact lens, no one know difference."

"She's just a kid!"

"You Grandma Moses?"

"She has five earrings!"

"Wing pierce her ears, Wing pierce yours. You cut hair, wear Tina's earrings, her glasses, no one know."

"This is ridiculous. We could *all* end up in jail, instead of just me!"

"No problem. Custom people overworked. Not bother with little Tina. We fool them. Wing know how to talk to English."

"When are you going to talk to them?"

"I go with you."

"What?"

"I go to Scotland. With you."

"Look, Mr. Wing. I'm a big girl. I can fight my own battles."

"Wing not fight your battles. Wing take business trip. You think U.S. have only banks in world? Wing check out international financing. Scotland good place to start."

Lucy felt a wave of hysteria approaching, but it quickly passed. She took a deep breath.

"I don't know why I'm getting upset," she said, managing a smile. "I'm not going to Scotland. And I'm certainly not going to let you go. It's absolutely out of the question, and that's final."

SIXTEEN

"NOW YOU BE CAREFUL, Lucy, you hear?" said Neal Bell, bending down to straighten Lucy's raincoat as Tina and Aunt Sally looked on.

Lucy nodded bravely, feeling like a little girl. It was strange having all these people fuss over her, but she didn't resist.

Only a few days had passed, yet here she was at J.F.K. with five earrings in her left ear, her hair cut short, brown contact lenses in her eyes, and a ticket to the Isle of Lis in her jacket pocket. How had she let Wing talk her into this harebrained scheme?

"Don't worry about a thing, girl," said Tina, Lucy's uncanny doppelgänger, giving her a pat. "You look great."

"I'm not kidding, Lucy," said Neal, a worried look crossing his face. "Don't tell anyone who you really are. You be Clark Kent. Superman doesn't have a secret identity for nothing, you know."

"I made some sammiches for you, Lucy," said Aunt Sally, shyly offering a paper bag.

Lucy took the bag and hugged the great hulking figure. Aunt Sally smiled and blushed. Lucy wondered again how she could let them do all this for her. Tina could go to jail if she got caught, for crissakes.

Tak Wing had finished supervising the loading of their luggage at the curb station and now swooped back down on the little group, opera cape flowing, teeth flashing, top hat cocked at a rakish angle. He seemed to be enjoying himself hugely.

"Mr. Wing," began Lucy urgently, "I still think this is..."

"Uh, uh, uh," said Wing sternly, shaking his finger. "Case closed. No more argument, please, thank you very much. You have glasses?"

"Yes, Mr. Wing," said Lucy, patting her pocket. Tina's spare glasses had lenses like the bottom of Coke bottles. Lucy was totally blind when she wore them.

"Wear glasses all the time."

"Right."

"Passport?"

"Yes, yes."

"Okay. Time to go," said Wing, shaking his pocket watch, then holding it to his ear as if the cold night air might have slowed it down.

"You be careful, Lucy," Neal said, bending down and giving her a brief, unexpected hug. "You hear me?"

Lucy nodded.

"Bye-bye, Lucy," said Aunt Sally and shuffled back toward the Cadillac, nervously wringing her hands.

"Do the Snicowskis proud, Lucy," said Tina, embracing her tightly.

"Are you sure you can manage?" said Lucy, genuinely concerned.

"They spend whole life without us before, yes?" said Wing, tapping his watch again. "Come, come. Time to fly away."

Lucy couldn't understand how Wing could still be so jolly after their meeting at First Connecticut on Friday. The loan officers had practically laughed out loud at the Neat 'n' Tidy balance sheet. They hadn't even had the courtesy to go through the motions of thinking it over.

"Frankly, Mr. Wing," said one of them, picking lint off his lapel, "Brazil is a better credit risk than you."

"New Jersey a lot closer."

"No thanks."

Wing had taken the rejection as gracefully as ever but Lucy knew the game was over. Wing wasn't sacrificing his remaining chances of raising money by going to Scotland with her; no bank was going to bail out Neat 'n' Tidy. And Scottish banks certainly weren't going to be any different. Scots were notoriously tight with a buck. Or so she had heard—she herself wouldn't know.

An L-1011 roared into the air above them. Lucy put her hand on Wing's arm.

"I still don't understand why you're doing this, Mr. Wing," she said quietly.

"Wing your friend," he sputtered. "This what friends do. We go now, okay?"

"Sure."

Wing turned and headed toward the departure area.

"Bye, Lucy," said Tina, tears welling in her eyes.

"Good-bye, honey," said Neal. "Be lucky."

Lucy impulsively kissed the old chauffeur on the cheek. She couldn't see the blush on his face, but she knew it was there. Tina bit her lip and waved. Aunt Sally played with a stuffed animal in the car. Lucy turned on her heel and followed Wing into the terminal.

Half an hour later she was scrunched into a window seat flying over the Atlantic.

This Sunday-night flight was the first one they could take and make the connection to Lis. Lucy had wanted to wait and plan things more carefully—after twenty-one days she could also have gotten a cheaper fare—but Wing had been adamant.

"Timing is everything, Rucy," he had declared. "Opportunity knocking now. No one home?"

It was true. Besides, if she had had more time to think about what she was getting herself into, she probably would have changed her mind. Still, Lucy wished Wing hadn't insisted they fly business class. One would think the man was a millionaire the way he spent her money.

"Take, please," said Wing, holding out an envelope, interrupting her thoughts.

"What's this?"

"Two thousand British pounds," said Wing. "Put in pocket."

"Mr. Wing, I…"

"I get at Barclays. You must have cash."

"I have everything I need."

"Ha. You think Wing stick to you like glue? Wing have other fishes to fry. You cannot use Rucy Trelaine credit cards because you are Tina Snicowski now. You take, please. Advance on salary."

"Thanks," Lucy said and reluctantly took the envelope, hoping the exchange rate wouldn't drop over the next few weeks, costing her more to pay him back.

"Take this, too," said Wing, handing her a thin, odd-sized volume.

"What now?"

"Is guidebook. You read. One of us should know where we going. Wing once get stuck in Australia without guidebook, not know where to go…"

Lucy tried desperately to fight off panic. Wing went on talking, but she barely heard him. The thought of going through British customs on a forged passport with this flamboyant character was suddenly terrifying. Lucy had spent years on the road learning how to be invisible. Traveling with Wing was going to be like being center stage in a purple spotlight. Naked. If only she could just forget MacAlpin, the brooch, everything. But Lucy knew she had come too far. She had to find out the truth. She had to know who Lucy MacAlpin Trelaine really was.

Eventually dinner came. Lucy wrestled with her tray table and pecked at the airline dinner. Wing attacked his meal with gusto. She tried to listen to his tall stories, but couldn't keep her mind on what he was saying. The in-flight movie was a Mel Gibson film. Wing loved it. After the first killing, Lucy couldn't bear to watch.

Wing finally dozed off, but Lucy couldn't even think of sleeping. The seat was too narrow, the engines were too noisy, she was too excited, too afraid.

She tried to read, but the guidebook gave little more sense of Lis than french fries give of France: Lis was one of the larger islands of the Hebrides, between Skye and Mull in location as well as size. Its population had been falling steadily since the nineteenth century. Dr. Johnson had visited in 1773 and called Lis "a place of cruel beauty." Boswell was less impressed, comparing it unfavorably with Rum and Eigg. There were mountains, wildlife, and some castles to see. There was a town called Dumlagchtat.

By the time the plane landed at Heathrow, Lucy had what seemed to be a permanent crick in her neck. Her watch said three o'clock in the morning, but local time was 9:00 a.m.

"Now aren't you happy we fly business class? Much more comfortable, yes?"

"Yes," Lucy agreed, looking at herself in the little mirror from her wallet. The dark circles under her eyes probably weren't permanent. Her hair would grow back, of course, but now she would have to go through the rest of her life with five holes in her ear.

"I gotta be nuts," she murmured to the window as she nervously filled out the check-in documents.

"You say something, Rucy?" said Wing happily. "I mean Tina."

"Not me."

Lucy had been practicing Tina's convoluted signature for the last three days, but it still didn't look right. It was too late to worry, however. The hatch was opening.

"Put on glasses, please."

Lucy took them out of her jacket pocket and complied.

"You ready?" said Wing.

"No."

"Good. Let's go."

Peering owl-like over the top of Tina's thick glasses, Lucy hung on to Wing's arm and hoped she wouldn't walk into a wall. They followed the crowd to the baggage car-

PLAY "LUCKY HEARTS" AND GET ...

★ **3 first-time-in-paperback mystery books just like the one you're reading—FREE**
★ **PLUS a surprise mystery gift—FREE**

THEN CONTINUE YOUR LUCKY STREAK WITH A SWEETHEART OF A DEAL

1. Play Lucky Hearts as instructed on the opposite page.
2. Send back this card and you'll receive brand-new, first-time-in-paperback Mystery Library novels. These books have a cover price of $4.99 each, but they are yours to keep absolutely free.
3. There's no catch. You're under no obligation to buy anything. We charge nothing — ZERO — for your first shipment. And you don't have to make any minimum number of purchases — not even one!
4. The fact is thousands of readers enjoy receiving books by mail from the Mystery Library Reader Service™. They like the convenience of home delivery…they like getting the best in mystery novels before they're available in stores…and they love our discount prices!
5. We hope that after receiving your free books you'll want to remain a subscriber. But the choice is yours — to continue or cancel, anytime at all! So why not take us up on our invitation, with no risk of any kind. You'll be glad you did!

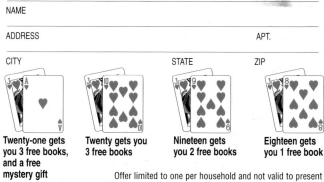

THE MYSTERY LIBRARY READER SERVICE: HERE'S HOW IT WORKS

Accepting free books places you under no obligation to buy anything. You may keep the books and gift and return the shipping statement marked "cancel". If you do not cancel, about a month later we'll send you three additional novels, and bill you just $4.19 each plus 25¢ delivery per book and applicable sales tax, if any. You may cancel at any time, but if you choose to continue, then every month we'll send you three more books, which you may either purchase at our great low price…or return to us and cancel your subscription.

*Terms and prices subject to change without notice. Sales tax applicable in N.Y.

ousel, retrieved Wing's suitcase and her two bags, then headed toward the exit station.

"Please, God, don't let him make a scene in customs," mumbled Lucy to her luggage, trying to follow Wing's advice and expect a miracle. The little Japanese Chinaman was calmly combing his goatee with his fingers as if he smuggled orphans through customs all the time.

Lucy expected giant, stone-faced officers to search through their bags, yell questions, perhaps wheel out a fluoroscope. Instead a little man in a blue shirt took their passports without even looking up.

"What is the purpose of your trip?" he said in a flat British voice. Lucy wondered if everyone could hear her heart pounding.

"Investigate investment opportunities in U.K.," replied Wing, who seemed to have taken over for both of them. He was very subdued, very matter-of-fact. Maybe he did have some survival sense after all, Lucy marveled.

"How long do you plan to be here?"

"Few weeks. Maybe less."

"And you, miss?"

"I'm Mr. Wing's secretary."

"Miss…Snicowski," said the man, looking up for the first time from her documents.

Lucy stiffened automatically.

"Yes, sir," she said, looking at the floor.

"Have a pleasant stay in Great Britain."

"Thank you very much," said Wing. Lucy bowed automatically. She had been hanging around a certain Oriental gentleman too long. The man stamped their passports and passed them back through the little window of his booth.

Wing was already speeding down the hall. Lucy followed at a run and didn't look back until she had cleared the international arrival area. No Royal Marines were in pursuit. There wasn't even a suspicious bobby.

"How you like England so far?" Wing finally grinned.

"I expected something more exotic," Lucy said, looking

around for the first time. The airport was like any other airport, the people still looked like people, the Muzak was Rodgers and Hammerstein.

"We must find shuttle plane to Scotland," he said, scurrying down the hall. "Have less than hour to catch flight." He pronounced it "fright," which Lucy found apropos. She had already caught fright. Now she took a deep breath and let her heart descend out of her throat and settle back where it belonged.

So far so good. She had successfully managed to gain entry illegally to Great Britain. She was now an international criminal.

SEVENTEEN

THE SHUTTLE PLANE BROKE through the clouds over Glasgow. Lucy stared out the window, disappointed. It looked like any industrial town in New England: narrow, red-brick houses, high-rise apartments, and office buildings. Only the chimneys were odd—tapering cannons pointing defiantly at the gray sky.

"You okay, Rucy?" Wing asked as they deplaned.

"I have an adrenaline headache, I have jet lag, and these damned contact lenses are destroying my eyeballs. Other than that I feel great."

"Still not want to wear Tina's glasses?"

"I can't believe that being totally blind is going to help my chances, Mr. Wing. In fact I think I should drop this whole ridiculous disguise."

"Better for fox to look like hound sometime," said Wing, wearing his favorite inscrutable expression.

"Just what every woman wants to hear," said Lucy.

"What if you don't like what you find? What if what you find don't like you? This way you have out."

"I'm sorry, Mr. Wing," Lucy nodded. "You're right. I didn't mean to snap. I'm just a little nervous today. Lord knows why."

"Wing understand. We find connecting plane, go to Lis, everything okay. Okay?"

Lucy nodded.

The Glasgow airport was old-fashioned, but familiar. It was still hard for Lucy to believe she was in another country. There were no men in kilts, no bagpipers. Young men in blue jeans and leather jackets stood around, their hands in their pockets. Women in tweed coats sat on benches.

Only when people spoke did the place seem foreign. Everyone sounded like he was choking on a chicken bone.

Everyone also seemed to be staring at them.

Lucy was sure it was because she looked so suspicious in her disguise until a thin, black-haired man in a short coat stepped out in front of them and jabbed Wing with his finger.

"What aire you supposed to be?" he said ominously in the strange guttural dialect, staring at Wing's top hat. Wing stared straight into the man's eyes for a moment, then smiled.

"Wing undertaker looking for new business. How you feeling?"

"I feel fine," said the man indignantly.

"Glad to hear that," said Wing, whipping out a business card. "Come see me when you kick bucket. I give you discount."

The man stood staring at the card as Wing walked briskly on, Lucy at his heels.

"Friendry place!" he said happily. Lucy didn't have the heart to argue. All she wanted was a shrimp cocktail and a hot shower. Did they have shrimp in Scotland? she wondered. Did they have showers?

The Island Air commuter terminal turned out to be simply a desk by a door. There were some folding chairs, but there was no one around. Lucy sat down and opened the bag of sandwiches Aunt Sally had given her the day before, a world away.

"Tuna or ham?" she said.

"Ham," replied Wing.

She handed him the soggy sandwich and they ate in silence. Lucy was really beginning to hate tuna.

"When does plane leave?" Wing yawned after he finished eating. Lucy checked their tickets.

"Another forty minutes."

"Wake, please."

Wing tilted his top hat over his face. In no more than

two minutes he was breathing heavily, obviously asleep. Lucy stared at the little figure, wondering how in the world the man could sleep at a time like this. Here they were, a million miles from nowhere—she illegally—headed toward a place with which their only connection was a dead man and a word on an old piece of jewelry. Was she the only one with enough sense to be scared shitless?

After a while an elderly couple, laden with suitcases, sat down across from her in two of the folding chairs. The woman smiled at Lucy.

"Going to Lis, dearie?"

"Yes, I am," Lucy said nervously, glancing at the sleeping figure of Wing. She was on her own.

"First time then?" The woman had a brusque voice and wore a tweed coat. Her accent was English.

"Yes. How did you know?"

"You don't exactly look like a local," said the woman and laughed heartily.

"What you put them things in your ear for?" said the man, equally enthusiastic and shaped like a beer can.

Lucy gulped. "Decoration?"

"We're the Pembles," said the woman, obviously pleased with the fact. "I'm Maura. He's Tim."

"I'm…Tina Snicowski."

"What kind of a name is that?" demanded Tim.

Lucy realized she had no idea.

"We're from Weehawken," she stammered.

Maura nodded. "Is that near Estonia?"

"You'll be just another white settler on Lis," chortled Tim.

"A what?"

"That's what the natives call you if you try to improve any island properties. They're a stupid, indolent lot, don't have the brains to appreciate the beauty of what they've got. We have a lovely vacation cottage, used to be a dump, practically. The little blighters treat us like dirt for fixing it up."

The woman nodded. "All they're interested in is a handout. You'll see. Made nothing of the place in a thousand years, but they resent anyone who tries to bring a little money into their economy. It's simply scandalous."

"And they're nasty, too," said Tim. "One of them threatened to give me a 'creepie' when I was down on my knees trying to paint our porch. A creepie, can you imagine?"

"What brings you to Lis?" said Maura eagerly.

"My boss is looking for investments," said Lucy nervously, certain the Pembles were spies for English customs.

"Him?" said Tim, gesturing at Wing with his chin.

"Yes."

"He's going to be disappointed then, he is. Just another white settler, that's all he'll be on Lis."

"Well, he likes new experiences."

"Where are you staying?" asked Tim.

Lucy dug into her travel folder. "In Iolair. At the Manor Lodge. Actually we hoped to stay in Dumlagchtat, but there doesn't seem to be a hotel there."

"There's nothing there at all," said the woman with a sniff. "Whatever did you want to go there for?"

"I have a friend whose people were from Dumlagchtat," said Lucy, carefully trying out the story she and Wing had invented. "I promised I'd look them up while I'm here. Do you know any of the local history?"

"Good God, no," snorted the man. "Waste of time. Nothing ever happened there."

"All of yiu fer Lis?" said a voice behind them. Lucy looked around. A slender boy in a leather coat was unlocking the door to the field. He looked about fifteen years old.

"I'm Ronnie MacPherson, yer pilot. If you hand me yer tickets we can get goin' afore the rain."

Lucy rose and shook Wing's arm, gently. He pushed his top hat back into place and was up in an instant, oblivious to the Pembles' open-mouthed stares.

"Are you a Chinaman or a Jap?" said Tim finally.

Maura nudged him in the side with her elbow.

"He can't help what he is, ducks," Tim chuckled. "No offense intended there, guy. So which is it?"

"Wing from Weehawken," said Wing, winking at Lucy and handing his ticket to MacPherson.

They all followed the boy out onto the tarmac toward an airplane that looked to Lucy like a Volvo station wagon with wings.

"Is this the plane?" she exclaimed.

"Aye. Dinna worry about not havin' enough room. We kin seat six when we put in t'other seat. Ah think here comes yer baggage."

An old man in a plaid shirt was wheeling out Wing's bag and Lucy's two suitcases on a cart. He and Ronnie threw them into the rear of the plane along with the Pembles' carry-ons.

"All aboard," said MacPherson.

"You sit up front with pilot, Tina," said Wing, taking the single seat at the very rear of the tiny cabin.

The Pembles took their places, chattering happily, as if flying in oversized juice crates was their idea of a good time. Lucy could hear thunder in the distance. Practically trembling with fear, she got in next to Ronnie MacPherson. He pressed a few buttons, the single propeller started to turn, they taxied.

MacPherson conversed incomprehensibly with the tower, then suddenly they were speeding down the runway. Lucy could feel the wheels leaving the ground and stared, horrified, as Glasgow receded beneath them.

"It's perfectly safe," smiled the boy pilot proudly, lighting up a cigarette. Rain clattered in sheets against the windows. Lucy felt every muscle in her body stiffen up, but no one else seemed to notice. Wing began telling the Pembles some lie about how he once had lived in Mayfair. MacPherson grinned like an idiot. Lucy put her hands in her lap and reacquainted herself with God.

The plane rose to cruising altitude and followed the coast

northward. Maura and Tim regaled Wing with unflattering stories about the Lis locals. The overcast sky made the farms and cliffs the same color as the sea. At one point Lucy shut her eyes and tried to sleep but couldn't. The tiny plane bounced wrenchingly through air currents and turbulence. After what seemed an eternity, they crossed a small body of water and banked over a strange island that looked like the back of an enormous sea creature.

"Lis," said MacPherson, winking at her.

Lucy looked down at the red mountains rising out of the ocean and at last felt like she was truly in a foreign land. The place below looked like the surface of the moon.

EIGHTEEN

LUCY WAS IN A LECTURE room at Harvard. Why hadn't she gotten around to studying for this test? How could she have been so lazy, so foolish?

The other students effortlessly filled out their blue books. The men were all ex-presidents of their suburban high-school classes and captains of their football teams. The women were cheerleaders with perfect features and extensive wardrobes. Lucy looked down at her clothes, covered with food stains from her job in the cafeteria. She didn't even know what the question was, for some reason. She tried to shrink in her seat, to be invisible.

"Lucy MacAlpin Trelaine."

She looked up with a start. The professor was right in front of her, staring at her blank test booklet.

"Why aren't you prepared, Miss Trelaine?" said the professor angrily. "Is this how you intend to live your life?"

"What are you doing at Harvard?" asked a well-dressed young woman with a tight smile.

"You just don't have what it takes!" a perfect-looking young man in a blue suit yelled from the back.

"You're not wanted here," said another. "You don't belong."

"Get out, get out!" chanted the class rhythmically.

Lucy opened her eyes and for a moment didn't know where she was. The walls were whitewashed, the ceiling was beamed. It was a large room with sunlight pouring through mullioned windows, catching dust motes in midair. A cherrywood highboy sat in the corner. A hooked rug was thrown over the wide planks of the flooring.

Lucy sat up with a start, shaking the dream from her

head. Suddenly she remembered. This was the Manor
Lodge. She was in Iolair. On Lis.

Lucy had had this dream before. No matter how much
she told herself she didn't care about flunking out of Harvard, she knew she had cared. It was awful not to measure
up, not to belong. She struggled into control of herself, then
walked to the bathroom to brush her teeth and sort out
yesterday's events in her mind.

There had been no taxi or bus service from the airstrip,
since most of the traffic onto the island was by ferry. The
Pembles had had their car parked at the remote landing
field, however, and had given Lucy and Wing a lift to the
hotel.

It was a twenty-minute drive. Maura and Tim had talked
nonstop, but afterward Lucy couldn't remember a word of
the conversation, just the stark glens of deer grass and new
heather, the twisted hawthorns and hazel bushes, the pink
granite cliffs and waterfalls, the black volcanic peaks
against the slate gray sky.

The huge old hotel sat atop a sheer escarpment overlooking Loch Hagstal. It was a stone building. All the
buildings she saw were stone, which was not surprising.
Except for a few carefully fenced areas, there seemed to be
no trees anywhere on Lis.

It had been midafternoon when they arrived at the Manor
Lodge and were shown to adjoining rooms. Wing had
wanted to get something to eat, Lucy told him to go on
without her.

She had badly needed to sleep, but there was something
that Lucy had to do first, something she wanted to do alone.
She had waited until Wing's footsteps disappeared down
the hall, then picked up the tiny island phone-directory. It
had taken her a long time to work up the courage to open
the book. This was the moment of truth.

There were no Trelaines.

There were no MacAlpins.

There wasn't even a Fingon.

Lucy had drawn a deep breath, not understanding why she felt so relieved. Then she had taken a long, hot bath in the huge, claw-footed bathtub—there was no shower—and fallen into a deep and instant sleep.

Now it was morning. Washed and feeling human again, Lucy put on a pair of slacks and a sweater and headed downstairs. Halfway down the hall she turned and dashed back to her room. She had forgotten to put in her contact lenses. Luckily, no one had seen her.

"Remind me to be more careful, will you?" Lucy said to a responsible-looking chair. Wing was right. It would be better to remain as Tina. At least for now.

Brown-eyed again, Lucy ventured down the vast staircase. A breakfast buffet was set up in the sprawling dining room.

"Good morning…Tina," said Wing, rising from behind a plate piled with eggs, smoked fish, and sausages.

"Good morning, Mr. Wing," Lucy said, suddenly realizing how famished she was.

"Go get food. You look hungry. You sleep okay?"

"Like a baby," she replied and headed for the buffet.

Though it was still early in the tourist season, the Manor Lodge was already crowded, which was not surprising considering that it was the only hotel on the south side of the island. It had once been a hunting retreat. Heads of stags graced the battered, dark, wood-paneled walls. Most of the accents Lucy heard at the tables around her were English, tourists on holiday. Several of the tourists were staring at Wing as if they had never seen an Oriental undertaker in an opera cape and top hat at breakfast before.

"So where we start?" said Wing, after Lucy finished her second helping of eggs and third cup of strong, black coffee.

"I guess we should rent a car," she said.

"We go to unpronounceable town?"

"Dumlagchtat."

"Okay. I drive."

"Maybe I better drive."

"You have Tina Snicowski driver license?"

"No," said Lucy, "but I'm sure it will be okay."

"Not okay," said Wing decisively. "You get ticket, cop ask for passport, we are in deep doo-doo. Wing drive."

"I suppose you have a license?"

Wing pulled one out of his pocket and grinned.

"Wing driver first-class. Used to be chauffeur for fish long time ago."

"Are you sure you can still handle a car?"

Wing nodded vigorously and signed the check.

"We have lots of fun. You see. Come, come, come."

Lucy followed him to the hotel desk with all the enthusiasm of a condemned murderer. The thoughts of careening around a strange country on the wrong side of the road with Wing at the wheel was about as appealing as menstrual cramps.

"We wish to rent car, please," said Wing, bowing to the clerk, a middle-aged man with sandy hair.

"I am sorry, but there are no rental caires on Lis," said the man, trying to conceal his surprise at finding such an unlikely figure before him.

"Hosanna," said Lucy.

"There aire a few local people with motors, however, who will hire their services. Shall I try to arrange something for you?"

"Please," said Wing. Lucy fought down the impulse to ask what it would cost.

"It may take some time," said the clerk. "If you'd like to return to your rooms, I can ring you up when your man arrives."

"Cannot come right away?" said Wing, tapping the counter with his finger. "We have important things to do, please."

"We'll be happy to wait," said Lucy, leading Wing away by the arm.

"So much to do, yes?" said Wing. "Not very efficient place."

"They just do things a little differently, that's all. Now here are some tourist brochures we can read and I'm sure the car will be here in no time."

"Okay," said Wing. "You read. Wing explore grounds."

"Don't go too far." Lucy sighed, watching the little man dart away. Wing had a metabolism like popcorn. He never sat still. If this took longer than a week, she reflected sadly, she might have to kill him, too.

Lucy went back to her room and threw herself onto the bed, still feeling sluggish from the long trip, still nervous about what she would find in this strange place. She opened a brochure entitled "The Glorious Past" and found herself reading about the three ruling families of Lis: the Mac-Donalds, the MacKinnons, and Lucy's jaw dropped open— the Fingons. If she were indeed a Fingon, Lucy realized, then she was descended from Scottish nobility!

Her excitement waned, however, as she read further.

The history of the Fingons was sickeningly bloody. Down through the centuries, Fingons had slaughtered their dinner guests, tortured their enemies, and massacred one another. And more than once—she read with horror—a Fingon father had murdered his own children, and vice versa! Not that such deeds were unusual for the nobility of Lis. The MacDonalds and the MacKinnons had equally grisly exploits to their credit.

The phone rang. Lucy jumped practically a foot.

"Your car is here, miss," said the desk clerk.

"Thanks," she replied. Sobered, Lucy proceeded down the staircase into the lobby, happy to leave the bloodshed of the past behind. The only history she should be concerned about, she told herself, was the events of thirty years ago.

Through the hotel's open door she could see a large, black sedan in the driveway, but no sign of Wing. Lucy wandered through the two small sitting rooms and then ventured out back. Still no Wing.

"Have you seen my friend?" she asked the desk clerk.

"No, Miss Snicowski," replied the man. For a moment Lucy didn't know who he was talking to, then remembered she was still supposed to be Tina.

Resolving to drop the disguise at the first suitable moment, Lucy ventured back into the dining room, where a few stragglers were still eating. Traveling with Wing was like traveling with a naughty child.

"Have you seen the Oriental gentleman that I was with this morning?" she asked a waitress.

"I believe he's in the kitchen, ma'am," the girl replied, gesturing toward a door. Lucy rolled her eyes and walked into the hotel's kitchen.

Wing was sitting on a chair in the corner of the ancient scullery, arms folded, watching a large, heavy woman dressed in white stir a gigantic pot of something.

"Excuse me?" said Lucy tentatively.

Wing looked up. The woman kept stirring.

"Our car's here, Mr. Wing."

Wing stood and bowed to the fat woman, who didn't look up.

"Thank you very much." He bowed again, turned on his heel, and headed for the lobby. Lucy followed.

"What was she making?" asked Lucy.

"Pickled herring. Wing get good idea for Neat 'n' Tidy."

"I don't want to hear," said Lucy, leading him out of the kitchen.

"Not for corpses!" protested Wing, reading her mind. "For Aunt Sally."

"You'd pickle Aunt Sally?"

"No, no, no. For Aunt Sally to cook."

They were now in the driveway and approaching the car.

"Hello, I'm Tina Snicowski," said Lucy, getting into the

large, black sedan, "and this is Mr. Wing, who is not going to go wandering off by himself anymore."

"Ranald Wharrie," said the driver, not looking up from his magazine. He was a large, red-faced man with bushy eyebrows and a battered cap.

"I drive. Okay, Mr. Wharrie?" said Wing, trying to open the door to the front seat.

"I am the driver or you nae ha' the use of my motor," replied Wharrie languidly, pressing down the door lock.

"I think we should respect the man's wishes," said Lucy, relieved. Wing shrugged and got into the backseat next to her.

"A hundred pounds per day," said Wharrie to Lucy, holding out his hand. "In advance. Ye also pay for my gas."

"That's outrageous!" exclaimed Lucy.

"Pay it or find another driver," said Wharrie.

"It's okay," said Wing, reaching for his wallet. Lucy grabbed his hand.

"Look, Mr. Wing. I appreciate everything you've done for me, but I'm not some charity case."

"Sure, Ruc...Tina," whispered Wing, eyeing the back of Wharrie's head. "Wing just want to help."

"I know. But this is my problem and I can pay my own way. You're just along for the ride, remember?"

Wing sat back silently in his seat and looked inscrutable. Lucy fished in her pocket for the money. A hundred pounds was practically a fortune at current exchange rates, but she wasn't in any position to argue right now. They could find a more agreeable (and cheaper) driver tomorrow. And she could always have Billy Rosenberg wire cash if, God forbid, she needed more than Wing had advanced. The important thing was to let Wing know who was in charge of this little expedition.

"Do you know where Dumlagchtat is?" Lucy said, leaning forward.

"Aye," said Wharrie.

"That's where we want to go."

Wharrie started the engine. Chills swept down Lucy's spine. For the first time the significance of their destination had sunk in. The answers to all her questions might be only a few miles away.

NINETEEN

WHARRIE TOOK the same road the Pembles had driven back from the airstrip yesterday, but in the opposite direction.

They climbed higher and higher into the mountains. Wharrie didn't speak and Wing was uncharacteristically silent, giving Lucy a chance to appreciate the strange scenery. She could see primroses and new bracken, and hear the call of cuckoos. The countryside stretched endlessly before them, an untroubled blanket of green, save for an occasional white cottage or farmhouse, a stark stand of trees, a naked boulder.

"It's beautiful!" she exclaimed as they rounded a curve and a spectacular open vista stretched out beneath them. Wharrie snorted contemptuously in the front seat.

"You don't think it's beautiful, Mr. Wharrie?" she asked, surprised.

"I'll chust drive, if ye doon't mind, lady," he said.

After a while, Wharrie pulled into a tiny town nestled in a glen under a huge mountain. It was no more than a few rows of houses facing each other across a cobbled street. The big Scot stopped the car in front of the largest house.

"This is Dumlagchtat. D'ye want me ta wait?"

"Of course you wait," said Wing, showing his annoyance. "We hire you for day."

"The lady hired me, and I'll hear only from her, if ye dinna mind, wee man."

Wing stared at Wharrie, his expression impossible to read.

"Please wait, Mr. Wharrie," said Lucy quickly, and she got out of the car, determined not to let the man get to her.

"Is there someone around here who might be able to tell me about local history?"

Wharrie shrugged. "I dinna ken."

"Well, is there a city hall or something?"

"Nae."

Wing scampered out of the car behind Lucy, glancing back at Wharrie, who had already buried his face in a magazine. Lucy was beginning to wonder if the Pembles had been right about the natives. Wharrie was about as friendly as acne.

They walked up one side of the short street and down the other, staring in silence at the small, chalk-colored houses with slate roofs. All the doors were closed. A few people were doing chores in the backyards, but no one gave them a second glance.

"I ask questions now?" said Wing brightly.

"Why don't I?" said Lucy.

"Okay. You boss."

"Excuse me," said Lucy, breaking off from Wing and approaching a woman in a plaid shawl who was hanging laundry. The woman did not look up.

"Excuse me," said Lucy again when she was only a few feet away. "I wonder if I might ask you a question."

The woman stopped what she was doing and stared as if Lucy were a pet dog who had just asked for a piece of pie.

"Aye?"

It must be her earrings, Lucy decided. Then Lucy noticed the woman's gaze had shifted. She was staring at Tak Wing, who was some thirty feet away inspecting a stone fence. Wing seemed to notice the woman's attention, for he touched his fingers to his top hat and smiled. The woman spat on the ground.

"I'm looking for some information," said Lucy brightly, hoping a good attitude would overcome the woman's obvious reluctance to talk to strangers. She looked again to Lucy but said nothing.

"Was there ever anyone named MacAlpin living around here?"

"I dinna ken," she said finally.

"Anyone named Trelaine?"

"Nae."

"People named Fingon?"

The woman squinted. "The Fingon all be dead."

"Is there someone who knows anything about them?"

The woman just stared at Lucy and didn't speak.

"Do you think one of your neighbors might remember the Fingons?"

"No one in Dumlagchtat remembers the Fingons."

"But didn't the Fingons live around here?" said Lucy awkwardly. "Weren't they important?"

The woman pointed toward the mountains looming up behind them.

"There they lived. A curse upon them."

"Thank you very much," said Lucy, a little frightened. "Have a nice day." The woman said nothing more and still hadn't moved when Lucy walked over and collected Wing.

"She says the Fingons are all dead but they lived up there," Lucy said, pointing at the mountains.

"We go there?"

"I guess so."

"Good, good," said Wing eagerly. "You make great progress already, Rucy, see?"

Lucy nodded and walked back toward the car, Wing bringing up the rear. As a homecoming, her visit to Dumlagchtat hadn't been very encouraging.

"Do you know a house up there in the mountains where people named Fingon used to live?" Lucy said to Wharrie after she and Wing had settled themselves again in the backseat.

"Aye," said Wharrie, not looking up from his magazine.

"Will you take us there, please?"

He shrugged and started his engine. Wing fidgeted in his

seat, craning around so that he wouldn't miss any detail of
the little village. In a few minutes they were on a road on
the side of the peak, heading toward a stone structure built
into the rock.

"Is castle!" said Wing breathlessly as they approached.

Lucy stared at the far-off structure, not knowing what to
say. It was a castle. Not a huge castle, but large enough to
astonish her. Its back was protected by the red peak, its
walls commanded a perfect view of the entire valley. It was
only when they were upon it that Lucy saw it was deserted
and gone to ruin. The windows were broken out. The roof
had holes in places.

They drove on in silence, through a crumbling gate, past
an ancient graveyard, and stopped in front of the boarded-
up door of the castle.

"Did the Fingons live here?" asked Lucy incredulously.
There was an oppressiveness in the air, almost a physical
presence of evil. The wind blew audibly against the cliffs.

"Aye," muttered Wharrie.

"What happened to them?"

"I'm a driver, not a guidebiuk," said the man.

Wing started to say something, but Lucy simply got out
of the car. There was no point in getting into a fight with
Wharrie. The man obviously had some kind of chip on his
shoulder and wasn't going to take it off just because they
found it annoying.

Lucy stared at the ruined castle looming so cold before
her. What was she supposed to do now? Who were these
people, these Fingons, who had lived in such an evil place?
What did they have to do with her? Finally she stopped
chasing her thoughts around in circles and got back into
the car.

"Let's see some more of the island, please, Mr. Wharrie," Lucy said with as much dignity as she could muster.

They drove for the rest of the day, stopping occasionally
to admire a waterfall or a cliff or a tourist attraction. Lucy
found the unspoiled landscapes and the bare glens where it

seemed man had never trod beautiful and eerily familiar. Wing enjoyed himself everywhere they went, despite the stares he received, but a New York cabby had more enthusiasm for scenery than Wharrie seemed to.

Lucy was finally able to learn something about the Fingons when they went through the island's major historic attraction. MacKinnon House was maintained by the Scottish Historical Trust and open to the public. The MacKinnon family had bankrupted itself in the 1930s.

"Yes," said the tour guide in answer to Lucy's query, "the Fingons were a powerful family on Lis for many years. They owned all the western coastlands and a fair portion of the rest of the island. Only the MacDonalds were more prominent."

"Are there any Fingons still living on the island?" Lucy asked hopefully.

"Nae. The last laird, Geoffrey Fingon, died many years ago," said the woman, a thin, hawk-faced biddy with gray hair.

"There weren't any children?"

"I dinna ken."

"Do you know if there's anyone who might remember the Fingons?"

"No one that I would ken," said the woman and resumed her historical commentary.

"I'd like to reserve a car again for tomorrow," Lucy told the desk clerk as they entered the Manor Lodge shortly after six that evening.

"Very well, Miss Snicowski," said the young woman at the desk.

"Other driver beside Mr. Wharrie, please," added Wing, after glancing respectfully at Lucy.

"I'm afraid Mr. Wharrie has the only available vehicle at present."

"He'll be fine," said Lucy, patting Wing on the arm. "Please ask him to be here at nine-thirty."

"More fun riding in hearse," muttered Wing.

They went upstairs to their rooms for an hour, then met for dinner at the hotel dining-room.

"What look good to you?" said Wing suspiciously, reading the menu. Lucy shook her head, not surprised that there were no shrimp cocktails, just sorry.

"What is jugged hare?" Wing asked.

"I think it's a rabbit in a bottle," said Lucy.

"Interesting concept." Wing nodded professionally. Lucy shuddered.

They settled on smoked salmon. Lucy had a glass of wine, which tasted sour and smokey. There was no club soda, so Wing settled for orange juice, which, to Lucy's astonishment, was blood red. Despite Wing's protests that oranges were red in Great Britain, she couldn't help feeling it was a bad omen.

"No, no, no," said Wing insistently. "Everything going fine."

"Sure," Lucy said.

"Cannot expect to find everything first day."

"I suppose. At least we know there were Fingons here once."

"Fingons rich people," said Wing proddingly. "Maybe other rich people remember Fingons. Rich people all know one another. What you think?"

"The MacDonalds!"

"Who, who, who?"

"The MacDonalds are the only ones left of the three ruling families of Lis. Mr. Wing, you're a genius. Of course the MacDonalds would have known the Fingons. I'll call them in the morning."

Wing smiled broadly, clearly pleased with himself.

Lucy said the name over in her head. The Fingons. Her family?

TWENTY

LUCY HAD an early breakfast the next morning and took a long walk down the grassy paths along the cliff, through the empty fields, and back again. Now she was bathed, changed, and sitting at the telephone in her room. Wing was due to meet her downstairs in fifteen minutes. The number for Fitzroy MacDonald, Sixth Earl of Mantach, was dialed and ringing.

"The Castle," answered a curt male voice.

"Yes, hello," said Lucy, launching into her cover story, trying to contain her excitement. "My name is...Tina Snicowski. I'm over here on vacation—I'm staying at the Manor Lodge hotel—and I promised a friend I'd look into her genealogy. She may be a Fingon, you see, and..."

"Excuse me, Miss...whatever you said your name was," interrupted the voice, "but why are you calling here?" The accent was British. The tone of voice was mildly incredulous.

"Well," said Lucy, trying to sound charming, "that's the thing. My friend wants to know about the last Lord Fingon and I thought one of the MacDonalds might remember something about...."

"I hardly think that his lordship would wish to involve himself in such a matter. Good day."

The phone went dead. Lucy stared at the receiver. It had never occurred to her that the MacDonalds wouldn't cooperate. Humiliated, she stomped downstairs and out into the driveway. Wharrie was reading a magazine in his ugly black sedan. Wing was already in the car.

"A hundred pounds in advance," Wharrie announced when she got in, holding out his hand.

"So what they say?" said Wing excitedly. "They remember? You find out everything?"

"Actually, they hardly knew the Fingons at all," Lucy lied. "They couldn't tell me a thing."

"You sure?" said Wing, looking surprised.

"Of course, I'm sure," Lucy snapped. There was no point in subjecting herself to further embarrassment.

"So sorry," said Wing, hanging his head.

"No, I'm sorry. It's not your fault."

"You will find someone else. Not to worry, please."

"Sure," said Lucy, feeling even worse. "How much did you say that was, Mr. Wharrie?"

"Hundred pounds," said the driver in a surly voice.

She counted out the bills.

"Feeling any friendlier today?"

He grunted.

"What we do now, Ru...Tina?" asked Wing soberly.

"We ask Mr. Wharrie," said Lucy, not having the energy to conceal her exasperation. "You know I'm trying to find some information about the Fingons, Mr. Wharrie. Do you have any suggestions about where to look?"

"Dinna ken any Fingons."

"Then do you know where administrative matters are taken care of for the island? A city hall or some place like that where they would have the birth and death records?"

"Goovernment business, ye mean?"

"Yes."

"Tha's all duin in Glasgow."

"Great," Lucy said. "Where on Lis haven't we been yet?"

"Skerrisay," said Wharrie.

Skerrisay, Lucy knew from her guidebook, was on the northern tip of the island and the island's largest city. With a population of less than two thousand, however, it was hardly a metropolis.

"How far away is it?"

"An hour and more. Diu you want to go there?"

Lucy looked at Wing. He shrugged.

"Why not?" Lucy said unhappily.

They drove up the north road again, through the bald mountains that rose in the center of the island. Several times Wharrie had to stop the car while flocks of black-faced sheep ambled across the road. Wild rabbits crossed the bracken and birds of every description filled the air.

"Why aren't we driving along the coast?" Lucy asked at one point. "Wouldn't that be quicker?"

"Tha' be the MacDonalds' lands, damn them all," said Wharrie, practically spitting out the words. "Commercial traffic to Skerrisay is routed through the interior."

"Landowners have rights, too," said Wing, obviously itching for a fight.

"What aboot our rights?" Wharrie shot back bitterly. "Lismen who enlisted in the army in World War I were promised land on the northern shore—land tha' once belonged to their ancestors afore they were evicted. When those who survived the trenches returned, they got nothing. The MacDonalds ha' pressured the authorities to sell them the coastlands so they wouldna lose the view from their precious castle."

"Very unfortunate," said Wing, "but if MacDonalds own land..."

"Oh, tha' makes it all right, I suppose," said Wharrie, anger apparently loosening his tongue. "Then you moost agree with the MacDonalds tha' a fish tha' was in the ocean yesterday belongs to them because it swam in their stream today. You moost agree, too, tha' the birds and the rabbits and whatever deer aire left on the island all belong to the MacDonalds because they happen to cross their lands. It's a wonder the bloody MacDonalds allow the rest of oos to breathe the air!"

Wing did not pursue the argument, which was fine with Lucy. She had had enough of the MacDonalds for a lifetime. And of Wharrie.

At last they arrived in Skerrisay, a quaint little place with stone houses and narrow roads. There were several souvenir stores near the water and Lucy could see one of the auto ferries from the mainland at a little dock.

"Is this undertaker, please?" said Wing, seeing a sign marked DIBBLE MCFEELY BURIALS as they stopped at a tiny intersection.

The dour Scot turned around slowly and stared at Wing.

"Ye ain't fixin' to expire in mi motor, aire ye?"

"Maybe Wing pay courtesy call," he said to Lucy, clearly uncomfortable. The tension between him and Wharrie had grown almost palpable.

"Good idea," said Lucy.

Wing opened the door and got out.

"We'll meet you back here in forty-five minutes, okay?" said Lucy, wondering if it would take even that long to size up the little town.

"Okay," said Wing. "Not mean to offend, Mr. Wharrie. Wing not understand about MacDonalds."

Wharrie didn't answer. Wing walked off toward Dibble McFeely, head bowed, opera cape drooping on the ground.

"He said he was sorry," said Lucy. Wharrie grunted and drove on in silence. At the next intersection, Lucy rolled down her window and motioned to a man carrying a basket.

"Excuse me," she said. "Is there a local historical society you can direct me to?"

The man walked over to the car.

"Eh?" he said.

"Is there some historical society that might be able to give me some information about the island?"

"There's the Island Study Group. Do ye ha' the Gaelic?"

"Pardon me?"

"He wants to know if ye speak Gaelic," snarled Wharrie.

"No, I don't know any Gaelic," said Lucy helplessly.

"Then that won't diu. They only converse in Gaelic. Ye might try the tourist bureau, oop the road past the kirk."

"Thank you," said Lucy.

They drove up the road, past a blackened church. The tourist bureau was marked with a prominent sign and occupied a small gray building with windowboxes full of little blue flowers. Lucy got out of the car and knocked on the door. After a minute a small elderly woman showed her in to a shabby waiting room with framed travel posters on the wall and the same tourist brochures Lucy had read at the hotel.

"Welcoom to Lis," said the woman.

"Thank you. I'm trying to find out some information about the Fingon family."

"Ooh, they be gone now."

"Yes, I know, but I'd still like to find out about them."

"Lived oop in the castle in Dumlagchtat, they did."

"Yes, I know that, too."

"But they're gone now. Not been a Fingon on Lis for years."

"Yes, but do you know what happened to them?"

"Nae."

"Do you know anyone who might?"

"Ha' ye tried the Island Stuidy Group?"

"Thanks very much," said Lucy and walked back to the car. How could she find out anything in a place where people either knew nothing, conversed only in Gaelic, or hung up in your ear?

For the next half hour, Wharrie drove slowly through Skerrisay. Lucy leaned out and asked pedestrians if they had ever known Trelaines or MacAlpins, if they remembered the Fingons. No one could or would help. Lucy began asking people to call her at the hotel if they ran into anybody who might remember the Fingons. Most looked at her as though she were mad.

By the time they returned to Dibble McFeely Burials, Lucy was discouraged. From the expression on his face as he got into the car, Tak Wing was discouraged, too.

"What's the matter?" said Lucy, not sure she wanted to hear the answer.

"Dibble McFeely very backward," said Wing sadly. "Have no use for modern equipment. Turnover not so good. Wing cremate more people in year than live on entire island."

Wharrie turned around in his seat, staring suspiciously at Wing for a moment but saying nothing.

"Well, we knew it was a small place," Lucy sighed.

Wing nodded. "You find something, maybe?"

Lucy shook her head. They drove back to the hotel in silence.

The next day Lucy and Wing continued their exploration of the island, stopping to ask about Fingons where there were signs of a town. None of the islanders had anything to say. Lucy wondered if they even knew where the Manor Lodge was, the way they stared after her.

By Friday morning Lucy was terribly depressed. She didn't have the nerve to quit so soon—they'd been here less than a week—but it seemed hopeless. No one on Lis seemed to know the Fingons. Or if they knew, they wouldn't tell Lucy. Nor did anyone remember any Robert MacAlpin or know the name Trelaine.

Tak Wing had been getting more bored and frustrated each day, barely talking, but unable to keep still—almost like a rambunctious child confined to a classroom. Wharrie had snapped at him several more times. So had Lucy, to her regret. She was therefore surprised when she came down to breakfast and found Wing all smiles, bouncing up and waving to her as she entered the dining room.

"What's the matter?" Lucy asked warily, sitting down at the table across from him.

"Wing have idea!" he said, pouring her a cup of coffee.

"Oh?"

"Wing go back to Glasgow," the little man said proudly. "No business for Neat 'n' Tidy here. Island too small.

Glasgow big city. Friendly place. Maybe find financing there. What you think?''

"What's this all about, Mr. Wing? You don't really think you're going to find financing in Glasgow, do you?''

"Sure.''

"You'd leave me all alone here?'' she asked sarcastically. It was too good to be true.

"What you need Wing for? He only come to protect you, but things look pretty safe, yes?''

"Safe enough for me to chuck this ridiculous disguise? I hate these contact lenses.''

"Maybe you keep just in case. Okay?''

"I promise you I can take care of myself, Mr. Wing,'' said Lucy indignantly.

"Good. So Wing go to Glasgow with clean conscience. But you stay as Tina, okay?''

Lucy frowned, but didn't move to take out the contacts.

"So why do you want to leave?''

The little man bowed his head.

"Wing no help to you, just get into hair.''

"You're helping a lot,'' said Lucy, trying to sound sincere.

"Wharrie sick of Wing. Rucy sick of Wing, too.''

"I'm not…''

"Wing have eyes, Rucy,'' he said, smiling and shaking his head. "Can see the handwriting on face. Maybe people start talking more when suspicious Oriental man is gone, yes?''

"Look, Mr. Wing…''

"But Wing murder two birds with one airplane, ha! Talk to bankers, yes, but also check birth records of Fingons. Government records for island kept in Glasgow, yes? Wing see if Fingon have baby daughter thirty year ago. Maybe find out about brooches from museums. Smart, huh?''

"Well,'' she said, feeling guilty to be so relieved, "if you're really determined…''

"Glad you agree.''

"You'll have to hurry," said Lucy, remembering the three-flight-per-week Island Air schedule. "If you can't book a seat out today, there won't be another plane until Monday."

"Not to worry. Have taken care of ticket already. Ronnie MacPherson arrive from Glasgow in two hours. Maybe you take Wing to airport?"

TWENTY-ONE

LUCY TOOK A BITE of toast and looked at the empty chair across from her. It was the next morning. Tak Wing was in Glasgow. She was finally alone.

Lucy had been elated to get rid of Wing at first, had reveled in her long lost privacy, had even enjoyed Wharrie's usual hostile silence after they dropped Wing off at the airfield and headed down the south coast of the island. Nor had she felt disappointed when again her questions about the Fingons were unanswered. She was free.

"What a relief," she had whispered confidingly to the salt-and-pepper shakers at dinner. "Nobody scrutinizing me for a change, nobody telling me what to do. I prefer my own company, you know. I'm set in my ways."

The salt and pepper did not reply. Lucy knew what they were thinking: she was talking like an old lady.

She had slept late—it was past eleven. Breakfast was no longer being served and it was too early for lunch, but one of the staff had taken pity on her and fixed her some toast, reheated some coffee.

Now, taking a final sip, Lucy had to admit that she missed the little man. Wing made for better conversation than inanimate objects did. With him here everything was like some kind of crazy adventure. Now that he was gone, Lis suddenly felt very lonely and forbidding.

Lucy put a five-pound note on the table and tried not to think about it. Wing had been right about his being no help to her here. He might actually turn up something in Glasgow.

"Would you like to leave your key, Miss Snicowski?"

asked the desk clerk, a beanpole in a tweed suit, as Lucy crossed through the lobby.

"No, thank you," she replied politely.

The man frowned disapprovingly but Lucy didn't care. She had been bringing her key with her whenever she went out, despite Wing's protestations that in Europe it was customary to leave one's key at the desk.

Such a custom was ridiculous, as far as Lucy was concerned. She had half a mind to give the Manor Lodge her professional opinion about their security. Desk clerks couldn't know every guest. Someone could just give her room number and get her key. After being burglarized in New York, Lucy was finished with being so trusting. She kept most of her cash in the hotel safe and the room key in her pocket.

"Did you get me another driver?"

"I'm sorry, no, miss."

Disappointed, Lucy walked down the gravel path toward the waiting car. Ranald Wharrie sat scowling, reading a magazine.

"How about giving me a discount rate, Mr. Wharrie," she said, getting in. "You're making a fortune and I'm going broke."

"A hundred pounds in advance," replied the big Scot.

"Thanks so much for your consideration," muttered Lucy.

"Ye people aire all alike," Wharrie shot back with vehemence. "My working season is three months and what I make has to last the year. Ah doon't drive because I laike it, ye know. There airen't any other chobs to be had."

Lucy had been on her best behavior the whole week, but this was getting ridiculous. She opened the car door and was about to tell Wharrie where he could drive himself when she saw the skinny desk clerk trotting down the walk toward her, motioning with his hands.

"Glad I caught you, Miss Snicowski," said the man,

puffing. "A pairty wishes to speak with you on the telephone."

Lucy bent into the car to address Wharrie.

"Do you think you can possibly wait for your hundred pounds until I take this call?"

"Aye."

"Thank you," she said with exaggerated politeness and followed the clerk back into the lobby to the house phone. It took her nearly twenty steps to realize what a phone call might mean. Could it be that one of her inquiries was about to pay off?

"Miss Snicowski?" said a man's voice on the line, a lilting voice with a soft burr.

"Yes?"

"I understand you're interested in the Fingons?"

"Yes, that's right," Lucy replied, frightened and thrilled at the same time. "Were you one of the people I talked with?"

The man chuckled. "It's a verra wee island, Miss Snicowski. Word gets around."

"Yes, of course."

"MacLean is the name. Angus MacLean. I ken a bit about the Fingons. If ye'd care to buy me a drink, I'd be happy to tell ye what I can. How's that?"

"That would be great," said Lucy.

"I'm callin' from a pub in Skerrisay called the Fairy's Egg. I'll be here all afternoon, if this is a good time for you."

"It's perfect. I'm leaving now."

Lucy hung up the phone. Skerrisay was the size of a postage stamp. If Wharrie didn't know the Fairy's Egg already, surely he would be able to find it—he had to be good for something.

She walked briskly back to the car and got in.

"A hundred pounds," said Wharrie, dropping his magazine and starting the engine.

Lucy counted out the bills into his hand.

"Do you know the Fairy's Egg in Skerrisay?"

"I can find it," Wharrie replied, recounting the money and putting it into his shirt pocket.

"Well, that's where we're going."

An hour and fifteen minutes later, they were again cruising the streets of Skerrisay. Wharrie's knowledge of the village, however, was less than impressive. Luckily Lucy happened to glance down a side street and saw a sign reading THE FAIRY'S EGG swinging in front of a small stone building.

"Stop the car!" she cried.

Wharrie pulled on the brakes, nearly sending Lucy into the front seat.

"Do you want me to wait?" said Wharrie, picking up his magazine.

Lucy satisfied herself that she had no broken bones and looked at the darkened doorway of the Fairy's Egg.

"Why don't you join me for a drink, Mr. Wharrie?" she said, giving it one last shot. "It'll take more than your driving to break my neck. Can't we be friends?"

"I'm renting my motor, not my company," he said, not looking around.

"Sorry. It's just that…I've come a long way and I haven't been finding what I need. Maybe this is it. I'm a little nervous. Do you understand?"

Wharrie glanced at her in his rearview mirror and pulled down his cap.

"Plenty of us dinna find what we need," he said.

"Mr. Wharrie?" Lucy said sweetly when she had gotten out of the car.

"Aye?"

"If you don't improve your attitude somebody is going to give you a creepie—and that somebody is going to be me!"

Lucy slammed the door with all her strength.

"Hey!" Wharrie cried out after her, but Lucy stalked into the little pub without looking back.

IT WAS A MOMENT before Lucy's eyes adjusted to the gloom in the Fairy's Egg. Everyone was staring at her. "Everyone" consisted of five rough-looking men and the bartender, a heavy man with a frightful scar extending from his temple to his chin.

Lucy sat down at a little table in the corner of the room and folded her hands in front of her, wondering if this had been such a good idea after all.

"Aire ye in the right place, lass?" asked the bartender finally.

"I'm looking for Mr. MacLean," she said, still feeling like an idiot for trying to befriend Wharrie.

"Why on airth ye be wantin' MacLean?" asked one of the men in a low voice.

Lucy swallowed hard.

"I'm looking for some information."

"What kind of information?" growled the bartender.

"Mr. MacLean said he knew something about local history."

The men on the barstools suddenly exploded into laughter.

"Now yer in fer it," said one.

"At last the MacLean has found his heaven," said another.

"Ye'll be one sorry lass ye askt," a third cried, pounding the bar in helpless mirth.

"Here, what's this commotion?" said a white-haired man with a black patch over one eye as he came out of the men's room, zipping up his fly.

"Is it your intention to torture this poor lass with yer miserable histories, Angus?" scowled the bartender as the others laughed uncontrollably.

"And wha's it to ye if ye can sell a drink?" said the man with the patch, toddling over to Lucy and flashing a crooked smile.

"You're Mr. MacLean?" said Lucy, wondering how she had managed to stumble into *Treasure Island.*

"Aye," he said, bowing at the waist. "Talisker, Jamie, for the lass and me."

The men at the bar howled and hooted. Lucy tried to maintain her composure. The bartender put shot glasses in front of them, filled them, and left the bottle.

"I'm Tina Snicowski," said Lucy to MacLean when the others had quieted down and returned to their own drinking. For the first time she was glad that she had listened to Wing and kept up her disguise. He really had picked a fine time to leave her on her own!

"Drink oop, Miss Snicowski," said MacLean, raising his glass and emptying it.

Lucy wasn't much of a drinker, but there didn't seem to be any choice. She tried to force down a swallow of the powerful golden liquid without choking. Smacking his lips, MacLean refilled his glass and topped off hers. Occasionally a patron would glance contemptuously over his shoulder at them.

"You're from Lis, Mr. MacLean?" Lucy said, taking another sip of the scotch whiskey and managing to smile in spite of it.

"Aye. My father was a crofter and his father afore him."

"What's a crofter?"

"Tha's a man who works a croft, a course."

Lucy must have looked blank, for MacLean squinted at her with his good eye and spoke in kindly tones.

"A croft is a wee wedge of land. Not enough to feed a family on."

"There's goin' t'be a quiz, lass," shouted one of the men at the bar, "so ye best take notes."

"Are you a historian, Mr. MacLean?" asked Lucy uncomfortably. He seemed friendly enough so far, but the Fairy's Egg wasn't exactly a place where a girl could relax.

"I chust ken a bit about local matters is all," said MacLean, oblivious to the laughter from the ugly throng at the bar. "Sairt of a hobby, ye might say."

"Why di' ye want to gie me a creepie?" said a voice

suddenly. Lucy looked up. Wharrie was standing menacingly next to her chair.

"Because you're an asshole, that's why," said Lucy, swallowing hard. She glanced at the door, calculating the best escape route in case things got out of hand.

"D'ye know what a creepie is, then?" said Wharrie slowly.

"No," she said, looking him right in the eye. "I heard the expression from a white settler."

"Tha' would explain it. Givin' a creepie to a person is not mooch of a threat. A creepie is a wee three-legged stool."

They stared at one another for a moment, until Wharrie's face broke into a grin. Lucy grinned back. MacLean watched the spectacle, frowning.

"I'll hae that drink wi' ye if yer still willin'," said Wharrie finally.

Lucy resumed breathing and gestured to a chair. The big man took off his cap and sat. Only a few strands of red hair still graced his broad skull. His presence was somehow strangely comforting. If Wharrie had decided to join the human race, maybe things really were looking up.

"This is Mr. Wharrie, who's been driving me around," said Lucy to MacLean. "Angus MacLean."

Wharrie's smile vanished as quickly as it had appeared. He nodded warily to MacLean across the table.

"I'm bringin' ye business, Jamie," MacLean called to the bartender.

"Mr. MacLean is going to tell me about the Fingons," said Lucy.

"Tha' so?" said Wharrie, obviously not impressed. Then he said something else that Lucy didn't catch. It wasn't until MacLean answered in strange guttural syllables that she realized they were speaking Gaelic. The bartender brought another glass. MacLean poured Wharrie's drink.

"To new friends," said MacLean, smiling his crooked

smile. Wharrie didn't smile back. They drank. Lucy's eyes teared, but she managed not to cough.

"So, what d'ye need to know, lass?" asked MacLean.

"Well, it's not me, actually," said Lucy. "I have this friend who may be related to the Fingons and I promised I would find out about them for her."

A glance passed between MacLean and Wharrie but neither man said anything.

"Fingon doesn't even seem like a Scottish name," Lucy said brightly, trying to get the conversation going.

"Oh, yes," MacLean grinned. "Ancient clan. Claimed to go back to a prince in the house of Alpin, they did."

"Alpin? Is that like Kenneth mac Alpin?"

"Aye. Ye diu ken some history then."

"No, not really. I just heard the name mentioned somewhere. Can you tell me about Kenneth mac Alpin?"

"Actually there were several Kenneths," said MacLean, taking a sip of his whiskey. "The first Kenneth mac Alpin was the king who united the Scots and the Picts in eight forty-three A.D."

"The Picts," repeated Lucy eagerly. "They were an ancient Scottish tribe, yes?"

"Nae," answered MacLean. "The Scots were na' even Scottish in the way ye mean. They were a tribe of pirates from Dalriada in Northern Ireland. In about five hundred A.D. Fergus Mor mac Erc, the first king of the Scots, invaded the Pict homeland—the area we call Argyll. Kenneth mac Alpin was Fergus's descendant."

"Scotland is named after a bunch of Irishmen?"

"Tha's right," MacLean nodded, fingering his eyepatch. Wharrie took a sip of whiskey and mumbled something in Gaelic.

"The Picts made jewelry, didn't they?" said Lucy, trying to contain her excitement. At last she had found someone who knew something and wasn't afraid to talk to her!

"Aye, the Picts were a very artistic race. They carved their weird symbols on gigantic stone pillars—ye still can find them around the countryside—as well as on jewelry and the like. The word *picti* is Latin for painted ones, so they might even ha' decorated themselves with paint or tattoos. Unfortunately we dinna ken mooch about them.''

"Why not?'' asked Lucy.

MacLean leaned forward.

"Because as soon as Kenneth mac Alpin became king, Pictish culture winked out of existence. The Picts vanished so ootterly it's thought that Kenneth secured his throne by massacring the entire Pictish nobility.''

"That's awful!''

"I'm not sure the Picts liked it either,'' chuckled MacLean. "Anyways, to strengthen his claim on Pictland—which came to be called Scotia, then Scotland—Kenneth moved his capital further inland, to Scone.''

"Skoon,'' repeated Lucy, wishing now that she had thought to bring a pad to take notes.

"Spelled S-C-O-N-E. The Alpin dynasty lasted a few hundred years until Kenneth's great-great-great-grandson Duncan was murdered by a fellow named MacBeth....''

"Is she dead from boredom yet, Angus?'' hollered one of the men at the bar. The others broke into laughter.

"Go on wi' ye!'' MacLean shouted back. Then he turned back to Lucy. "Anyways, the Fingons claimed descent from the House of Alpin.''

"The Fingons were rich, weren't they?'' said Lucy.

"In a manner of speakin','' said MacLean easily. "The Fingons owned the castle outside Dumlagchtat and most of the crofts on Lis, as well. They were the landlords.''

"What happened to them?''

Wharrie suddenly stood up. Lucy had nearly forgotten his craggy, silent presence across the table.

"I'll tell yiu wha' happened to them,'' Wharrie said in a murderous voice. "The bastards bled the island dry, then died out of their own wickedness, tha's wha' happened to the Fingons.''

TWENTY-TWO

"THEY PREACHED against you on Sunday at the Glen Tobar Bridge," said Roderick Beaton, standing uncomfortably by the breakfast table.

The time was seven o'clock in the morning. The place was Dumlagchtat Castle. The year was 1846.

"Again?" exclaimed Henry, Eighth Baronet and Sixth Lord Fingon, sipping his China tea. "I don't understand why these crofters prefer to stand in the rain than sit in a comfortable church. What's wrong with the Church of Scotland that they need to start their own?"

"The minister you appointed, your lordship, keeps telling them that their problems are due to their own wickedness."

"And so they are," said Lord Fingon, his huge blue eyes flashing with anger. "My actions are merely evidence of God's wrath. I should evict the lot of them, famine or no."

"I don't know that such a step would look good now, m'lord," said Beaton mildly, "in view of your pledge to the relief people to postpone further clearances."

Lord Fingon snorted and brushed his thin lips with a napkin. What were they to do with all these starving crofters? They hadn't always been a problem, of course. Fifty years ago Henry's grandfather, Iain, had created the crofts for his clansmen after evicting them from Fingon lands because sheep farmers could pay higher rents. Iain's true genius, however, lay in locating the crofts on the coasts, near the kelp beds.

The crofters couldn't feed their families off their miserable slivers of land, and so to make ends meet they had no choice but to take on the brutal work of harvesting kelp, a

leathery seaweed rich in the alkali so vital for the burgeon-
ing industrial revolution.

Kelp profits had paid for the fabulous castle in which
Henry enjoyed his breakfast today, thanks to the crofters'
cheap labor. A single window in the castle cost more than
a hundred of Iain's kelping tenants could earn in a year.

In a pathetic gesture, the crofters had petitioned old Iain
to stand by them in their hour of need—as if this were still
the days when Fingon was laird of the clan and cared about
these peasants! When the old man ignored them, the crofters began to purchase passage to the New World.

It had been a dangerous oversight. The price of passage
was cheap enough that even the impoverished crofters
could afford it. A startling number began to leave.

Iain issued conciliatory statements urging his crofters to
think twice about leaving their ancestral lands. He halted
evictions and promised that crofts would be enlarged.

This action temporarily stemmed the flight, giving Iain
time to organize with the other landlords and press for leg-
islation in Parliament that would raise the cost of transat-
lantic passage far beyond the crofters' means. Those foolish
enough to remain had to accept even smaller crofts.

After the kelp market collapsed, however, the crofters
became a liability. Henry himself had halved their crofts,
halved them again, raised the rents, but still some crofters
had stayed. Now they starved.

"More tea, dear?" asked Lady Fingon icily, breaking
Lord Fingon's train of thought.

"No," he snapped angrily. "What else, Beaton?"

Lord Fingon knew his wife hated these meetings with
Beaton, but there was nothing to be done about it. Henry
wanted to get to an early start on this morning's hunting,
and seeing his factor now was the most efficient scheduling.

"Another emigrant ship was lost last week, m'lord."

"How many does that make this year?" groaned Henry,
going to work on his egg.

"Four m'lord."

Lord Fingon was disgusted. At least the ships weren't expensive. In fact, they were the least costly and least seaworthy vessels money could buy. Their useful cargo life over, these ancient craft shipped from Canada full of lumber that didn't need to be kept particularly dry. They returned with departing crofters, who paid in advance, of course. Even slave vessels were a safer way to travel. After all, the slaver suffered if his cargo arrived in poor condition. With emigrants it didn't matter.

"Is there no good news in the world?" said Lord Fingon when he finished chewing.

"There has been an interesting development, m'lord," said Beaton, fingering his little moustache.

Henry Fingon didn't much like his factor, but he had to admit the man was clever. And effective. There had been hardly any resistance to this year's evictions. Of course Beaton was also the sheriff clerk's deputy and owned four of the largest sheep farms that would replace the evicted crofters, so he was well motivated.

"And what would that interesting development be, pray tell," said Lord Fingon, putting down his fork. Beaton had his attention, which was obviously why he had produced so much bad news first.

"You may recall the cargo of meal we bought in Liverpool to feed the crofters."

"I do not care to be reminded, Beaton."

"I agree, your lordship, that we were pressed into taking this step by the government's relief program."

"Well, they certainly can't blame me for the potato famine. If the crofters are starving, then it is through their own stupidity. They should have had the good sense to get out before this."

"Exactly, m'lord, but about the cargo of meal…"

"Yes, what about it?"

"It seems that due to the famine, meal prices have risen sharply. If we were to sell now on the open market, we could reap a handsome profit, I think."

"Can we do that without causing a stir with the relief people?"

"We've promised to halt the clearances, m'lord, but isn't this simply a matter of business?"

Lord Fingon put down his fork and beamed.

"Beaton, my dear fellow. Have some tea. You don't mind, do you, dear?"

He motioned to a servant for another chair, ignoring Lady Fingon's glare.

"Thank you, m'lord," said Beaton humbly, and sat.

"Tell me, Beaton," said Lady Fingon, pouring the factor a cup of tea, "how long is it going to take you and Henry to destroy this godforsaken island?"

"Beg pardon, m'lady?"

"Certainly that's what you're doing, isn't it? Wasn't Lis once covered with trees? There are only a few forests left."

"That be the sheep, m'lady. They graze closer than the cattle the crofters kept. And the red deer in the woods we set aside for stalking—they eat the young shoots, too."

"Well?"

"Well, what, your ladyship?"

"Well," answered Lady Fingon, "the older sheep farms are failing. The kelp business is dead. Most of the people are gone. Where is Henry's income going to come from when the remaining pastures are ruined and there are no more crofters to pay rent?"

Beaton just stared stupidly into his tea.

Henry threw down his napkin. "Really, Gwendolyn. I don't understand why you concern yourself with these matters. You know nothing about business."

"You haven't thought beyond next week, have you, Henry?"

"There will always be something, Gwendolyn. There's plenty of land. There's fish, game. Things are fine."

"Things are fine with me, I assure you. I can't wait to get back to England and civilization."

"The future is a long way off, my dear. I'm afraid there will be more than enough for our lifetimes."

"Is that what you say, Beaton?" inquired Lady Fingon pointedly.

"I shouldn't think your ladyship would have to worry, what with the Fingon treasure," said the factor with a wink.

"What's this, Henry?" said Gwendolyn Fingon perking up. "You've never mentioned a family treasure."

"A pointless legend," said Lord Fingon poisonously and squinted at his factor until Beaton buried his face in his teacup.

"Tell me about this Fingon treasure, Mr. Beaton," said Lady Fingon sweetly.

"Go ahead, Beaton, tell us," said the lord evenly.

"It's just that they say that the Fingons have held a treasure since ancient times, m'lord," said the factor nervously. "Some say it was given them by the mac Alpin himself."

"Is there any truth to this, Henry?" said Gwendolyn, obviously intrigued. "You never mentioned a treasure to me before."

"There is, actually," said Lord Fingon. "The Fingon treasure was said to be wealth beyond a person's dreams."

Lady Fingon's eyes widened—obviously she was stunned. Lord Fingon smiled and leaned across the table, addressing her in a conspiratorial voice.

"My great-grandfather, Alan Fingon, divided the treasure between his two sons, Rorie and my grandfather Iain, after Culloden so it would be safe."

"Please go on, Henry," said Lady Fingon eagerly.

"Each half was said to be useless without the other," said Fingon, his blue eyes wide. "Alan and Rorie took one half of the treasure to Nova Scotia in the seventeen-eighties. Iain stayed here with the other half. I still have it."

"You do?" asked Lady Fingon. Beaton tried not to look interested, but he unconsciously licked his lips.

"Yes. You've seen me wear it at funerals. It's the Fingon brooch."

"That horrid thing?" gasped Gwendolyn. "Really, Henry!"

"I suppose I should go to Canada one day and see if the cousins have another one like it," said Lord Fingon, bursting into laughter. "Two of them together might be hideous enough to defoliate a continent!"

Lady Fingon threw her napkin on the table and stormed from the room in disgust. Her husband smiled and poured himself a fresh cup of tea.

"Sell the meal, Beaton," he said. "We might try Ireland to get the best price."

"Aye, m'lord." Beaton nodded and left hurriedly before he put another foot in his mouth. Lord Fingon sat back in his chair and quietly sipped his tea.

Fingon treasure, what rubbish!

When he was younger, Henry had even been fool enough to write the Canadian Fingons and inquire whether they knew of the family legend. They hadn't known what he was talking about. No, thought Lord Fingon, the Fingon treasure—if there had ever been such a thing—was long gone.

As for the miserable brooch with its huge terminals and hideous carvings—well, Henry was ashamed to wear the thing in polite company. It was the sort of item that was handed down from generation to generation merely because it would bring nothing in a sale. Someone had even defaced the reverse side with incomprehensible mottos.

"Dumlagchtat mac Alpin Bethoc, indeed," the Sixth Lord Fingon muttered in disgust to a candlestick. "And who the devil is Lucy MacAlpin Trelaine?"

TWENTY-THREE

"Until the last Laird Fingon died thirty years ago," said MacLean, tamping his pipe. "The family lands were auctioned off, the castle fell to ruin as ye saw, the Fingon brooch was never seen again."

Lucy sat for a moment, speechless, then took a sip of the whiskey in front of her. For the past hour MacLean and Wharrie had been telling her about the Fingons, about two centuries of exploitation and misery: starving people evicted from their homes to make way for sheep; emigrants packed into lumberships; an ecology mismanaged into oblivion. No wonder Wharrie and the other islanders she'd met were bitter and suspicious. No wonder the very mention of name Fingon brought icy stares.

"There was no male heir, ye see," MacLean was saying, "chust a daughter who was cut oot from the will."

"A baby?" said Lucy, looking up.

"A young woman," said MacLean.

"Barbara Fingon," nodded Wharrie.

"What happened to Barbara Fingon?" Lucy asked, afraid to hear the answer.

"Went to America, I heard," said MacLean. "She was the last of the Fingons."

Lucy took another drink. A daughter who went to America thirty years ago. A Pictish brooch. It all fit. But Barbara Fingon hadn't been the last of the Fingons when she died on a country road in Massachusetts. There had been one more of these monsters. A daughter. A daughter with big blue eyes.

"Tell me more about this Fingon treasure," Lucy said, hoping her voice didn't reflect the turmoil inside her. At least one thing finally made sense. Robert MacAlpin's risking everything for an ugly brooch was incomprehensible, but for a treasure…

"Like I said," said MacLean, pouring himself another drink from the bottle, "legend has that it was given the Fingon for protection in ancient times by Kenneth mac Alpin himself. It's said…"

"What is it you're really after, lass?" interrupted Wharrie in a gruff voice.

"I told you," said Lucy, turning to the big man who sat frowning at her side. "I have a friend in the States who thinks she might be related to the Fingons. I'm just checking it out for her, that's all."

"I dinna think so," said Wharrie, leaning forward.

"Why would I lie?"

"Because you're after the Fingon treasure, tha' wha' I think. You're after the treasure, chust like the other American."

"What's this?" said MacLean, suddenly very interested.

"What other American?" said Lucy blankly. Wharrie broke into a broad smile for the first time, revealing a mouth full of crooked, yellow teeth.

"The one who showed up last week with the Fingon brooch, a course," he said. "Called himself Fraser."

"Fraser!" exclaimed Lucy, nearly falling out of her chair.

"This Fraser had the Fingon brooch?" said MacLean, rubbing his stubbed chin and regarding Lucy with a new interest.

"Aye," said Wharrie. "And this lass ken the man. See how she's ashakin'."

"I know him," Lucy said softly and took a big slug of scotch. She swallowed it without even wincing.

"So ye aire after the treasure," declared Wharrie triumphantly. Now that he had found his tongue, it seemed he wouldn't shut up.

"I'm not," she protested helplessly.

"Then how do ye ken Fraser?"

"He's trying to find me."

"And why be he trying to do that?"

"Because I killed his partner," she said softly.

MacLean and Wharrie looked at one another, then at Lucy, then drained their glasses. Lucy took another sip, too. Somehow the scotch was getting much smoother.

It was pointless to hide the truth any longer, she knew. Fingons had been lying to the people of Lis for too long. The game was over. Fraser was bound to catch up with her now. She knew too much for him to let her get away.

"My name isn't Tina Snicowski," she said solemnly. "You can call me Lucy, though that's probably not my name either. I think I may be Barbara Fingon's daughter."

"A Fingon?" exclaimed Wharrie.

"You canna know wha' you're sayin' lass," said MacLean, shaking his head skeptically.

"I know exactly what I'm saying," said Lucy. She took another drink and told them the whole story. When she described how Robert MacAlpin had tried to kill her for the brooch, MacLean looked like he had been punched in the stomach. After she finished, Wharrie pulled his chair over and awkwardly put his arm around her shoulder.

"Well, I dinna see how yer accountable, though Fingon blood runs in your veins," he pronounced gently.

"Get on wi' ye!" said MacLean, giving Wharrie's thick arm a punch. "Hasna the lass suffered enough?"

"Well, I canna speak for Lis," said Wharrie, downing his scotch and pouring another, "but I forgive ye."

"What's she done to forgive?" said MacLean, "other than pay you to drive her aboot?"

"Well, I forgive her tha'."

MacLean scowled at him and patted Lucy's hand.

"It's okay, lass. You're with friends now."

"Will you tell me about Fraser, Mr. Wharrie?" said Lucy, feeling better somehow, feeling like she had always wanted to feel after confession when she was a child but never had.

"He coom in last Thursday," said Wharrie. "My cousin, Sorley MacRae, drove him around. He was stayin' in a vacation home near Dumlagchtat, owned by a college professor from London, it is."

"And he had the Fingon brooch?" said MacLean.

"He showed it to Sorley that first day," said Wharrie in tones of amazement mixed with contempt. "'Ha' ye ever seen anything like this afore?' says he. A course Sorley dinna say tha' he had, but it was clearly the Fingon brooch. The next day Fraser spent two hours walkin' at Dumlagchtat Castle. Then he left for Glasgow."

"Glasgow!" said Lucy.

"Aye," nodded Wharrie. "Said he needed to check some records."

"That's where my friend Mr. Wing went—to see if he could find a record of my birth."

"Who's this?" said MacLean.

"Little bastard she's with," Wharrie said and spat.

"Don't call him that," said Lucy angrily. "What do you have against Mr. Wing?"

"The Japs killed me faether in World War II."

"Well, for your information, Mr. Wharrie," Lucy said indignantly, downing another swallow of whiskey, "Mr. Wing isn't Japanese at all. He's Chinese. And the Japanese killed his whole family."

Wharrie looked down. "I dinna ken."

"Well, you ken now," said Lucy. "And if Fraser's in Glasgow, Mr. Wing may be in danger."

"They'll not run into one another if tha's wha' you're worried aboot,' said Wharrie, shaking his big head. "Gooverment offices aire closed on the weekend and Fraser is flying back tonight. Sorley's supposed to pick him oop at the airstrip. A charter."

"If he's coom all the way from America with the

brooch,'' said MacLean in a low whisper, ''there's only one thing he could be after.''

''Me,'' said Lucy sadly.

MacLean shook his head.

''Not you, lass. Ranald's right. He moost be after the Fingon treasure. And if you're really the last Fingon like ye say, then the treasure rightfully belongs to you!''

''Now YE GO ON OOP to yer room and have a wee nap,'' said MacLean as they pulled up in front of the Manor Lodge.

''I don't wanna go to my room,'' protested Lucy, her tongue thick, her eyes watering. ''I wanna be with you guys.''

Lucy was sandwiched between MacLean and Wharrie in the front seat of the big sedan. She couldn't remember the ride back from Skerrisay except for the place where they had gone into the ditch. That had been great fun. And then there was all the singing. Lucy had never known how much fun singing could be.

''Be a good lass, now,'' said Wharrie, cutting the motor. ''Go on wi' ye.''

He looked so cute with his bright red nose. It was hard for Lucy to believe there was ever a time when they hadn't been buddies.

The three of them had spent the entire afternoon in the Fairy's Egg, trading theories and sympathy, drinking single-malt whiskey. Lucy was ashamed of herself for ever thinking ill of Wharrie. The man had legitimate grievances! He had to live in a trailer because vacation homes had raised all the real-estate prices beyond the reach of the locals. His poor wife had to hire out as a maid.

She liked MacLean, too. The man was a real character. He seemed to know the story behind everything, regaling them with history and jokes and irreverent observations about himself, the island, Great Britain, the world.

''I don't care about any stupid old treasure, but you're

still going to help me get back my brooch, aren't you?" she said now, dimly aware that MacLean had opened the car door and was helping her out. The world was spinning round and around in a most unfortunate way.

"Sure, we will, lass," said MacLean. Wharrie had gotten out of the car and was taking Lucy's other arm. They led her very gently into the hotel, which was lucky since her legs seemed to have turned to Jell-O. They were the best friends a girl ever had!

When they got to the lobby, Lucy momentarily fought free of their support. How would it look to all these tourists if she needed to be helped to her room? Even if she was a lousy Fingon, she still had her pride.

"Maybe you should ha' a wee bite to eat," said MacLean looking concerned. "It's not good to drink on an empty stomach."

"No, thank you," Lucy said politely, feeling nauseous at the mere thought of food, "but you go ahead."

They must not have been hungry either, for they kept walking.

"Why dinna we see you oop to yer room?" said MacLean. "I'll get the key. What's your room number, Lucy?"

"I got that little sucker right here," Lucy said, smugly patting the key in her pocket. "Never trust a hotel. I know, believe me, I know."

MacLean and Wharrie gently closed ranks around her and started up the stairs. The stairs were not sturdy at all. They seemed to be moving all over the place, in fact.

Lucy wondered for a moment whether she might not have had a little too much to drink after all, then dismissed the thought. She hadn't had any more than MacLean and Wharrie, and they didn't seem drunk or anything. Hadn't Wharrie's nose always been that shade?

The only difference in MacLean she could see was tiny flecks of white foam in the corner of his uncovered eye.

No, they weren't drunk. And she had only had...how many drinks had she had? Lucy couldn't remember.

At last they reached the room.

"So we'll all meet here tomorrow," she said, blowing each word out of her lips like a soap bubble, "and we'll figure out something and we'll call the cops on Fraser and everything will work out okay, okay?"

MacLean nodded gravely, helping her get the key into the lock. Lucy grabbed him and hugged him, then hugged Wharrie.

"You guys are great," she said. "This is what having friends is all about."

They looked at one another, perhaps comparing blushes.

"Good night, Lucy," said MacLean.

"Go to bed, lass," said Wharrie.

Lucy grinned and slowly closed the door.

She felt pretty good. She had friends everywhere now, even on Lis. They didn't care that she was a dirty rotten Fingon. They'd help her get her brooch back. She might even find the treasure. That would be nice, too. It was only a matter of time before everybody would be living happily ever after.

Lucy lay down on the bed and closed her eyes. The world spun. There was a very peculiar sound, a ringing in her ears. The room continued to spin. The ringing wouldn't go away. Lucy was considering the possibility that maybe she didn't feel so well when she realized that the ringing was the telephone.

"Hello?" she said tentatively, barely managing to get the receiver out of its cradle.

"Herro, herro."

"Mr. Wing!"

"You not forgot me. Good, good, good. So how things going for you?"

"Fine," said Lucy, trying to figure out when her head had grown to the size (and shape) of a watermelon. "Why are you calling? Did you find something in Glasgow?"

"No. Government office closed for weekend. I just call to say hello. See how you doing."

"That's sooooooo sweet!"

"Hello?"

"No, I really mean it," Lucy said, her eyes welling with tears. "You've been so kind, everybody has been so nice I just don't know what to say. Thank you, Mr. Wing, thank you from the bottom of my heart. Thank you, thank you, thank you."

"You okay, Rucy? You sound crazy."

"I'm fine. I'm great."

"You sure? You need anything, maybe?"

"No," said Lucy musically. "I've hooked up with some new friends and they're helping me. They're great. Everybody's great. Except those MacDonald bastards. Why won't they talk to me, Mr. Wing? Why don't they like me?"

Why did her eyeballs feel like they'd been wallpapered?

"You tell me MacDonald don't know nothing."

"They know plenty, only they're too important for the likes of us. You gotta have references from the hoi polloi or else the MacDonalds won't give you the time of day. You don't happen to know the Queen, do you?"

It was those damn contact lenses, Lucy decided. They were shrinking. Or were her eyeballs getting fatter? How did you lose weight in your eyeballs? Stop looking at food?

"You been drinking, Rucy?"

"Me? Ha! Yes."

"You take two aspirin and go to sleep. What you drink?"

"Scotch whiskey."

"Oy yoy yoy. You feel terrible in morning. I know. Hope you learn your lesson."

"I'm fine. I feel great," she protested, though the room was revolving at increased speed and the little holes in her ears were beginning to itch. "Have the Queen give MacDonald a call, will you?"

"Okay. I tell her. You drink water. Go to sleep. Eat eggs for breakfast, vitamin B. Okay?"

"Okay."

"I come back on Monday plane."

"You find my birth certificate first. I gotta have a birthday. Everybody's gotta have a birthday. Can't have a birthday cake without a birthday."

"I look Monday morning for birth certificate. Come back Monday afternoon, you hear?"

"Please find my birthday, Mr. Wing," said Lucy. "I love you." Then she hung up. Wing was the sweetest, kindest man in the entire whole wide world, she decided. Even sweeter than MacLean and Wharrie, though they were sweet too. Everybody was sweet. Except the MacDonalds. And Fraser.

Fraser!

He had stolen her brooch and chased her through the park and now he was here, trying to steal her treasure, the son of a bitch! Lucy didn't care if he was handsome and looked like a little boy with those big, brown glasses. He was nothing but a common criminal and just the thought of him made her want to throw up.

And she did.

TWENTY-FOUR

WHARRIE AND MACLEAN were standing at the bottom of the hotel staircase, grinning from ear to ear.

A tidal wave of nausea swept through what was left of Lucy's gastrointestinal tract. She held on to the handrail and tried to maintain her dignity. And her balance. Somehow she reached ground level intact.

"What time is it?" she croaked. All they had said on the house telephone was "Come downstairs."

"Nine o'clock," said MacLean smugly.

"Evening or morning?"

"It's Sunday morning, lass. I told ye to go easy on the whiskey yesterday, dinna I?"

"Why, Lucy," said Wharrie, his mouth dropping open. "Yiu've droonk so much, yer eyeballs has turned blue!"

Startled, Lucy raised a hand to her face, then remembered. She had somehow managed to remove the contact lenses last night before passing out. She hadn't given them a thought this morning, not that it would have been possible to get them back in, anyway.

"I think I'm supposed to eat an egg," she mumbled and made for the dining room. The two men looked at one another, then followed.

"Maybe ye should try some oatmeal," said Wharrie gently, sitting down at her left, across from MacLean.

"You don't have to yell," said Lucy.

"A kipper would be better," said MacLean. Lucy didn't even have the strength to shoot him a dirty look. They sat in silence, occasionally sipping strong, black coffee. Finally Lucy's breakfast arrived.

She stared at the two yellow orbs looking up at her from

the plate and would have thrown up if there had been anything left in her stomach. The nausea passed after a few minutes, and she managed to choke down a slice of dry toast, washed down with two glasses of water.

"Better?" said MacLean, finally.

Lucy nodded.

"How d'ye diu tha' with yer eyeballs?" asked Wharrie, unable to take his eyes off hers.

"All Americans ha' red, white, and blue eyeballs," said MacLean, winkin' at Lucy. "Dinna ye ken anything?"

"Oh," said Wharrie, but still looked confused.

"Come on, Lucy," said MacLean, standing. "We ha' somethin' to show ye."

"Can't it wait a few weeks?" said Lucy nibbling the other slice of toast.

"Ye'll be pleased," said Wharrie.

"He's right," nodded MacLean.

Lucy shrugged, signed the bill, stood carefully. The floor seemed fastened on a bit more securely now. She followed the two men out to Wharrie's car. They were on one of the island's bumpy roads before Lucy had time to consider how wise a journey in her present condition would be.

"Where are we going?" said Lucy, desperately trying to keep her stomach out of her throat.

"Ye'll see. It's a surprise."

She didn't feel up to arguing.

After a few miles, details of yesterday's conference at the Fairy's Egg drifted back into her consciousness. Lucy felt foolish and vaguely ashamed. Why had she drunk so much? It had been a terrible mistake to confide so much to these men. She didn't really know anything about them. How could she have felt so close to them yesterday?

Neither MacLean nor Wharrie spoke as they drove along, past Dumlagchtat and up the mountain, finally pulling into the long drive of the ruined Fingon Castle. Instead of going through the gate, however, Wharrie turned the car onto an access road that led down the slope. They drove in silence for a few minutes more, then stopped.

Lucy was getting worried. She was miles away from any other living soul. Why should these men help her? What were they really after? Would her head feel like a kettle drum for the rest of her life?

"What's here?" Lucy asked, trying to sound unconcerned as they got out of the car.

"You'll see," said Wharrie, opening the trunk and taking out an old, black shotgun and a large basket.

"What's that for?" Lucy gasped when she saw the gun.

"Ye'll find oot," said Wharrie, a mirthless smile on his face.

"It's not far." MacLean grunted, producing a short billy club from his pocket and testing it on his palm. "Chust walk down there."

Lucy walked nervously down the path MacLean had indicated, the two men directly behind her. A wave of fear swept through her. They were after the treasure, of course. Why had she told them she was a Fingon? How could she have been so naïve? What were they going to do to her?

The path led through a rocky formation ringed by a few stunted trees. Beneath the hill was a small stone cottage, practically a ruin. The thatched roof was incomplete, the windows were knocked out, and the yard was littered with rusted farm implements.

Suddenly Lucy understood. This was it—the people of Lis's just revenge against the last Fingon. They were going to rape and/or kill her in this remote place and no one would ever know. She turned to them, her eyes brimming with tears, but Wharrie just grinned callously.

Her body would never be found, Lucy thought, desperately looking for some way to escape, finding none. Wing would probably think that she had run out on him and kept his two thousand pounds. The thought of hurting him after all he had done for her was unbearable. What did Wharrie have in that little basket? The stuff they used to dissolve bodies? Quicklime?

MacLean opened the door of the cottage and nudged her into the darkness. Lucy tried to steady herself, to muster some dignity. If she had to die here in this godforsaken place, without a name, without a birthday, she would at least die bravely. She steeled herself for the blow.

Nothing happened.

After a moment Lucy's eyes began to adjust to the gloom and she finally understood what she was seeing. There, next to the crumbling chimney, bound hand and foot to a chair, his mouth gagged with tape, was Michael Fraser.

"Mmmrpphhshharggh!" said Fraser, wiggling his legs.

"What's he doing here?" asked Lucy, totally bewildered.

"We've kidnapped him," said MacLean, obviously delighted.

"You've what?"

"Snatched him," said Wharrie proudly.

"Aye." MacLean nodded. "Ranald's cousin was supposed to pick Mr. Fraser oop at the airstrip last night, but we got him instead. Now ye can do with him as ye please."

Lucy didn't know whether to be relieved or hysterical.

"Mmmgshhhfhfhtwwww!" said Fraser. His legs were rubbing together furiously, like a cricket's.

"Shut oop, you," said Wharrie, shaking his club.

Fraser stopped making noise, his leg-wiggling giving way to occasional twitches. Lucy pulled both men to the door by their sleeves.

"Are you people crazy? Why did you do this?" she demanded.

MacLean looked hurt.

"It seemed like a good idea last night."

"Aye," said Wharrie. "We thought yiu'd be pleased."

"Pleased to be a kidnapper?" she hissed.

"We found this in his pocket," said MacLean, digging

into his own pocket and producing a large, silver object, which he placed in her hand. It was her brooch.

"What should we do with him, then?" asked Wharrie, fingering the trigger of the shotgun.

"Why are you asking me?" said Lucy dumbly, clutching the brooch in her hand.

"We did it for you, Lucy," said MacLean quietly. "So you could have your brooch. So you could find your treasure."

"We chust wanted to help," said Wharrie.

Lucy snorted, paced a few steps, and finally sat down at an ancient stool by the dusty table. She felt ashamed of herself. How could she think these dear men would harm her, when they merely wanted to make her an accomplice to a kidnapping? As if she hadn't broken enough laws already!

"Aire ye angry, Lucy?" said Wharrie, confused.

Lucy rolled her eyes, turned the brooch over in her fingers, and looked at the familiar inscriptions. At least it was a chance to get some answers. If she found a treasure, too, so be it.

"What are you doing here with my brooch, Mr. Fraser?" she said evenly.

"Mmmmghghththhhatt!" said Fraser. He was very angry and needed a shave. Lucy thought it made him look quite sexy, the son of a bitch.

"Should I take the tape off?" asked MacLean.

She nodded. MacLean ripped the tape from Fraser's mouth. For a moment Lucy thought it might have taken the man's lips off, the sound was so disgusting. It served him right.

"Ouch, goddammit!" said Fraser.

"Answer the lady's question, mister," said Wharrie, prodding Fraser's ribs with the shotgun.

"I've got to pee so bad I think I'm going to die!" said Fraser in a high voice.

"Don't try that funny business with oos, Jack," said

MacLean, shaking his club in the man's face. Fraser leaned over to catch Lucy's eye.

"What kind of a person are you?" he said urgently. "I've been holding it all night long, for crissakes!"

Wharrie and MacLean both started to talk, but Lucy held up her hands and shouted them down.

"All… All right! Let him pee."

"Why canna he go in his pants?" said Wharrie.

"How would you like to go in your pants?" demanded Fraser.

"Let him pee, for goodness' sakes," said Lucy.

MacLean shrugged, took out a pocket knife, and cut the rope that was holding Fraser's feet and arms to the chair. He stood shakily, his hands still tied behind his back with a separate rope.

"Aren't you going to untie my hands?" he said incredulously.

"And have you pull something?" said Wharrie with contempt. "What kind of fools do you think we aire?"

Fraser looked from one man to the other.

"I have to pull something, know what I mean? Or does one of you want to pull it for me?"

Suddenly the situation didn't seem so menacing. Lucy put a hand over her mouth, trying not to laugh. MacLean shot her an angry look with his single eye.

"All right," he said. "Keep him covered, Ranald."

Wharrie raised the shotgun. MacLean cut the rope. Fraser rubbed his legs with his freed hands and trotted for the door.

"Don't go anywhere," he said over his shoulder to Lucy as he left, Wharrie and MacLean at his heels. "I want to talk to you."

Lucy looked around the broken cottage, smiling at the picture of Michael Fraser trussed like a chicken, wondering how many years you got for kidnapping in Scotland and what the jails were like.

After a few moments the men returned. The furrows were

gone from Fraser's forehead and he had brushed the mop of red hair from his eyes and put on his glasses. He never took his eyes off Lucy, even when MacLean pushed him back down into the chair he had been bound to.

"Feel better, Mr. Fraser?" she asked self-consciously. What was he staring at?

"Thank you, I feel relieved. Literally."

"Doon't be smart, you," said MacLean, making a bony fist. Wharrie raised his shotgun.

"All right, Fraser," Lucy said, trying to sound tough. "What are you doing here?"

"It says Dumlagchtat on the back of your brooch."

"Why are you so interested in my brooch?"

"I think it tells where a treasure is buried, actually."

"Dinna I say so!" exclaimed Wharrie.

"And where might that be?" said Lucy slowly.

"Why should I tell you?"

"Because this lass is Barbara Fingon's daughter," said Wharrie, motioning with the shotgun. "She's Lucy Fingon."

"Oh. So it's Lucy Fingon, now, huh?" said Fraser, sarcasm dripping from his voice. "I guess that justifies everything."

"You're in no position to be rude, Mr. Fraser," said Lucy testily.

"Well, I don't like to be kidnapped, Miss…Fingon. And it's *Dr*. Fraser, actually. Dr. Michael Fraser of the New York Metropolitan Museum of Art. But you can call me Mike."

TWENTY-FIVE

MIKE FRASER WAS FAMISHED. He hadn't eaten since breakfast yesterday morning in Glasgow, figuring to have something once he got back to Lis.

The two Scotsmen had picked him up at the airstrip, claiming that the fellow who had been driving him had a cold. Mike had thought nothing of it, just told them to take him to the best restaurant on the island. He had a lot to celebrate. Instead they had brought him to this leaky shack and left him tied to a chair all night.

Mike took another huge bite of the cheese sandwich MacLean had produced from his picnic basket. There was also hot tea from a thermos, which the others were drinking from plastic cups.

Mike was still pretty angry, but a part of him couldn't help enjoying the excitement. Nothing like this ever happened at the museum. He hadn't had such a ridiculous adventure since his frat brothers at Yale had dropped him off on a country road at 2:00 a.m.

"You were talking about Robert MacAlpin," said the girl.

Mike grinned. She was a tough little number. He almost hadn't recognized her at first; she looked all of twelve years old with her hair cut short like that. And her ear looked like a traffic light! What could have prompted her to do such a thing? Then he remembered she had also had him kidnapped. Obviously, sanity wasn't one of her top priorities.

"I swear I'd never met the man before that day, Lucy. We talked on the phone. He told me his name was Scott."

Even though they were all politely having lunch, Mike

knew the situation was still precarious. The best policy was to stick as close to the truth as possible, without jeopardizing his or the museum's interests. Except for the tremendously uncomfortable night he had just endured, no real harm had been done. Yet.

"If you didn't know MacAlpin, then what were you doing at Trump Tower?" she asked angrily.

Mike looked up from his sandwich and studied the girl. The way she had been talking to him, one would think that he was the criminal, not her. How could she expect him to believe that she hadn't known what her friends were up to? Still, she had him in a ridiculous position. He would have to play his cards very carefully indeed.

"I don't usually do appraisals, but the man was a real salesman," Mike shrugged innocently. "He said he had an artifact that might lead to a whole trove of Celtic treasure. If I authenticated the piece, he said he would give the museum right of first refusal to whatever he ultimately found. It sounded a little crazy, but I figured there was nothing to lose. That's all there was to it."

The girl looked skeptical. Mike took another bite of his sandwich, wondering if he should feel flattered. Apparently she couldn't believe he had been so stupid. He had let himself be kidnapped by the Scottish Mutt and Jeff, hadn't he?

"Why did you chase me through the park?" she said.

"I wanted to talk to you about the brooch," he answered truthfully. "It belongs to you, doesn't it? The museum can't go around playing finders-keepers like we could in the old days, you know."

She looked quite pale, almost greenish in this light. Like she was ready to throw up or something. Could be guilt, Michael theorized, taking another sandwich from the basket and biting into it. He was beginning to feel sorry for her. Maybe she had a conscience after all.

"You expect me to believe you were just there to appraise my brooch?" she said, hands on her hips, her enormous blue eyes flashing. "Then why did you keep it?"

Michael waited to answer until he had swallowed the food in his mouth. This was no time to forget his manners.

"I wanted to return it. Every time I tried to, you ran away. I didn't know where to find you. I didn't even know your real name."

She smiled wryly. "What did you tell the police?"

"I didn't think it would be prudent to involve the museum in Mr. MacAlpin's unfortunate…accident," Mike said carefully, "so I didn't stick around."

"It *was* an accident," she said quickly, as if she had read his mind.

"I believe you," he said, chewing. She didn't really look like a killer. She looked kind of cute, in fact. Mike's thoughts were interrupted by a twangy voice from the corner. It was the older man with the patch over his eye, the one Lucy had called MacLean.

"Excuse me, Dr. Fraser," he said, sipping his tea, "but why dinna we return to the subject of the treasure?"

"Since MacAlpin was dead and I had the brooch—" Mike shrugged, "I thought I might try to find this treasure he spoke of. Dumlagchtat was the obvious place to start looking, since it's written on the back of the artifact. Professor Lackey told me the legend of the Fingon treasure. I'm staying at his cottage. But while we're on the subject, I might ask Lucy what brings her here?"

The girl flushed. "I'm looking for my family," she said quietly.

"But there aren't any Fingons left on Lis, are there?" asked Mike. She looked at her shoes. The other man, Wharrie, leaped in to change the subject.

"Ye said the brooch told where the treasure is. So where is it?"

Wharrie was the big, red-faced one. He had barely spoken at all since they arrived, but neither had he relaxed his grip on the shotgun.

Mike couldn't help but smile. He'd lived so long in the institutional world of government bureaucracy and museum committees that it was refreshing to find someone who still believed life was so simple.

"You just want to go and dig it up, I suppose," he said gently. "It's not as easy as that, my friend."

"Why not?" said Lucy.

Mike finished the second sandwich and rubbed his hands together to dispose of the crumbs.

"First, there may not be a treasure at all," he said, trying not to sound professorial, but counting the point off against his finger nevertheless. "Just because I think it might be here, doesn't mean that I'm right.

"Second," he continued, counting another finger, "there's the question of ownership. Let's say there is a treasure and let's say it is buried where I think it is. To whom does it belong?"

"To whoever finds it," said Wharrie.

"Not under Scottish law," said Mike. "In fact it belongs to the property owner, who in this case is one Julius Fingon of Nova Scotia, Canada."

"A Fingon?" blinked Lucy, looking genuinely surprised. "In Nova Scotia?"

"Julius Fingon bought the castle after the death of his distant cousin, Lord Geoffrey." Mike nodded. "That's what I went to Glasgow to find out. I've written for Julius Fingon's permission to excavate, but it could be months before the legalities are ironed out.

"Of course," said Mike, counting a third finger, "since the treasure may be connected with Kenneth mac Alpin, the government may try to claim it under the Historical Artifacts Act."

"Not if we dig it oop first an' doon't mention the fact," said Wharrie humorlessly.

"Fourth," said Mike, ignoring the interruption and happily finishing with his hand, "you can't just go out with a spade and dig up something like this. Part of the treasure is its archaeological value. An excavation must be planned and carefully executed to properly document the site for historical purposes. That could take years.''

''Not if we dig it oop first an' doon't mention the fact,'' repeated Wharrie.

Mike was getting a little annoyed. It was frustrating to deal with people who couldn't understand reality, even when you took great pains to illuminate it.

''I told you,'' he said levelly. ''You can't...''

''Yer the one who canna, Dr. Fraser,'' said MacLean. ''Ye canna come here and steal our treasure and turn it over to some foreigner in Canada, tha's wha' ye canna do.''

''But, there's the question of ownership...''

''Ownership be damned, man,'' growled MacLean. ''What's in this for you, then?''

''Well,'' said Mike reasonably, ''the museum might possibly propose to buy what it could from the proper owner....''

''And so Lucy and the rest of us would be cut out entirely!''

Mike bit his lip and looked at Lucy, who seemed lost in thought. She was smart enough to understand the subtleties of the situation. Surely she could explain the facts of life to these rustics.

''There are legal remedies Miss...Fingon...could apply if she believed she had a claim,'' Mike declared with annoyance when Lucy didn't come to his rescue. ''The case would proceed through the courts. It might take some time, of course, but there's a right way to do this and there's a...''

''Do we have a shovel?'' the girl said suddenly.

Mike couldn't believe it. How could she even consider such a step? He tried to rise to his feet, but MacLean pushed him back.

''There's one in the boot o' the car,'' said Wharrie.

''You can't destroy a historical site,'' Mike said as reasonably as he could manage. ''It's unethical. Think of the knowledge that would be lost.''

"I don't care about knowledge," said the girl, almost breezily.

"Look," he said in the most patient voice he could muster. "You're obviously an intelligent person. You must have some respect for scholarship..."

"I'm not going to let another Fingon steal anything from this island."

"That's incredibly naïve," said Mike, suddenly furious. "You're a Fingon yourself, aren't you? Or was that all bullshit? What sort of game are you playing, lady?"

"Let's get the shovel," said Lucy, turning to her companions, her eyes blazing, her jaw set. Mike started toward her, but both Wharrie and MacLean stepped forward to stop him.

"I can't believe you would really do something like this!" he exclaimed.

"Well, believe it," she said defiantly.

Mike was genuinely angry now. How could she be so stubborn?

"Well, I won't tell you where it is," he said, folding his arms in front of him. "It's too important. It's a matter of principle. Shoot me if you must."

Wharrie raised the shotgun. "Shall I shoot him then, Lucy?"

Mike immediately felt like an idiot. Was he really going to die for the art museum? Had the sandwiches gone to his brain? There might not even be any treasure.

"You're not going to let him shoot me, are you?" Mike asked, his voice wavering now.

"No," the girl announced after what was an excruciatingly long pause for Mike. "That won't be necessary."

"I knew you'd see reason," he said, breathing again.

"Aire ye sure?" said Wharrie, obviously disappointed.

"We're not going to chust give oop, aire we, lass?" said MacLean, his jaw slack, his fist tightening around the club, his gray eye watery.

"No," she said with a smile. "We just don't need Dr. Fraser to tell us where to look."

"Why not?" said MacLean.

Wharrie stared at her. Mike stared, too.

"Because I already know."

MIKE WAS CONVINCED that the girl was trying to trick him until she led them to the precise spot he had in mind.

"How did you figure it out?" he asked unhappily.

"You told me yourself," she replied.

"When?"

"You said you came here because Dumlagchtat was written on the back of the brooch. You said the treasure might be connected with Kenneth mac Alpin. The name mac Alpin is also on the brooch, Dumlagchtat mac Alpin Bethoc. There's only one other word of the inscription, and you said in New York that Bethoc was an old family name from the house of Alpin. I just asked myself where would an old family name mark the place to dig? You did say it had to be dug up, didn't you?"

They all stared at the worn gravestone in front of them in the little cemetery by the entrance to Dumlagchtat Castle. Amidst all the stones marking the final resting places of five hundred years of Fingons, there was only this one without dates and just a single name—Bethoc.

Mike felt like a fool for underestimating this Lucy Scott or Fingon or whatever her name was—again. First she had outrun him, then she had outmanned him, and now she had outthought him.

"I can't believe it took me so long to figure it out," she said, adding insult to injury.

Now that they were out of the gloomy cottage Mike could get a better look at her. Why had she done that to her hair? he wondered. She didn't look so pale anymore, but she wasn't his type at all, too short, too flat, definitely too smart. Why did she look so appealing then, fists clenched, jaw defiant, those idiotic earrings in her ear?

"Start digging, Dr. Fraser," said MacLean, handing him the shovel. Mike stared at it, but didn't move.

"Shall I strike him with my cloob?" said MacLean, looking to Lucy.

"We're going to dig here whether you like it or not, Dr. Fraser," she said coolly. "And if Mr. Wharrie does the work, I don't think he'll be as careful as you."

"Kidnapping is a crime, you know," Mike said in a final attempt to get her to see reason. "Or do you propose to kill me, too, when I've done your dirty work?"

Wharrie looked to MacLean, who looked to Lucy. Mike was instantly sorry he had brought the subject up.

"Employees of the Metropolitan Museum aren't supposed to steal people's jewelry, Dr. Fraser," she said innocently. "You didn't want to be involved with Robert MacAlpin's accident, but you left the scene and removed evidence as well. Think what a mess I can make of your reputation if you press charges against us."

Mike tried to smile. She didn't have to involve the police to hurt him. Just the details of this sordid kidnapping—if he were crazy enough to report it—would be enough to make him look an idiot to his colleagues. Brickwall would eat him alive.

Mike took the shovel. He had said his piece. If she wanted to take responsibility for this, there was nothing more he could do. She had him over a barrel and she knew it.

The ground was hard-packed peat. Mike took off his shirt after an hour. MacLean went back to the cottage and brought out chairs. The others sat and drank tea and watched him dig for three hours in the hot sun. The hole was more than six feet down when they finally gave up.

There was nothing buried under the gravestone. Not even a body.

TWENTY-SIX

WHARRIE STOPPED THE CAR in front of Dr. Lackey's cottage. Fraser pushed open the door and got out. His face was smeared with dirt, his red hair was tangled and matted, his eyebrows knitted together over his horn-rimmed glasses. To her dismay, Lucy thought he looked adorable.

"No hard feelings," said Fraser, throwing his jacket over one shoulder. His hands were dirty, blistered.

"Thanks," she said, feeling confused. She tried not to look as lost as she felt. She hadn't come here to find a treasure, hadn't even known one existed. Why, then, did she feel so disappointed?

Lucy still couldn't believe Fraser wasn't going to press charges. He could nail them to the wall if he wanted to. Why was he being so decent? He couldn't really be worried about being involved in Robert MacAlpin's death, could he? The police were bound to take his word over hers. He was a Ph.D., for crissakes. How could she ever have been gullible enough to believe he was a fence?

"What are you going to do now?" Fraser said, leaning over the car.

Lucy shrugged. "Go back to New York, I guess. There's not a lot more I can do here."

"Yer not going to give oop yet, girl?" said MacLean unhappily from the backseat. "We're all havin' such a grand time, airen't we, Ranald?"

"Aye," said Wharrie, staring straight ahead, gripping the wheel tightly.

Lucy smiled. "Thanks, guys."

"Will I see you again, Lucy?" asked Fraser.

"Why would you want to?" answered Lucy, bewildered.

"Because I'm out of my mind, obviously. And because I had fun this morning, God help me."

"I dinna approve," said MacLean from the back, sticking his nose into the air.

"I don't think it would be such a good idea," Lucy said, dropping her head to hide her blush. "But thanks, anyway."

"Why not?"

"Oh, it never works out when you kidnap a man for the first date."

"Maybe this time will be different," he persisted.

"Let's go, Ranald," Lucy said, feeling herself weaken, fearing to make herself any more of a fool than she already had. Wharrie started the engine.

"Call me if you change your mind," shouted Fraser as they pulled away. "I'm in the Manhattan book. On East Seventy-ninth Street. Michael Fraser. F-R-A-S-E-R."

Lucy couldn't help looking back over her shoulder. Michael Fraser, Ph.D., was standing in the middle of the road watching them drive away.

IT WAS NEARLY three o'clock in the afternoon when Wharrie pulled the sedan up in front of the Manor Lodge.

"When aire ye goin' back to New York, Lucy?" asked MacLean, struggling out of the backseat to open the door for her.

"I don't know," she said wearily. "Maybe Mr. Wing will turn up my birth certificate in Glasgow and I can get a real passport."

"But yer goin' to see the Fingon oop in Canada?" MacLean pressed.

Lucy felt her muscles tense. She had longed for a family all her life, but after hearing about the Fingons she had been relieved that they were all gone. The thought of another branch of these monsters thriving anywhere in the world was unbearable.

"I don't want anything to do with the Fingons," she said quietly.

"Have ye thought of stayin' here?" said Wharrie gently. "It's where yer roots aire and ye'd be welcome, even though yer name is not."

"This is no place for a young person," said MacLean. Wharrie shook his head. "No, I suppose not."

"Thanks for all your help, both of you," she said sincerely. "What would we have done if there had been a treasure in that grave?"

"Kept it," said MacLean with a big smile.

"Something was there once, I'll wager," said Wharrie, snapping his fingers. "Else why dinna we find bones? It was dug oop, it was."

"Let me know if you ever find it," said Lucy, getting out of the car.

"Say, why don't we all have a wee drink?" said MacLean.

"Naught be open on Sunday," said Wharrie.

"We'll go to my place. What do ye say, Lucy?"

"I don't think so," she laughed, having learned her lesson well enough.

"At least let me buy ye both a farewell dinner," MacLean twinkled. "For *auld lang syne*."

"All right," Lucy smiled.

"We'll pick ye oop at seven. There's a place I ken but a few miles from here. Now how aboot that drink, Ranald?"

They smiled at one another and drove off singing. Lucy walked through the lobby, fishing in her pocket for her room key, feeling sorry for herself. She wanted to be Lucy Trelaine again, not some Fingon. Even if there had been a treasure, it could never have been enough to compensate her for descending from such people.

Abruptly she stopped. Where was her key? She remembered taking it with her this morning. Could it have fallen out of her pocket somehow at the little cottage?

Lucy nearly jumped into the air when she felt the hand tap her shoulder. Whirling around, she found herself facing the tall, skinny desk clerk in the tweed jacket.

"I'm terribly sorry, Miss Snicowski," he said, blushing. "I called your name three times, but ye dinna seem to hear me."

"Yes," said Lucy, rattled, the pretense of Tina Snicowski entirely forgotten. "What is it?"

"These messages came for ye," said the man. She realized he was staring. It took her a moment to remember that her eyes had changed color since last he saw her.

"Thanks." She smiled and gave him a pound note from her pocket. "And can you get me another room key? I seem to have misplaced mine."

"Certainly." He swallowed and walked away, casting glances back over his shoulder.

Lucy made a thorough inspection of her room when she got upstairs. Nothing seemed to be out of place. Surely the key had fallen out of her pocket in the excitement today. Still, perhaps it would be wiser to change rooms. Or was she being paranoid?

Lucy glanced at the message slip in her hand. Wing wanted her to call him at the Glasgow Hilton. There was also a small envelope addressed to Tina Snicowski. Lucy tore it open.

Dear Miss Snicowski,
 I understand you wish to see me. Perhaps you can stop by for tea today. My driver will collect you at 3:30 if that is convenient.

Cordially yours,
Fitzroy MacDonald of that Ilk

Lucy had never ridden in a Rolls-Royce before. It was nice, though not so much different from normal cars. She was separated from the gray-uniformed chauffeur by a glass panel.

Wing had been out, but Lucy had left a message for him to check the Lis birth records under the name Barbara Fingon. She barely had time enough to wash her face and put on a clean dress before MacDonald's chauffeur announced his presence.

For the past fifteen minutes they had been driving within the boundaries of the MacDonald estate. Practically the entire eastern coast of the island belonged to them. Out of the window Lucy could see the castle now, an enormous stone structure looking out over the sea. There were actually a few trees around it.

She didn't like the MacDonalds on principle, but she was too curious to turn down the invitation. Lord MacDonald might still be able to fill in some of the details about the Fingons, her sordid family. What had changed his mind about seeing her? she wondered.

The Rolls pulled up in front of the castle. The chauffeur got out and wordlessly opened her door. The massive walls made the building seem like a small city. Lucy followed a walk toward a portcullis. When she turned around, the car was already driving away.

Lucy followed simple stone steps through an inner courtyard to a bleak wooden door with a huge iron knocker. Forbidding gray stone rose on all sides. No doubt the MacDonalds had needed this protection against their kinsmen if the Fingons were any guide. She clasped the knocker and swung it three times against the door. Nothing happened for a full minute, then a thin man with an enormous nose emerged. He was wearing a black suit and a winged collar.

"Mr. MacDonald is expecting me," Lucy said, gaping at the man's getup. Did the MacDonalds think they were in an old movie or something?

"*Lord* MacDonald will see you in the drawing room," said the butler in a pompous voice. "Follow me."

He turned and led her down a hall with a black-and-white-checked marble floor. Suits of armor and portraits lined the walls.

"How big is this place?" said Lucy, amazed.

"The castle has one hundred twenty-seven rooms," replied the man with curt disapproval.

They passed through several other rooms, all packed from floor to ceiling with paintings, ornate furniture—obscenely superfluous riches compared to the island's prevailing poverty. They finally stopped in a gigantic chamber with a three-story ceiling and a fireplace larger than a New York City apartment. A huge staircase at the end of the room rose to a second-floor gallery.

"I shall summon the earl," said the butler, and left through a studded door on the other side of the room.

There were several dark chairs with high backs and a long leather sofa, but Lucy stood in the center of the room, her hands folded in front of her. She wasn't going to be intimidated by these people's stage sets.

Suddenly a man appeared at the top of the stairs in a kilt, with two golden retrievers at his side. Lord MacDonald strode purposefully down the stairs until he was right in front of her, a thickset, balding figure with thin lips, sallow skin, and a bushy mustache.

"Hallooo!" he suddenly roared. "You must be Miss Snicowski. Am I pronouncing that right? Snicowski? Are you related to the people who make the helicopters? No, that was Sikorsky. I have it. The conductor."

"Actually my name isn't Snicowski at all, Mr. MacDonald," said Lucy, damned if she was going to address him as Lord.

"Then what it is, pray tell?" he harrumphed, looking her straight in the ear.

"I don't know, exactly," said Lucy, reaching involuntarily toward her earrings, wondering if the little holes would ever knit back together. "But I think I'm Barbara Fingon's daughter."

"Eh wot? Barbara? Nice girl. Whatever happened to Barbara, I wonder?" His accent was not at all like Mac-Lean's or Wharrie's. In fact, he sounded distinctly British.

"If I'm right, she was killed in a car crash when I was a baby."

"Is that so?" he said.

"Yes," said Lucy.

They stared at one another for a few seconds. Finally MacDonald spoke again.

"So how is old Hewby?"

"Huh?" said Lucy, baffled.

"Bartlett Hewby. He called yesterday. Said I should see you. How is he?"

"He's fine, I guess," said Lucy, wondering if MacDonald often got calls from basset hounds.

"We had some good times. Made some money. Do you see him often?"

Lucy shrugged helplessly. "I take him for a walk every once in a while." Obviously Tak Wing had something to do with this.

"Old boy must be eighty-five. Still walks with young girls, eh? Good show."

Lucy nodded, realizing finally that Wing must have named his dog for a real man, a real man with connections, and one whom Wing could call on for a favor.

"About the Fingons," said Lucy, determined not to miss this opportunity, no matter how bizarrely it had come about. "I wonder if you might tell me…"

"No, sorry, 'fraid not. Must run to the mainland. Business, you understand. Have tea with my daughter on the east terrace. Catriona. She was Barbara's best friend. Charming girl. She's living here between divorces. Rackine will show you there. Rackine!" he hollered and the pickle-nosed butler reappeared.

"Show this young lady to my daughter."

"Yes, m'lord," said Rackine.

MacDonald vanished down the hall, the dogs at his heels.

TWENTY-SEVEN

THE EAST TERRACE of MacDonald Castle was a wide veranda thoughtfully landscaped with boxed rosebushes and blooming fruit trees. The day was mild enough to eat outdoors and the table was set with crisp, white linens, crystal, old silver.

Catriona MacDonald poured the tea herself, adding milk at the same time. A manservant stood a few feet away, his hands demurely folded behind his back. The earl's daughter was a slim, elegant woman—in her late forties, Lucy estimated. She wore a yellow dress, a broad-brimmed hat, and carried herself with such poise that Lucy felt like a hairy-underarmed peasant in comparison.

"One lump or two?" asked Catriona in a musical soprano.

"Two," croaked Lucy. She didn't even like tea, but it would be lunacy not to go along with this for a while.

"I'm so glad you came to see me," said Catriona, passing the cup and saucer to Lucy, who grabbed them awkwardly. "I always felt very hurt that Barbara never wrote, but of course now I see there was an excellent reason. She was dead, of course. Tea cake?"

Catriona indicated an assortment of cakes and cookies with a silver knife.

"Yes, please," said Lucy. She hadn't had anything since the dry toast this morning at breakfast. Her hangover was a mere dissonance now, following her around like an afternoon shadow.

"The Prince of Wales is particularly fond of my tea cake," said Catriona. "When he comes to visit he always is sure to compliment me. But there I go again, dropping names. I'm such a silly chatterbox."

For ten minutes, Catriona had gushed details about her ex-husband's polo partners and her children's exclusive schools. How strange, Lucy thought, that after all the years of searching for her family this silly woman could clear up everything in the time it took to have tea.

"Do you make it yourself?" asked Lucy.

"Beg pardon?" said Catriona pleasantly.

"Do you make the tea cake yourself?"

The woman looked genuinely puzzled.

"How on earth would I do that?" She smiled.

"Tell me about Bar...about my mother," said Lucy.

"Oh, she was quite the best person around." Catriona giggled. "Rather wild, of course, but great fun. She had wonderful clothes, always a clever thing to say, a fabulous seat...."

"Seat?"

"Horses, don't you know? We used to do the shows together. She was famous for her riding tricks. Do you know she could pass her hands over her head from back to front without unclasping them?"

Lucy nodded and gave up what few doubts she still harbored about her mother's identity.

"Yes, Barbara was a glorious girl," said Catriona wistfully. "I miss her terribly. You look like her, you know."

"I do?"

"Indeed. You have her coloring, those same marvelous blue eyes. It's a shame you wear your hair so short. Still, sneaking into Britain disguised as a punk rocker—that's what you're supposed to be, isn't it?—it's quite the sort of mad thing Barbara would have done. Yes, you take after her strongly, indeed."

Lucy braced herself and asked what she had wanted to ask for the last ten minutes.

"Do you know who my father was?"

"You don't know? Oh. Of course you don't, you poor dear. His name was Robert MacAlpin."

Lucy felt no sudden pain, no sensation like her heart breaking. She just felt empty inside, sad, resigned. She had killed her own father, after all. Her own father had tried to kill her. And all for a treasure that was not there—for an empty hole in the ground.

"Tell me about him," Lucy said quietly.

"Robbie was one of the grooms at Dumlagchtat Castle," said Catriona, her eyes turning toward an ancient memory, a smile crossing her lips. "He was a very sweet boy, quite adorable, really."

"Grooms?"

"For the horses, don't you know? His people had been with the Fingons for generations, but they were all dead and Robbie was alone in the world. Barbara didn't like to see the boy so lonely—that's how it started. She used to sneak out at night to his cottage on the estate."

"A thatched cottage at the foot of the castle?" said Lucy with a start, wondering if the ruin where they had held Fraser had been the very place where she had been conceived.

"Wasn't it wicked?" Catriona nodded impishly. "Are you sure you want to hear everything?"

"Please," said Lucy, taking a sip of tea. It was sickeningly sweet.

"Well," said Catriona, leaning forward confidingly. "Barbara's father, Lord Geoffrey, was furious about the relationship. Forbade Barbara to have anything to do with the boy. Barbara was a very headstrong girl, though, absolutely hated being told what to do. She not only kept seeing Robbie, but managed to get herself pregnant as well. Never one for halfway measures was Barbara. I say, I suppose that was you, wasn't it?"

"I suppose," said Lucy, unhappily.

"Yes. Well, anyway. Barbara being Barbara, she announced she intended to marry Robbie. They were going to run off to New Zealand or some such godforsaken place. They even took out passports. I remember it all so clearly. It was quite the best scandal we had ever had on Lis.''

"They got married?" Lucy asked hopefully.

"No, actually they didn't," said Catriona, looking a little embarrassed for the first time since she had begun her story. "You see, Lord Geoffrey promptly disinherited her. He was always rewriting his will to keep people in line. Barbara was only nineteen and didn't have any money of her own, so she had to stay on at the castle.''

"Nineteen!" exclaimed Lucy, her eyes welling with tears. "She was only nineteen?"

"Yes, it's wonderful to be young," sighed Catriona. "I suppose Barbara thought she could wear the old boy down sooner or later. Then two terrible things happened."

"What happened?" said Lucy, her resolve not to care shattered beyond repair. Catriona daintily took a sliver of tea cake between two perfectly manicured fingers and slipped it into her mouth. Lucy took her elbows off the table self-consciously.

"First Robbie ran away," said the woman after a moment of suspense and a sip of tea. "One night Barbara went down to his cottage, but instead of Robbie she found one of his friends, who told her that Robbie had changed his mind about them and had left the country. Barbara was certain her father had something to do with Robbie's disappearance—had bribed him or even had him kidnapped, can you imagine?"

Lucy could imagine, but didn't say so. Catriona continued blithely.

"Well, Barbara promptly confronted Lord Geoffrey. He denied everything. There was a terrible row. Barbara was so upset she came to stay with us. Father had his friends at the foreign office look into things and they discovered that a Robert MacAlpin had indeed been passed through customs in America. As if this weren't enough of a heartbreak for Barbara, Lord Geoffrey suffered a massive stroke the very next day. Out of guilt, I expect.''

Catriona shook her head and continued in a more sober voice.

"Barbara returned home and cared for her father for several months, but he never regained his senses. I think she expected him to come around long enough to put her back into his will, but he never did. The irony was that the estate turned out to be bankrupt. There would have been nothing left for Barbara to inherit even if she had been in the will. Everything had to be sold to satisfy the death taxes. Some distant relative of Lord Geoffrey's, a Canadian lumberman, bought the castle and all the lands.''

"Julius Fingon," said Lucy quietly.

"Yes, that's right. In fact Julius Fingon was the reason that Barbara went off to America.''

"What?''

"Well, you see, Julius Fingon had written Lord Geoffrey about wanting to buy an old family heirloom called the Fingon brooch.''

"The Fingon brooch," repeated Lucy, afraid to breathe.

"The whole affair was very irregular," said Catriona. "I mean, no one had ever even heard of this man until he writes from out of the blue offering ten thousand pounds for the brooch. Of course Lord Geoffrey sensed that something was up and wouldn't part with it. So when her father died and left her nothing, Barbara decided to go to Nova Scotia and sell Julius Fingon the brooch.''

"I thought you said she didn't inherit anything," said Lucy.

"Well, the Fingon brooch didn't count," said Catriona indignantly. "It had been in her family for centuries. Barbara just took it. I remember she was wearing it when I took her down to Southampton to board the *Queen Elizabeth* for New York—aeroplanes were the only things on this earth she was afraid of. That was the last I saw of her.''

"I think I finally understand," marveled Lucy.

"Bar...my mother...must have hired a car and been on her way from New York to Nova Scotia when she was killed."

"I suppose it was a silly plan." Catriona sighed. "But Barbara was most unhappy and it was all she could think to do, you see. She had no home of her own, no money, no husband. And she was quite pregnant."

"Then I wasn't born here?"

"No, it must have happened in the States."

Lucy bit her lip.

"I guess that makes me a U.S. citizen, after all."

"Yes, aren't you?"

"I didn't know. Until now, I mean. I guess I thought I might have been born in Scotland. Then maybe I could have gotten a British passport to get back to New York with."

"I'll be happy to have father speak with one of his friends about it, if you like."

"I don't know what they could do."

"Nonsense, my dear. You're the granddaughter of a peer. Surely that still counts for something."

"I don't even know what she named me."

"Well, there must be a record somewhere. We'll see what we can find. This is such fun. Like a detective mystery."

"What happened to Dumlagchtat Castle?" asked Lucy, wanting to change the subject, ashamed of being alive. "Did Julius Fingon live in it at all?"

"Gracious, no. None of us ever saw hide nor hair of Julius Fingon, though father corresponded with him on business matters. Still does, I believe. The man owns half of Lis. Everyone thinks he's a terrible scoundrel."

"Why?"

"Because of what he did to Dumlagchtat Castle, of course. Father wanted him to turn it into a hotel. The Scottish Historical Trust offered to make it into some sort of horrid museum. But Julius Fingon had the castle stripped and the entire contents auctioned. He sold the glass in the windows, the lead on the roof, even the copper plumbing. Left the place a complete ruin. Just disgraceful, don't you think?''

"Of course," murmured Lucy. How could a Fingon be anything but disgraceful?

"Now," said Catriona, pouring them each another cup of tea. "I want to hear more about you."

"There's not much else to tell," said Lucy. "I grew up in foster homes. I never knew I was a Fingon."

"But how did you find your way here, then?"

Lucy dug the brooch out of her purse and passed it to Catriona.

"It was on the blanket around me when my mother was killed in the car crash I told you about."

"The Fingon brooch," whispered Catriona, turning the heavy silver ring over in her hand.

"It only came into my possession recently."

"Barbara always thought the brooch had some special meaning to her destiny," said Catriona. "It was one of the reasons that she got involved with Robbie. He was the only MacAlpin she had ever met, you see, and the name macAlpin appears on the brooch. Twice, in fact."

"Lucy MacAlpin Trelaine was always written on the brooch?"

"Yes, though we never knew what it meant. Why?"

"Nothing," said Lucy.

"So how did the brooch lead you here?" said Catriona breathlessly, handing it back to Lucy. "This is so mysterious."

"I ran into Robert MacAlpin in New York."

Catriona's eyes opened very wide. "You did?" she whispered. "You found Robbie? Why did he run away? Did he tell you?"

"No," said Lucy. "He said that my mother was the one who ran away."

"Nonsense," sputtered Catriona. "Why would he tell such a lie? He certainly wasn't the boy we thought he was.

Did Barbara find him when she was in New York, I wonder?''

"It would have been difficult. He was living in New Jersey."

"New Jersey," said Catriona pensively. "That's near Chicago, isn't it?"

"Not really."

"But don't keep me in suspense. What was Robbie doing in America?''

"Selling insurance."

Catriona burst into laughter.

"What's so funny?" asked Lucy, annoyed.

"It's just so hard to picture Robbie selling anything. He was so tongue-tied, so shy. Is he still so handsome?"

"He's dead," said Lucy.

"Oh, dear," said Catriona.

Lucy took the obituary clipping out of her wallet and handed it to the woman.

"You can see he was very successful," said Lucy bitterly. "He was a member of the Golden Circle. I guess that meant he sold a lot of insurance."

"Yes, I see."

"I suppose I should be proud of him," said Lucy, nibbling a cookie.

"Yes," said Catriona, handing back the clipping. "Only there's just one thing."

"What's that?" said Lucy.

"This isn't Robert MacAlpin."

TWENTY-EIGHT

"WHAT HAPPENED TO Mr. Wharrie?" asked Lucy, looking at the peaceful figure snoring softly in the backseat of the long, black sedan.

"I'm afraid our laddie finally discovered his tolerance level for fine whiskey," chuckled Angus MacLean, pushing his cap up on his head and cranking at the unfamiliar gearshift.

Lucy had returned from MacDonald Castle an hour before and had taken a hot bath and changed, but now it looked like their dinner plans would have to be postponed. Lucy didn't really mind. After what she had learned from Catriona MacDonald, she didn't feel much like celebrating anyway.

"Is he all right?" asked Lucy, concerned. Wharrie let out a snort.

"Nothin' that a night's sleep and a kipper in the mornin' willna fix," said MacLean. "Get in and we'll take him home. If I can get this infernal contraption to work, tha' is."

"Maybe I better drive," Lucy said. License or not, she trusted her driving more than MacLean's. He looked sober enough but had the same white flecks in the corners of his eye that he had had yesterday at the Fairy's Egg.

"Dinna ye relish a wee drive over mountain roads with a droonken one-eyed man at the wheel?"

Lucy smiled.

"Suit yourself," MacLean shrugged, moving out of the driver's seat.

Lucy hadn't driven a car with a manual transmission for years, and it felt strange having the steering wheel on the right side of the car. Finally she succeeded in engaging the gears and pulled out of the Manor Lodge driveway onto the road toward Dumlagchtat.

"We'll have our wee celebration tomorrow," said MacLean lazily. "You'll be stayin' tha' long, won't ye?"

"Sure."

At least she wasn't hungry, having eaten two slices of Catriona MacDonald's tea cake and several cookies. After this morning's hangover, Lucy was surprised her appetite had returned at all.

MacLean shut his eye and seemed to doze off. Lucy tried to enjoy the drive, memorizing the stark countryside, the crumbling stone fences, the tall grass, the endless sky. Driving on the wrong side of the road didn't turn out to be much of a problem, since the road was virtually one lane. It was past seven o'clock in the evening, but the sun wouldn't go down for hours. It had been a very long day.

Though Catriona MacDonald's story left no room for doubt that Lucy was Barbara Fingon's daughter, it had left many questions unanswered. If the man Lucy had killed in New York wasn't Robert MacAlpin, then who was he? Was her father still alive after all? Why had he deserted Barbara Fingon?

The Canadian, Julius Fingon, troubled Lucy as well. Why had he wanted to buy the Fingon brooch? How had he even heard of it? Why did he destroy Dumlagchtat Castle?

"Take that steep road there, next to the sea," said MacLean, apparently not asleep after all. Lucy followed his directions.

"I finally talked with the MacDonalds this afternoon," she said as the road began to climb.

"Yes, I know," said MacLean.

"You do?" she said, surprised.

"Well, I know ye went to the castle. Ranald found yer room key on the seat and dinna want ye to worry. We called. Desk clerk said Lord MacDonald's car ha' picked ye oop.''

MacLean dug into his pocket and produced the key.

"Thanks," said Lucy, relieved. MacLean tucked the key into her pocket. The drive was getting steeper and there was no guardrail. The cliff seemed only inches away from the road. Lucy's hands were beginning to ache from gripping the wheel. The car had no power steering.

"So," said MacLean, "did ye learn anything from the MacDonalds?"

"I did, in fact," said Lucy and briefly outlined the revelations concerning Robert MacAlpin.

"Verra curious, indeed," said MacLean when she had finished.

"Do you remember Dr. Fraser mentioning a Canadian named Julius Fingon who owns Dumlagchtat Castle?" said Lucy.

"Aye."

"Well, Julius Fingon once tried to buy the Fingon brooch."

"Lord MacDonald knew this?"

"His daughter Catriona told me. She was best friends with my mother."

"So what do you intend to do, then?" said MacLean quietly. The cliffs were very high up now. The ocean breakers were barely audible against the rocks far below.

Lucy shrugged. "I guess I'll have to see this Julius Fingon after all. I don't know if there's any connection between him and the real Robert MacAlpin, but…"

"Pull over to the side, Lucy," said Maclean.

"Is something wrong?"

"Please, chust pull over."

Lucy pressed down on the brake. The car came to a gentle stop on the deserted road. MacLean reached over, switched off the ignition, and removed the key.

"Ye canna see Julius Fingon, Lucy," he said.

"Why not?" said Lucy. "Why did we stop?"

"Ye chust canna, tha's all."

Lucy stared at the man. His face was ashen. His hand was trembling.

"It's nae good," MacLean mumbled. "There's nae point to it anymore."

"What's wrong, Angus?" said Lucy, concerned. "Please tell me what's bothering you."

He looked up and spoke in a low voice.

"I havna been telling you the truth, lass. I havna been telling you the truth at all."

"About what?"

"Aboot things tha' happened long ago. It's a complicated tale, one I'm not proud of."

"We don't seem to be going anywhere," said Lucy, trying to smile reassuringly. MacLean began to speak, staring out over the sea with his single eye.

"'Twas thairty years ago," he said. "I was doin' wha' I be doin' all the time since—sittin' in the Fairy's Egg, drinkin' my whiskey, borin' everyone with my stories."

"I don't think your stories are boring, Angus," said Lucy. MacLean seemed not to hear.

"A stranger coom in," he went on. "A huge, angry-lookin' man, he was, an American by his accent. The lads wouldna ha' naught to diu with him, but I stairts talking about local matters, chust like I done wi' you. Well, we have a few whiskeys and after a while the man says he's a collector of antiquities, Pictish brooches in particular."

"Pictish brooches!" exclaimed Lucy.

"Aye," nodded MacLean. "The man dinna look like no collector to me but I was eager to show off mi knowledge, so I says, 'Diu ye know then the famous Fingon brooch tha' be pairt of an ancient treasure?'"

"'Know it?' he replies. 'I've been tryin' to buy it off Laird Fingon for years, only he willna sell. I'd pay five thousand pounds to the man who brought me the Fingon brooch. No questions asked.'

"I almost fell out of mi chair. Five thousand pounds was

a fortune thairty years ago, Lucy, and I ha' dreams. I knew wha' the man was suggestin' and I knew tha' such a opportunity would not coom my way again.

"'If the Fingon brooch was somehow to coom into my hands,' I says to him, 'where might I be able to find ye?'

"'I ha' business in London,' says he, 'but I'll be back one month from this day. Bring the Fingon brooch to me here and ye shall ha' your money.'

"The next day I paid a call on a friend of mine, Hugh Grimmon. Hugh was from Dumlagchtat and knew the ways of Fingon Castle. He was also more experienced in these matters than I was, having had several run-ins with the law afore. I told Hugh I'd split the five thousand pounds with him if he could help me break into the castle. I was dead serious. I even bought this billy for the caper.''

MacLean reached into his pocket and took out the club he had threatened Fraser with that morning. Lucy shivered, astonished at the thought of this old, gentle soul concocting such a plan.

"Hugh had a better idea,'' continued MacLean. "He had heard that a friend of his, a groom at the estate, was lookin' to raise some money so's he could run away with Laird Geoffrey's daughter.''

"Robert MacAlpin?'' said Lucy, intrigued.

"Aye.'' MacLean nodded. "So Hugh and me, we goes to MacAlpin's wee cottage, the same place where we took Fraser t'other nicht, and we offer the lad five hundred pounds to persuade Barbara Fingon to get us the brooch.

"'I willna,' MacAlpin says. 'Isna honest,' he says. We offer him a larger share, but still the lad refuses. Then he says, 'Tha' man from Nova Scotia put you oop to this, dinna he?'

"'Wha' man?' says I.

"'The one Barbara told me aboot,' says MacAlpin. 'The one who wrote Laird Geoffrey and offered ten thousand pounds for the brooch. Julius Fingon.'''

"Julius Fingon!'' said Lucy.

"Aye." MacLean nodded. "Julius Fingon. Suddenly everything made sense to me. It wasna an American I ha' talked with, but a Canadian. And I knew why he wanted the brooch. Hugh understood, too, of course. Everyone on Lis has heard the stories about the Fingon treasure.

"'Dinna ye see, lad?' Hugh says to MacAlpin. 'We dinna have to settle for a few thousand pounds. Julius Fingon is after the Fingon treasure. The brooch must be the key to it—or else why would he be willin' to pay so much? If we get him the brooch, then he'll ha' to give us a share of the treasure itself!'

"'Barbara is all the treasure I want,' says the lad, gettin' hot under the collar.

"'You still need money to take her away,' says Hugh.

"'I already ha' all the money I need. I dinna want any pairt of yer foul scheme. Now get out afore I call the sheriff constable on ye.'

"Hugh grabs MacAlpin by the shirt and stairts shouting at him. MacAlpin pushes him away. Hugh strikes the lad with his fist. MacAlpin falls backwards. It happened so quick, Lucy, chust a matter of seconds. Hugh is standin' over MacAlpin, yellin', but the lad doesna move. He ha' hit his head on the hearthstone. He was dead. It was an accident, lass. I swear."

Lucy stared, unable to speak. MacLean was telling her that he and his friend had killed her father thirty years ago. Thirty years ago! MacLean continued, his eyes moist.

"We dragged the body oot back behind the cottage and dug a hole to hide wha' we ha' done. Then Hugh remembered wha' the lad had said about havin' all the money he needed to run away with Barbara Fingon.

"'It must be in the cottage,' says Hugh. 'Let's go look for it.'

"I refused. I was sick from wha' we done already. Hugh shrugged and went inside to find what he could steal. I'm coverin' the lad with earth when I heard voices. I put down my shovel and go to the window to see wha's happenin'.

There in the cottage with Hugh is a young lass, a young lass that looked chust like you, Lucy.''

"Barbara Fingon?" asked Lucy, numb.

"Aye," replied MacLean. "I couldna make out all the words, but she was sayin' something like, 'Nae, it's not true! I dinna believe you!' and Hugh is answerin', 'I swear, Miss Fingon. Robbie changed his mind. He couldna face ye. Tha's why he ha' me come here to tell ye.'

"'My faether had something to do with this, dinna he?' says the girl. 'Did Laird Geoffrey pay Robbie to go away?'

"I can see that Hugh dinna ken what to do, tha' he's makin' it all oop as he went along. He chust stands there silent.

"'Tell me! Tell me!' she shrieks, and then she slaps him across the face.

"'You Fingons aire all alike,' Hugh says back, and I was feared he would kill her, too. But suddenly she storms oot of the cottage and runs back toward the castle.

"'What will we diu now?' says I, rushin' in.

"'We make it all come true,' says Hugh, cool as can be, and shows me Robbie MacAlpin's strongbox.''

"What was in it?" said Lucy evenly. Hugh Grimmon's accusation—You Fingons are all alike!—was still ringing in her ears.

"Three hundred eighty pounds," said MacLean. "And Robbie MacAlpin's passport. Hugh was the same height and build as MacAlpin. He said he'd take the money and the passport and leave the country. Said I ha' to help him, or he'd swear I struck the blow. Said everyone would think the lad ran away. And tha's wha' happened.''

"Then the man who tried to kill me in New York was the same man who killed my father," said Lucy softly.

"Tha's right," said MacLean, nervously rubbing the short billy club still in his fist. "It was Hugh Grimmon."

Lucy sat dumbfounded.

"The way I figure," MacLean went on sadly, "when Hugh heard tha' you ha' found a Celtic brooch with the word *Dumlagchtat* tha' had been missing for thirty years, he guessed it wa' the Fingon brooch. He probably couldna believe his luck. If it wa' genuine, then he knew where to sell it.''

"To Julius Fingon of Nova Scotia."

"Aye."

"And he knew that if I went to Lis I might turn up the truth and destroy the life he had built for himself as Robert MacAlpin.''

"But it was the brooch he wanted," said MacLean. "The brooch and the Fingon treasure.''

"Did Julius Fingon know of this?" said Lucy. "Of what happened to Robbie MacAlpin?"

"Nae," MacLean shook his head, unable to meet Lucy's eyes. "When the month ha' passed, Julius Fingon come back to the Fairy's Egg like he promised.

"'Have you got the brooch for me?' says he.

"'No, Mr. Julius Fingon,' says I.

"'How did ye ken my name?' says he.

"'It doesna matter,' says I. 'But I think perhaps ye should pay me something anyhow, to insure I willna tell Laird Geoffrey wha' ye were oop to.'

"'Come wi' me back to mi hotel,' says he.

"When I follow him outside, he throws me into an alleyway. He was a giant man, Lucy. I couldna break free. He holds me against a wall and with his thumb, he scoops out my eye.''

Lucy recoiled in horror. MacLean reached up and touched his patch, the thirty-year-old pain still fresh in his face.

"'If ye get me the brooch I'll make ye rich, MacLean,' says Julius Fingon. 'If ye tell anyone about me, I'll be back for your other eye.'

"He leaves me bleeding in the dirt, Lucy. The irony of it was tha' Laird Geoffrey had been stricken and never was conscious again. I had no one to tell.''

Lucy shook her head. MacLean stared out over the sea.

"Ye dinna kill Hugh Grimmon, Lucy," said MacLean. "It was the hand of justice that struck him down, as sure as it was the hand of justice that took my eye. I spent the last thirty years hopin' tha' the brooch would come back to me so I could dangle it in front of Julius Fingon and make him pay for wha' he done to me. To show him justice."

"I don't think that anyone will find justice here," Lucy said sadly.

"I should chust stand aside, then, and let you go to him, I suppose?" said MacLean. "Let two Fingons split the treasure and leave me with nothing to show for my life?"

"But Angus..." began Lucy, reaching out a hand, the anger she had been feeling turning toward pity.

"Give me the brooch, lass," he said quietly. "I know ye ha' it with ye."

Lucy stopped, surprised, hurt.

"Is that what this was all about? Was everything you've done and said just to get that brooch?"

"It cost me my eye. I will ha' the brooch, Lucy."

"It's back at the hotel," she said.

MacLean's lips curled into a grim smile.

"Never trust a hotel, isna tha' what you said yesterday? Of course, I took tha' key from ye and searched your room when you were at MacDonald Castle, chust to be sure."

"Why didn't you just keep the brooch after you took it from Fraser?" said Lucy, stalling, trying to figure out what to do. "You had it in your pocket."

"I could hairdly do that with an unpredictable lad like Ranald standin' over me with a shotgun," he said, smiling sadly. "And besides, it seemed better to wait and take the whole Fingon treasure if we happened to find it."

"But we didn't."

MacLean said nothing. Lucy felt the tears welling up in her eyes.

"I thought you were my friend, Angus," she said, her teeth clenched.

MacLean's smile abruptly vanished.

"GIVE ME THE BROOCH!" he shouted and slammed the club into the dash in front of her, denting the metal, producing a fearful noise.

Lucy's hand scrambled into her pocket and held out the Fingon brooch. MacLean tore it from her fingers, not taking his eye off her.

"Now put your hands in your lap in front of you," he commanded.

Lucy put her hands in her lap. MacLean glanced briefly at the silver ring in his hand, then tucked it into his front pocket, not lowering the club.

"I'm sorry, lass. Now turn around. I'll hit ye once on the back of the head. You'll nae feel a thing. When they find the car, the accident will speak for itself. Wharrie had a bit too much to drink. He took ye for a ride in the mountains, lost control of the car. Case closed."

Lucy looked desperately behind her.

"Ranald can't help you, I'm afraid," said MacLean humorlessly. "I put enough chloral hydrate in his whiskey to knock out a elk. Turn around, Lucy."

MacLean was perspiring freely, clearly building up his nerve. Lucy tried to think of something to do, but nothing came to mind. The man was old, but still a lot bigger than she was. And he had the club.

"Turn around," he rasped.

"So you don't have to look at me when you do it?"

"Aye," he whispered. "It's a bonnie face, Lucy. I dinna want to…"

His voice trailed off.

"If you think I'm going to make this easy for you," said Lucy angrily, "you're nuts."

The man wet his lips and swallowed. He lowered the club marginally.

"You can still stop, Angus. You haven't killed anybody yet."

"Nae."

"Then put down the club."

"I canna. Dinna ye see?"

"If it was the hand of justice that killed Hugh Grimmon," she said desperately, "then what will happen to you if you do this now?"

"Turn around, Lucy."

"Please, Angus."

"Turn around!"

"No!"

"Turn around, damn you!"

MacLean raised the club over his head, grazing the car's upholstered ceiling. Lucy's hands involuntarily went up in front of her face and she grabbed his hand as it descended, deflecting the blow. The club crashed into the dashboard. Lucy tried to hold on to MacLean's hand, but he was too strong. The club rose again.

MacLean's teeth were clenched, his face strained. Lucy heard a shrill scream, realized it was hers. Time seemed to slow down as she watched the club descending forever toward her face.

In the instant before it struck, she seemed to see a shadow passing overhead like the angel of death. She involuntarily closed her eyes, waiting for the impact.

It never came.

Instead she heard a terrible sound, the sound she thought would have been made when the club struck her flesh. When she opened her eyes, however, she saw that it had been the sound of Wharrie's boot smashing into the side of MacLean's head.

The big Scot struggled to right himself, pulling his foot back from the unconscious form of MacLean. Then he boosted himself up in the backseat and, ignoring Lucy's cowering figure, he stared at the shattered dashboard in disbelief.

"Look wha' tha' daft coof's doon to my caire!" he groaned.

TWENTY-NINE

IT WAS THREE DAYS LATER. The entire Lis police force, all four officers, augmented by a dozen volunteers, had been digging for the past few hours in the hard ground outside the cottage at the foot of Dumlagchtat Castle. A few locals had gotten wind of the grim activity and stood under umbrellas, watching the constables.

Lucy sat, sheltered from the light drizzle, in the backseat of the single island police car. With her was Catriona MacDonald. Tak Wing sat in the front next to Chief Constable Gordon Livingstone, a large Britisher with a lined, gray face.

"...but our department doesn't run sophisticated tests on accident victims," Chief Constable Livingstone was saying. "There would have been no reason to suspect foul play if MacLean had been able to carry out his plan. It was certainly lucky that Mr. Wharrie came around."

"Wharrie turn out to be okay guy," marveled Wing. "Save Rucy even though drugged, pick Wing up at airstrip—even apologize for World War II. What come over him, Rucy, you think?"

"You were the one who told me to expect miracles," said Lucy, turning away from the window. She had been eyeing the crowd, hoping to see Michael Fraser, but there was no reason to believe Mike would even hear about this search, let alone still be on the island. What would she say to him, anyhow?

"Well, it's all too morbid even to think about," said Catriona MacDonald. "It's simply unbelievable that these horrible men could get away with Robbie MacAlpin's murder for thirty years."

"No one would have even known there was any murder," said Livingstone sadly, "had not Miss Fingon looked into things."

Lucy winced. She still hadn't adjusted to being called Fingon. It wasn't a name she was proud of.

"The thing that surprises me about this whole affair," the chief constable continued, looking down at his notebook, "is that this...Hugh Grimmon...was able to sneak through customs using another person's passport. That still strikes me as very hard to believe."

Lucy swallowed hard. Tak Wing grinned.

There was a tap at the window. Lucy looked up and saw Lord MacDonald. He was accompanied by one of the constables, whose blue uniform was covered by a wet slicker.

"Afternoon, m'lord," said Livingstone, opening the door and tipping his hat.

"Livingstone," said Lord MacDonald.

"Well, I should get over and see how the lads are doing," said the chief constable, departing the sedan. Lord MacDonald brushed the rain off his coat and plopped down in the empty seat next to Tak Wing.

"I say, bit damp out there. Don't think I know you," he said, staring at Wing.

"Tak Wing," twinkled the little man, bowing as well as he could manage from a seated position. "American entrepreneur."

"That so? I'm a bit of an entrepreneur myself."

Catriona patted Lucy's hand.

"We're all frightfully sorry about this, Lucy," she chattered. "Poor Robbie. He was such a sweet boy. All these years we had thought so ill of him, when all along he was..."

"Bit rough for you, eh wot?" said MacDonald heartily, turning around in his seat to face Lucy. "You don't have to be here, you know. They'll send word if they find anything, I'm sure."

"No," sighed Lucy. "It's all right. I feel relieved it's over. I really do."

"You poor dear," said Catriona. "You must come stay with us until this whole dreadful mess is settled."

"No, thanks," said Lucy. "I have to get back to New York and help Mr. Wing with some financing."

As nice as the MacDonalds were being now, Lucy knew they wouldn't give her the time of day if her name weren't Fingon. Friends like that she could live without.

"Do a bit of finance, too, Mr. Wing?" said MacDonald.

"Wing very experienced in art of deal," said Wing with a very strange expression on his face. "Can see that you involved with big deal right now."

"I say, that's amazing!" exclaimed MacDonald. "I am involved in a big deal, in fact. Selling one of my Inverness factories. How did you know?"

"You try to get better price, they say take it or leave it."

"By George, that's uncanny!"

"They bluffing," said Wing triumphantly. "You can get much more."

"You mean they'll increase the offer on the table? Are you sure?"

"Father, please," said Catriona. "Do you have to discuss business at a time like this?"

"No," said MacDonald cheerfully. "Quite right. But you must join me for lunch, Mr. Wing. I'd be very interested to hear more about this."

"Father has some news that might cheer you, Lucy, darling," said Catriona pointedly. "You did get it, didn't you, father?"

"Yes, indeed," chortled Lord MacDonald, turning to Lucy, clearly pleased with himself. "The foreign office has located your birth certificate, my dear. In New York."

"You're kidding," said Lucy with an involuntary laugh.

"Quite serious. It gave the embassy staff a devil of a time. They checked every possible date after Barbara landed, found nothing, were totally stymied. The Yanks are so damned clever with their computers that they're lost entirely unless you can give them the exact information they're looking for."

"I know," said Lucy. "But they found it?"

"Very nearly gave up, but then some bright lad thought to check the dates before the *Queen Elizabeth* docked." Macdonald sniffed. "Seems you were born at sea."

"Then I'm not a U.S. citizen after all?" said Lucy, totally confused.

"On the contrary. Your mother was Scottish, but the ship was in U.S. territorial waters at the time of your birth, so you are technically a dual national. The foreign office is working on a U.K. passport for you right now. Should have it ready in a few days."

"Did you get a copy of the birth certificate?" Lucy asked quietly.

"No, but I have all information right here."

"Can you tell me my birthday?"

Lord MacDonald pulled out a fax and placed reading glasses on his nose.

"Now let's see. Date of birth: September twenty-ninth. Mother: Barbara Fingon. Father: Robert MacAlpin. Weight: six pounds, four ounces."

September 29. Lucy was even older than she had thought. For some reason she didn't care.

"Don't you want to know your name?" asked MacDonald.

Lucy looked up, afraid to ask.

"It's Lucy," he bellowed happily. "Lucy Fingon."

"Dear Barbara," said Catriona taking a handkerchief out of her patent-leather bag and dabbing her eyes. "She must have named you Lucy because it was on the Fingon brooch. The brooch said MacAlpin, and she loved a MacAlpin. It said Lucy, and she named you Lucy. The poor darling. So sentimental. So sweet."

"Pleased to meet you, Rucy Fingon!" exclaimed Wing, pumping her hand enthusiastically.

Lucy felt numb. Lucy Fingon. It wasn't as pretty a name as Lucy MacAlpin Trelaine, but it was hers. It belonged to her by right of birth. And she was still Lucy. Thank God Barbara Fingon hadn't gone with Bethoc!

"I have another surprise for you, my dear," said Mac-Donald, looking incredibly smug.

"I think I've had all the surprises I can manage for a while, thank you," said Lucy.

"I spoke to Julius Fingon in Canada this morning," said MacDonald as if she hadn't spoken. "You can't imagine his surprise when I told him about his long lost cousin Lucy Fingon. He had no idea Barbara was pregnant when she disappeared, of course. People were very discreet about that sort of thing in those days. He wants very much to speak with you. What do you think of that?"

Lucy didn't say anything. When she was a little girl she had dreamed of this moment. She would finally find her real family. They would be rich and beautiful. They would take her away from the poverty, the cruelty of the world. It hadn't worked out the way she thought.

MacDonald and Catriona looked at her expectantly. Wing was smiling ear to ear. The rain was falling harder now. It beat insistently on the roof of the car.

"I have Julius's number right here," said Lord Mac-Donald, digging into his jacket pocket. "You can call him any time after…"

"I'm not going to call him," said Lucy.

"You can't possibly blame him for what happened to your father, old girl," said MacDonald, rubbing his hands together. "He knew nothing about what MacLean had done. Was terribly angry when I told him. He's a wealthy man, Lucy. Seems eager to make it up to you."

"I think he's done enough," said Lucy.

"But you're a Fingon," said Catriona, looking to her father. "Blood is thicker than water and all that."

Lucy didn't say anything. Julius Fingon had set in motion the events that had made her an orphan. His pursuit of the Fingon treasure had cost Robbie MacAlpin and Barbara Fingon their lives, to say nothing of what had happened to Hugh Grimmon and Angus MacLean. She had nearly been killed herself.

No, Lucy wanted nothing from the Fingons. She would build her own life, meet the world on her terms. She wasn't going to be swept along anymore. She was going to choose what was important and what was not. Lucy smiled. For the first time in years she didn't feel like a failure.

"But what will you do?" sputtered Lord MacDonald.

Suddenly she felt a gentle hand on her shoulder.

"We go home now, Rucy?" Tak Wing said.

Home. Lucy had never been homesick before; she had never had a home to miss. Now she thought of her rooms in the silly house in Weehawken and smiled.

"Yes, Mr. Wing," said Lucy and smiled. "We go home."

Chief Constable Livingstone suddenly appeared out of the rain at the window. MacDonald reached over and opened the door.

"I'm sorry, Miss Fingon," said Chief Constable Livingstone, leaning in. "I think we've found your father."

No one said anything for a moment. Lucy wondered why she didn't feel like crying. She had been crying at the drop of a hat lately. Perhaps she was all cried out.

"You poor lamb," said Catriona, putting her arm around Lucy's shoulder and squeezing her gently. "All this has been too much for you."

"No," said Lucy. "I'm fine. But it's funny, don't you think?"

"What's that, dear?" said Catriona.

"I came here to find out who I was, and now I have. But I still don't know the first thing about Lucy MacAlpin Trelaine."

THIRTY

"YOU WILL NOT," said Lucy quietly.

"But Rucy," protested Wing, his little hands bunching into fists.

"You are not going to open any new branches until your cash flow improves, and that's final."

"But Teaneck such good location."

"It will still be a good location a year from now. I don't know how you tricked Lord MacDonald into bailing out Neat 'n' Tidy, but I'm not going to let you blow it now."

"Wing not trick MacDonald," protested Wing. "Wing teach MacDonald how to play poker. What you think, Neal? We start new Neat 'n' Tidy in Teaneck, okay?"

"I just drive the car," said Neal from the front seat. "My executive decisions are road decisions."

The car smelled like coffee. There was a Maxwell House plant in Hoboken, a Hills Bros operation in Edgewater, Savarin had a location in Ridgefield. The aroma of coffee smelled like home to Lucy. Even the closed windows and air conditioning couldn't block it out.

"I don't know how you can even take the man's money," said Lucy. "The MacDonalds extorted it from the people of Lis over generations, you know."

"Money have no conscience," said Wing. "Money just trapped energy. Wing set it free. Make new jobs for poor people of Teaneck."

"What about the poor people of Lis?"

"Poor people are poor people everywhere." Wing shrugged. "Wing no believe in discrimination. So we expand to Teaneck, yes?"

"Not until the cash flow improves. And if I hear one

more word about Teaneck, I'm going to give you a creepie.''

''Boy, Rucy,'' sighed Wing, ''you get tough in Scotland.''

Lucy smiled and touched the Fingon brooch at her throat. She had been wearing it a lot lately, settling into her new identity. She was a different person now, one she liked a whole lot better. She even had a new name. Lucy Fingon.

The name Fingon didn't have to represent greed and cruelty and despair, Lucy had decided. She could make it anything she wanted it to be and would start by repaying some of Wing's kindness—whether he liked it or not.

''To what do you owe your tremendous self-confidence, Miss Fingon?'' asked imaginary reporters in Lucy's daydreams.

''Justifiable homicide, leaving the scene of a crime, illegal entry into Great Britain, grave robbing and kidnapping, thank you very much.''

And that wasn't all, Lucy thought with a self-satisfied grin. But she wasn't telling all her secrets. Not even to Wing. At least not yet.

The car pulled into the driveway of the Weehawken Neat 'n' Tidy.

''What about we at least buy building in Teaneck, maybe?'' said Wing as they got out of the car and headed toward the side door. ''In case property values rise.''

''You're asking for it.''

''Leave her be, Taki,'' said Neal. ''She's trying to do you a favor.''

''You think Wing going to make it easy for her?'' said Wing with a twinkle.

Lucy punched him in the biceps and reached for the back screen door. Before she could open it, Tina stepped out.

''There's a guy here who wants to see Lucy,'' Tina said quietly, her eyes large behind the thick lenses. ''I think he's that man from Canada who keeps calling and sending the letters.''

Lucy nodded. Lord MacDonald had given Julius Fingon her address. Even though Lucy had returned the Canadian's letters unopened and not taken his calls, the man apparently wasn't going to give up.

"What you tell him?" Wing asked Tina, suddenly very serious.

"I said Lucy wasn't here, but he insisted on waiting. I put him in the front room."

Tina looked worried, but Lucy patted her shoulder.

"You did fine, Tina."

"Neal, you take Rucy away in car," said Wing, tilting his top hat to a combative angle. "I get rid of man."

"No," said Lucy. "It's okay. I guess I'll have to talk with him sooner or later. I might as well get it over with."

"You no have to…" began Wing, but Lucy just smiled and walked into the house.

Julius Fingon was examining a framed picture on the wall of a black man in an army sergeant's uniform. A small woman wearing a brown coat stood next to him. As Lucy entered the room, Lucy's relative turned and stared at her with milky blue eyes larger than her own.

Lucy understood how MacLean had been helpless against Julius Fingon. The man was a giant, at least six foot seven inches in height. He was broad-shouldered, dressed in a black suit, and supported his not inconsiderable weight on a burled cane. His most stunning feature, however, was his snow-white hair. It ringed his head like the corona of the sun and burst from his face in a flowing beard. Julius Fingon looked like nothing short of the Michelangelo edition of God.

"You can wait outside, Louise," he said in an unexpectedly high, squeaky voice. The little woman in the brown coat nodded and walked past Lucy, closing the french doors behind her.

"My nurse," Julius Fingon grinned. "Treats me like a baby. I'm old enough to be her grandfather."

Lucy didn't say anything, just folded her arms in front of her and stared.

"MacDonald sent me a copy of your birth certificate," the giant continued easily. "You're Barbara Fingon's daughter, Lucy."

"That's right," she replied quietly. "And you're Julius Fingon."

"Why didn't you take my calls?" he said, his face a granite mask. "Why did you return my letters? I've had to journey here at considerable inconvenience to see you. It's a long way for an old man to go."

"What do you want, Mr. Fingon?"

The old man smiled. A crafty, humorless smile, it seemed to Lucy. He made a menacing black silhouette against the luminous backdrop of Manhattan.

"I want to get to know you, Lucy," he said.

"Well, I don't want to know you, Mr. Fingon."

"I'm your flesh and blood, child. What do you have against me?"

"For a start I don't like men who gouge other people's eyes out."

"You mean MacLean. I wasn't proud of myself for that, but the man was trying to blackmail me. He was dangerous."

"Were you really so frightened?" said Lucy, determined not to be intimidated by this bully.

"There's a certain rough justice in the world that you obviously don't understand, young lady."

"What right do you have to talk about justice?"

"What right?" thundered Fingon, pounding the floor with his cane. "I'll tell you what right. My wife died one month after I did that to MacLean. Within a year my son and his family were killed in an airplane crash. Within five years both of my daughters died, childless. For twenty-five years the only love I've gotten is from my cats. That's what gives me the right to talk about justice."

"What are you doing here, Mr. Fingon?" said Lucy softly.

"For twenty-five years I thought I was the last Fingon. But I'm not. You are."

"So?"

"So under the terms of my will, you'll inherit all my worldly goods, the loot of a thousand years of Fingons."

The old man's eyes sparkled, perhaps with greed.

"I don't want it," said Lucy uncomfortably. How much was he worth? she wondered.

"Maybe I should leave it to my cat." Fingon's voice dripped sarcasm, his lips worked themselves into a sneer.

"Do whatever you want," Lucy shot back, aware of what he was after, wanting to hurt him, "but you're never going to get the Fingon brooch."

"The Fingon brooch," the old man repeated slowly, chewing each word. "I once wanted the Fingon brooch very badly. Very badly indeed. Legally it belongs to me, you know."

"How do you figure that?" Lucy asked. If Julius Fingon recognized the brooch clasped at her throat he made no sign.

"I bought Lord Geoffrey's entire estate," he said, walking slowly across the room, supporting his weight on the cane. "I paid a fortune for it."

"My mother was on her way to sell you the brooch when she was killed."

"Your mother stole it," hissed Fingon, now right next to her, his eyes blazing. "It was my property. Your mother was a thief."

"And you're a murderer," Lucy said, glaring up at him. "If you hadn't made your slimy little deal with MacLean, my mother would be alive today. So would my father."

"MacDonald told me they dug up a body," he sniffed, lowering himself into a chair. "MacLean did it, I gather."

"He and another man, Hugh Grimmon," said Lucy,

clenching her teeth. "Grimmon tried to kill me for the Fingon brooch. He's dead, too."

"Lord God, how I wanted that brooch," cackled Fingon, slapping his knee, oblivious to Lucy's fury. "When I think of the money I pissed away..."

"Why, Mr. Fingon?" said Lucy, desperately wanting to puncture his smug indifference. "Why did you want the brooch so badly?"

"The treasure, of course," said the old man. "When I was a boy, growing up, my daddy told me all about the Fingon treasure. Riches beyond your wildest dreams, he said. Riches beyond your wildest dreams. I thought it was a lot of crap, until I found this little item in dad's papers after he died."

Julius Fingon reached into the inside pocket of his jacket and pulled out a yellowed piece of parchment, folded in quarters.

"What is it?" asked Lucy, curious in spite of herself.

"It's a letter from Henry, Eighth Baronet and Sixth Lord Fingon to my great-grandfather, dated May fourteen, eighteen thirty-two," he said. "Would you like me to read it to you?"

Lucy bit her lip. Fingon took a pair of glasses from another pocket and unfolded the letter.

"'Dear Cousin Duncan,'" he read in a rapid, perfunctory voice. "'I am writing to inquire whether you are aware of the legends concerning a priceless treasure which the Fingons were supposed to have been given for safekeeping in ancient times. With father's death an artifact known as the Fingon brooch has passed into my possession. This brooch allegedly contains half the secret to the treasure, while your branch of the family is supposed to possess the other half. I would consider putting my brooch together with whatever it is that you possess in exchange for an equal share of any treasure we may be led to. Yours very truly.'"

"So what did they find?" asked Lucy cautiously, remembering the empty grave in Dumlagchtat. Julius ignored the interruption, continuing in a low voice.

"My great-grandfather scrawled this in the margin: 'Grandfather did speak of a family treasure. Our half may have been lost in fire of '07. I pretended ignorance to Henry. Will try to get brooch on next trip to Lis.''

Julius refolded the paper and put it back into his pocket. Then he looked over the rims of his glasses at Lucy.

"But my great-grandfather never made it back to Lis," he said. "According to dates in the family Bible, he died in a logging accident within three months after receiving this letter. No one else was curious enough to do anything about the brooch, apparently."

Fingon paused, momentarily out of breath. Lucy waited. The old man finally went on.

"But when I found the letter, I dreamed of treasure. I wrote Lord Geoffrey asking to buy the Fingon brooch. He turned me down flat. This convinced me that the brooch was indeed the key to a treasure, an immensely valuable one, or else why wouldn't Geoffrey sell? The old boy was stone broke. Now I realize that it was my own greed that convinced him that the damned thing had any value. You're not the first Fingon who didn't trust a relative."

"What made you think you could find the treasure even if you had the brooch?" said Lucy.

"Arrogance." Julius shrugged. "Stupidity. I was rich already, of course, but the treasure became my obsession. Even though the Fingons of Lis had possessed the brooch for centuries without finding anything, I was convinced that I could take one glance at it and decipher its secret. The Fingon brooch made a total fool of me. That's it, isn't it? At your neck?"

"Yes," Lucy said.

"It's odd," Julius said sadly, not moving. "Even ten years ago, I would have torn the thing from your throat. Now I look at it and feel nothing at all. I'm eighty-five years old, Lucy. My heart is failing. My arteries are crumbling. No brooch, no treasure, not all the money in the world will save me from the grave.''

"You really don't want it?'' asked Lucy, unbelievingly. The old man shook his head.

"The treasure was just a dream. My life was just a dream. All dreams come to an end.''

"There was a Fingon treasure," said Lucy quietly after a moment. The old man didn't seem to hear her, apparently lost in his memories. Then he looked up.

"What?'' he said absently.

"I said there was Fingon treasure. It was buried where the brooch said it would be, but when we looked, someone had already dug it up.''

"What are you talking about?'' said the old man, squinting, his face a thousand wrinkles.

"See for yourself,'' said Lucy, unfastening the silver ring from her scarf, holding it out to Julius. Maybe justice would be served if he at least knew that all his scheming had been for nothing.

The old giant pushed himself up to a standing position on his cane, stepped over, and took the brooch from her hand.

"Look at the inscription on the back,'' said Lucy, sitting wearily on the sofa. "Dumlagchtat mac Alpin Bethoc. There was a grave marked BETHOC in a little cemetery at Dumlagchtat Castle. In it was supposed to be a treasure given to the Fingons by Kenneth mac Alpin. The grave was empty.''

Julius Fingon turned the brooch over in his bony fingers and stared at the inscription.

"What's this written on the pin?'' rasped Julius, squinting through his spectacles. "I can't make it out.''

"Oh, that's nothing,'' said Lucy wistfully. "It says Lucy MacAlpin Trelaine. That's who I used to think I was. Now I know the truth. You don't know any Trelaines by any chance, do you?''

Julius turned to face her. His mouth was open, but he

seemed lost in thought, his great blue eyes stared blankly ahead. A strange gurgling noise seemed to come from his throat.

"Mr. Fingon? Are you all right, Mr. Fingon?" said Lucy, rising from the sofa. She didn't even hear herself scream when Julius Fingon crashed facedown into the polished hardwood floor, as rigid as a felled tree.

THIRTY-ONE

"WHERE ARE YOU GOING, Miss Fingon?" said the lanky officer in the customs booth at the Halifax airport.

"Little Skye," said Lucy.

"How long do you plan to stay?"

"A few days, I think. I'm making arrangements to settle a cousin's estate."

"Are you a U.S. citizen?"

"I have a dual U.S./U.K. nationality." Lucy pulled out her passport with pride and handed it to the man. He barely glanced at it.

"Are you bringing anything with you that you plan to leave behind? Any gifts?"

Lucy dug into the left-hand pocket of her jacket.

"Just this paperweight," she replied, holding up a gray cylinder with the name Julius Fingon engraved upon it in gold letters.

"Welcome to Canada," said the man.

"Thank you very much," Lucy said, popped Julius back into her pocket, and walked down the aisle toward the exit. Transporting the compact deceased could become a huge new profit center for Neat 'n' Tidy, Lucy thought with a smile. She was beginning to think like Wing. She didn't know whether to celebrate or shoot herself.

"*Mademoiselle* Fingon?" said a thin man tentatively as Lucy passed the gate. He looked to be in his thirties, but his thick hair was gray. He was dressed in a taupe-colored summer suit.

"Yes, Mr. Dessault?"

"*Oui.* Welcome to Nova Scotia."

"Thank you."

"The baggage claim is this way and my car is just outside...."

In a few minutes they were in Dessault's Mercedes, heading south along the coast.

"...leaving funds available *immédiatement*," the lawyer was saying in a musical French accent. "The estate is a very large one and probate procedures, they are complicated. It will be years before everything passes into your name. As executrix, however, you control the estate and can invest in a responsible manner, *n'est-ce pas?*"

"And the others?" said Lucy, still shaken by what had happened. She had spoken to Dessault several times in the two weeks since Julius Fingon's death, but the reality of the situation still had not entirely sunken in.

"There was a special account to take care of the nurse, *Mademoiselle* MacGilvry the housekeeper, and the gardener, *Monsieur* Warrick. I say to Warrick he can continue to work for the time being, I hope you do not mind."

"No, not at all."

"He is a nice old fellow. He comes three days a week. He is off now for the weekend. You can meet him next Monday. How long, then, will you plan to stay?"

Lucy shrugged. "You tell me."

"There is quite a bit of paperwork we must encounter. You are sure you wish to sell the house?"

"I think so," said Lucy.

"Well, you are the executrix. But you will change your mind about the house when you see it, perhaps. Julius loved this house. The property has been in your family for generations."

Lucy didn't say anything. What would she do with a house in the middle of nowhere?

They drove for nearly two hours. The passing countryside ranged from thick forests to grassy, rolling hills reminiscent of the stark landscapes of Lis. At one point Lucy heard the sound of bagpipes and looked out to find a field full of men in kilts.

"Are there many Scots here?"

Dessault grinned. "Nova Scotia, it means New Scotland."

"Of course," said Lucy, feeling foolish.

"After the Jacobite forces have lost at Culloden," Dessault explained, "the Scottish diaspora began. Your ancestor, Alan Fingon, came to Little Skye in seventeen eighty-four. During the clearances of the nineteenth century, fifty thousand Highlanders have settled in Nova Scotia."

"Fifty thousand!"

"*Oui.*"

"You certainly know a lot about Scottish history."

"Canadians, they try to be good neighbors."

Lucy nodded, not knowing what that really meant. She had never had neighbors.

As they neared Little Skye, Lucy was struck with déjà vu, the rocky coast was so like the one near Dumlagchtat. Perhaps this was why Alan had chosen this place to make a new life.

Dessault turned the car off the meandering highway, onto a road that cut across the belly of a small peak. As they turned the final corner, Lucy's heart leaped in her chest. Ahead of them sprawled a meadow exploding with wildflowers, framed with mountains and the sea. The most astonishing feature of the picture, however, were the trees. A row of them soared a hundred feet into the sky on either side of the road, which ended at a sprawling stone house.

Dessault stopped the car in front of the house and they both got out.

"Here are the keys to the house and garage," said Dessault, placing them in her hand. "There are three vehicles; the keys for them are also upon this ring. I understand from the housekeeper that there is plenty of food in the refrigerator for you. If you need anything, however, Little Skye is only a few minutes away."

Lucy nodded, speechless with the quiet wonder of the place. The sun shone down golden on the flowers and the gray slate roof of the house. She could hear the sea lap faintly at the rocks below. The Fingons could not have been all bad to have created such a place.

"W-would you like to come in for a drink or something?" she finally stuttered.

"Perhaps I come back on Monday. I think maybe you wish to be alone now, yes?"

Lucy nodded, her eyes following the gentle curve of the huge trees back over the ridge, wondering how she could bring herself to sell this miracle.

"I never dreamed it would be so beautiful."

Dessault merely nodded.

"Is it always this beautiful?"

"In the winter its beauty is considerably more colder," said the lawyer gravely. "But yes, it is always this beautiful."

"Those trees are incredible," said Lucy, awed by the feeling of the place, as warm and good as the castle at Dumlagchtat had been cold and severe.

"They are the Fingon oaks. Julius told me that his ancestor, Alan Fingon, planted them when he built the house."

"I believe it," said Lucy.

"They are certainly the tallest in this area. The original forests here were cut for lumber long ago, much of it exported back to Scotland, in point of fact. But these oaks, they remain forever. They give the house its name."

"What?" said Lucy, barely listening.

"The lane of trees. Of course the spelling is obscure, but it is for the trees that people call the house. Trelaine. Tree-lane. *Mademoiselle* Fingon? Are you all right?"

LUCY FOUND THE graveyard on a promontory behind the house, looking out over the sea. It was small—barely twenty stones—surrounded by a short, white, picket fence and shaded by a huge, beautiful oak.

After Dessault drove away, Lucy had dropped her bags

in the house, barely noticing the low-beamed ceilings hung with dried flowers, the warm wooden paneling, the rich upholstery and leather. She had changed into jeans and gone outside to the garage.

When she didn't find what she was looking for, Lucy tried the shed behind the house. The door wasn't locked. It was full of gardening implements. Lucy took a shovel.

Now she stood in front of a flat, rectangular stone in the little graveyard beneath the beautiful tree, afraid to move. The other stones all bore the names of Fingons, the dates of their births and deaths. Alan. Rorie. Duncan. This stone, however, had only a single name chiseled deep into the well-worn granite: LUCY.

Lucy stood on the grass, piecing together the story in her mind.

Some ancient treasure had been consigned to the Fingons for protection centuries ago. It had been buried at the Castle at Dumlagchtat, its secret location engraved on a brooch. There it had lain until the Fingon line split at the end of the eighteenth century.

Alan Fingon had exhumed the treasure, brought it here to Trelaine, and buried it in this grave. Then Alan had deeded the house to one son, but conveying the brooch with the location of the treasure to the other son, still in Lis. The secret was then forgotten over the years.

If Barbara Fingon had reached her destination, Julius would have understood the message on the back of the brooch. He had understood instantly when Lucy had told him what was written there. The insight had exploded into his ancient brain with such a strong flash of greed—or justice—that it had killed him.

Now Lucy stood here, shovel in hand, above a grave in which wealth beyond dreams was buried. Dared she dig? She knew she had to. She knew that here lay the secret of her life. Here, at last, was Lucy MacAlpin Trelaine.

Lucy pressed her foot on the metal rim and the spade cut into the grass. The ground was thick clay, studded with rocks. After only a few minutes, Lucy grew discouraged. She returned to the gardener's shed and brought out a pickax, which she raised over her head and crashed into the grave. Half an hour later, her hands blistered and already aching, Lucy went back to the shed again, returning with gloves.

She began digging again, alternating the ax and the shovel. She returned twice to the house, once for water, once to get something to tie around her forehead to stop the sweat from drizzling into her eyes. She settled for a knee sock from the drawer in Julius's incongruously charming bedroom—all lace curtains and chintz.

After three hours, Lucy's arms felt like lead, her legs like rubber. Still she dug, grimy, sweating, her blisters beginning to bleed. Images of Michael Fraser, slick with sweat and anger, kept invading her mind. She wished he were here now. Had the ground at Dumlagchtat been this hard, cold, unyielding?

Lucy dug and she sweated, and the world seemed to become one vast, deep hole from which she would never escape until suddenly she swung her ax from the shoulder—she could no longer lift it over her head—and it struck the ground with a cracking sound. She had found something!

Lucy grabbed the shovel and dug furiously until she found what she thought was the source of the sound. There in the grave were tiny bones and a skull, surrounded by red earth that must once have been a coffin.

Lucy sank to her knees, assembling the brittle shards of what centuries ago had undoubtedly been a baby.

"Poor, dear Lucy," she said quietly and began to sob, not sure which Lucy she wept for. Could this be all there was? Was this the famous Fingon treasure that generations of her ancestors had kept hidden? That her father had died for? The bones of a child who had never lived?

"No!" shrieked Lucy. Furiously she threw the bones down, whatever natural squeamishness she'd had long gone from working with Wing. She grabbed her pickax and swung it with all her strength into the grave.

To her astonishment it met the earth with a clang.

It took twenty more minutes for Lucy to excavate the box and drag it out of the hole, bracing her back against the mud to support it on the way up. The baby's remains had been only a final red herring, she realized with disgust, the kind of red herring only a Fingon could think up.

Nearly five hours had passed since she had begun, and Lucy lay on the grass between headstones for a moment, aching to her bones, her sweat drying in the setting sun, before examining what she had found.

It was an iron box, a foot square. The metal was barely visible through corrosion and mud. This, she knew, was what she had been searching for. This was the Fingon treasure.

Lucy pushed herself up on the handle of her ax and swung it against the lock. It held. She struck again, this time above the hinge, and the whole front of the box broke off. Lucy pried open the lid and dumped the contents out onto the grass beside her. Then she stared at the Fingon treasure with a mixture of awe and disgust.

It was about the size of a loaf of bread and was covered with dirt and rust. It was a rock.

THIRTY-TWO

LUCY FELT A LITTLE BETTER.

She had dragged herself and the rock back into the house, peeled off her sweat-drenched clothes, and taken a long, hot shower. Then she had sat down in the tub and soaked for another half an hour.

Tomorrow she would lay Julius Fingon to rest in the hole she had dug, there with the bones of her namesake, there beside the rest of her family, there beneath the beautiful tree. Now Lucy lay on the white spread of the huge, four-poster bed in the old man's room, propped up by pillows.

Julius's cat, a white Persian with one green eye and one blue, was curled up in her lap, apparently bearing no resentment over being left out of the will.

Lucy could see herself in a mirror across the room, looking like an Oriental potentate in Julius's oversized terry-cloth robe, a towel wrapped around her hair.

The rock lay next to her.

Now that she had scrubbed the centuries of dirt from it with Julius's bath brush, the rock looked better. It was white, smooth, oval-shaped—slightly flattened on top. Lucy thought it might be marble. Carved into its face was an inscription, which Lucy recognized from her Catholic childhood as being in Latin:

Ni fallit Fatum, Scoti, quocunque locatum
Invenient lapidem, regnare tenetur ibidem.

Lucy fingered the letters, mystified. Did *Scoti* have something to do with Scotland? Lucy certainly didn't have the knowledge to translate the words. Was it an explanation of where a real treasure was hidden? It was lucky that Lucy happened to know someone who understood Latin. At least she hoped he did.

Lucy reached over, pulled the phone onto the bed with her. The cat looked over with an expression between boredom and annoyance.

"Sorry," Lucy murmured and dialed a now familiar number.

"Hello?" answered the voice after a few rings.

"Hi, it's me."

"Lucy!" A warm voice filled her ear. "I was waiting for your call. You get in all right? How was the flight?"

"Fine," she said, happy just to hear his voice again.

Lucy had been seeing Mike Fraser since the day after she returned from Lis. Wing knew something was up, even though Lucy hadn't mentioned how serious the relationship was getting. She couldn't keep her happiness a secret much longer. Nor was there any reason to anymore, now that she was sure of how she felt about Mike.

"I miss you already," he said.

"Listen, Michael. I've come across this Latin inscription that I need you to translate for me."

"No 'I miss you, too'?"

"I miss you, too, silly man. You do understand Latin, don't you?"

"Just want me for my mind, huh? You know what they say: *Mens sana in corpore sano.*"

"What is this? A little Ph.D. humor?"

"That's Latin. A sound mind in a sound body."

"Yes, I know."

"All right. So what's your quotation?"

Lucy read the inscription on the rock as best as she could. Halfway through, Mike stopped her with a chuckle.

"Where did you come across that?"

"An old book," Lucy said. She didn't want to say anything about the rock, even to Mike, until she knew what it was she had found. "Do you know what it means?"

"Sure. It's the inscription that was supposed to be on the Stone of Destiny."

"The what?"

"The Stone of Destiny, the Palladium of the Scots, the Stone of Scone. All the kings of the Scots were supposed to be crowned seated on it."

"Come on," said Lucy. "You're kidding me, right?"

"Why would I kid?" asked Mike. "Wait a second."

Lucy was glad he had put down the receiver. She was too stunned to think straight. The cat had begun to purr happily in her lap. In a minute Mike returned.

"I had to get a book," he explained.

"You mean Ph.D.'s don't know everything?"

"That's right," he said. "But we know where to look everything up. Listen to this:

Unless the Fates are faithless found
And prophet's voice be vain,
Where'er this monument is found
The Scottish race shall reign.

At least that's the way Sir Walter Scott translated the verse."

"I don't understand. What was this stone? Where did it come from?"

Mike chuckled. "Got a little while? Its a great yarn, but a bit involved."

"Go ahead."

"The Stone of Destiny," he said, savoring the words. "According to legend it was the stone that Jacob used as a pillow at Beth-el."

Lucy stared at the receiver, trying to remember the story of Jacob's pillow, which the nuns had told her so many years before. Could this stone beside her be the same stone that was in the Bible? The room seemed to spin.

"After Jacob's death," Mike continued, "his sons are

supposed to have carried the stone—some of ancient texts describe it as a marble seat—to Egypt.

"When Moses brought the plagues upon Pharaoh, the stone came into the possession of Scota, Pharaoh's daughter, and her husband, King Gathelus, son of Cecrops, the legendary builder of Athens. They took it with them to Spain. From there the stone was carried by the Spanish king's son, Simon Brech, on his invasion of Ireland in seven hundred B.C."

"My God," said Lucy.

"Anyway that's one story," said Mike. "Another version makes the stone the capstone of the first temple in Jerusalem. After the death of Zechariah, the prophet Jeremiah is supposed to have taken it to a colony in Ireland. Actually, this version's quite intriguing. On Devenish Island in Lake Erne there's a man-made cave which has been called Jeremiah's Tomb by the local inhabitants from ancient times. What do you think of that?"

"Very interesting," Lucy said, surprised that she could still speak.

"In either event," Mike continued happily, "the stone was then placed on the sacred hill of Tara, where it became an integral part of the coronation ceremony of Irish kings. You know the Scots were an Irish tribe?"

"Yes," she whispered.

"Ireland is where the stone picked up another nickname," he continued. "*Lia Fail*, the Fatal Stone."

"It fell on somebody."

"No, not at all," he laughed. "During these ancient coronations the stone was said to roar when a claimant of royal race sat on it. It remained silent for a pretender, which presumably was fatal.

"Anyway," Mike continued, "when Fergus Mor mac Erc invaded Scotland he brought the stone with him. All of Fergus's descendants were crowned seated upon it, including your friend, Kenneth mac Alpin. Kenneth moved his capital further inland to Scone and, of course, he brought the stone with him, hence the name, the Stone of Scone. All the MacAlpin kings were coronated seated upon it. Kenneth, in fact, is the one who was supposed to have carved those Latin verses.''

"Where is this Stone of Scone, Michael?" said Lucy, after a breath.

"Edward I of England carried it off to London after he invaded Scotland in twelve ninety-six. The Latin prophecy was still fulfilled, however. No other king ruled on Scottish soil. But a Scottish king, Mary Queen of Scots's son, sat on a coronation chair containing the Stone of Scone to be crowned James I of England. His descendants down to the present monarch were crowned rulers of Great Britain, Scotland included, seated on that same coronation chair.''

"You mean the Stone's still in England?" Lucy exclaimed, glancing at the marble object beside her, totally confused.

"Yes. At the Shrine of Edward the Confessor in Westminster Abbey.''

"Are they sure it's the right stone?''

"Well, there are people who think Edward was duped into taking a phony in twelve ninety-six." Michael laughed.

"Did he?''

"It's possible, I suppose. There are no Latin verses carved into the stone at Westminster Abbey. It's not made of marble. In fact, it's just an unimpressive chunk of sandstone. A few years ago some geologists tested it. They expected to find an origin at least as exotic as Irish Dalriada, but it turned out to be calcareous sandstone identical to that quarried in Scone. So, yes, the real Stone of Destiny might still be out there somewhere.''

"What would happen if it turned up?''

"Who knows?" laughed Mike. "What would happen if somebody found the Holy Grail or the True Cross? A lot of trouble, most likely.''

"Yes, I suppose." Lucy marveled, smiling at the

thought. Trouble was practically her middle name these days.

"So how long are you going to be up there?" asked Mike.

"I'm not sure. A week, maybe more."

"When you come back I have all sorts of Latin words I'd like to try out on you."

"Sounds interesting."

"So why did you want to know about the inscription on the Stone of Scone anyway?" asked Mike.

"One day after you've plied me with shrimp cocktails I might tell you," said Lucy.

They made their good-byes. Lucy put down the phone and ran her hand over the stone.

There was an old family Bible on Julius's bedstead. Lucy hadn't touched a Bible since she was sixteen. Now she extricated herself from the sleepy cat and picked up the heavy book.

In the front was a page listing the births and deaths of Fingons going back to 1715. Lucy stared at the lines that had led to her feeling connected to the world at last. Then she leafed through Genesis until she came to the passage she was looking for.

And Jacob went out from Beer-sheba and went toward Haran. And he lighted upon the place, and tarried there all night, because the sun was set; and he took one of the stones of the place, and put it under his head and lay down in that place to sleep. And he dreamed, and behold a ladder set up on the earth, and the top of it reached to heaven; and behold the angels of God ascending and descending upon it. And behold the Lord stood beside him, and said, "I am the Lord, the God of Abraham thy father, and the God of Isaac. The land whereon thou liest, to thee will I give it, and to thy seed.... And, behold, I am with thee, and will keep thee whithersoever thou goest, and will bring thee back into this land; for I will not leave thee, until I have done that which I have spoken to thee of." And Jacob awaked out of his sleep, and he said: "Surely the Lord is in this place; and I knew it not." And he was afraid, and said, "How full of awe is this place! this is none other than the house of God, and this is the gate of heaven."

Lucy closed the book and put it back on the table. What would Mike say when she told him about the stone? Should she tell him? Should she tell anyone?

Lucy touched the cold marble. Why had she been given this treasure? What in God's name was she supposed to do with it?

The cat had returned to her lap and was again purring happily. Lucy smiled. She didn't have to decide right away. She would think about it, listen to her heart, find the right thing to do.

Lucy had already figured out the right thing to do with Julius's money, the Fingon loot. She was going to follow Wing's example and release its trapped energy. She was going to plant trees on all the Fingon lands on Lis—millions and millions of trees until the whole island was once again the vast forest it had been before there were any Fingons. And she'd hire all the unemployed people of Lis to do the planting.

Lucy read the words in the Bible again:

The land whereon thou liest, to thee will I give it, and to thy seed.... And, behold, I am with thee, and will keep thee whithersoever thou goest, and will bring thee back into this land.

Dare she believe it? Could God really not be angry with her? The thought made her want to keep Trelaine after all. It would be a good environment in which to raise children—about as far from the slums of Boston as you could get. Perhaps this was where she was meant to be.

Lucy looked up at the big oak beams in the ceiling and smiled. She had a wonderful man in her life, a family in Weehawken, a new home—but most important, she had herself. Lucy Fingon was ready to claim her destiny.

With her heart full and her mind roaring with dreams, she put the stone beneath her head and went to sleep.

Take 3 books and a surprise gift FREE

SPECIAL LIMITED-TIME OFFER

Mail to: The Mystery Library™
3010 Walden Ave.
P.O. Box 1867
Buffalo, N.Y. 14240-1867

YES! Please send me 3 free books from the Mystery Library™ and my free surprise gift. Then send me 3 mystery books, first time in paperback, every month. Bill me only $4.19 per book plus 25¢ delivery and applicable sales tax, if any*. There is no minimum number of books I must purchase. I can always return a shipment at your expense and cancel my subscription. Even if I never buy another book from the Mystery Library™, the 3 free books and surprise gift are mine to keep forever.   415 BPY A3US

Name	(PLEASE PRINT)	

Address		Apt. No.

City	State	Zip

* Terms and prices subject to change without notice. N.Y. residents add
  applicable sales tax. This offer is limited to one order per household and not
  valid to present subscribers.
© 1990 Worldwide Library.

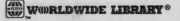